WHEN WITCHES WAKE

HANKS HOLLOW SERIES BOOK FOUR

RACHELLE KAMPEN

Editor: Red Adept Editing

Proofreader: Red Adept Editing

Cover designer: MiblArt

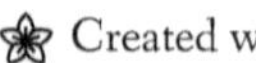 Created with Vellum

ONE

ROSIE

Rosie knew she was sleeping. The world around her was like a low background buzz, never completely reaching her. Wrapped in a fog that kept her drowsy, she didn't really feel a desire to try to find her way out of it. Sometimes, a voice reached her, and she tried to claw her way toward it, but she always ended up sinking back into the fog.

Time was obscure. She couldn't tell whether she had just gone to sleep or she had been sleeping for days. Sometimes, the fog felt blissful, like finally being able to sink into bed after an exhausting day. Other times, it was terrifying, like waking up from a nightmare and not knowing what was real.

"You've been sleeping long enough, Rosie." Her grandma's voice cut through the fog and pulled Rosie toward her. "Come on now, dear. It's time to wake up."

The fog slowly lifted, its embrace letting her go. It felt like going into an air-conditioned home on a hot, humid day. Cool air kissed her cheeks, making goose bumps rise on her arms.

"Oh my God, is she waking up? Get the doctor! Hurry!"

Rosie didn't recognize the voice, but it was close by. Cold fingers pressed into her wrist.

"Rose." The woman spoke intimately, as if they knew each other. "The doctor is on his way, honey. Everything will be okay."

Rosie's eyelids peeled apart slowly, as though they'd been glued together, and the blur of a person standing over her came into focus. Purple scrubs, stethoscope hanging over the neck, hair pulled into a ponytail. Rosie realized the voice she'd heard a moment ago belonged to the nurse standing over her. She looked at Rosie with concern and something else. Her energy brushed over Rosie like a whoosh of air, enormously surprised and apprehensive.

Rosie's eyes wandered over the rest of the hospital room, and when she tried to turn her head, plastic tugged at her cheek. Something filled her mouth. It forced air into her lungs and sucked it back out again, breathing for her. She tried to breathe on her own, but she couldn't. Panic overwhelmed her. When she raised her arm to try to rip it out, she was frustrated to find the limb heavy and uncooperative.

"No, honey, we need to leave that there until the doctor can take it out." The nurse calmly took Rosie's hand and laid it back at her side then smiled pleasantly, but Rosie could feel the woman's apprehension grow.

Rosie's panic heightened as she tried to remember what might have happened to bring her here, but she couldn't focus on anything but the tube in her mouth. Memories assaulted her brain in flashes, like lightning striking her over and over. Her father. Lucas. The cliff. Machines screamed with piercing, blaring alarms. The woods. Her mother. The gods. Stuart...

"She needs a sedative! Where's the doctor?" The

nurse's fake calm disappeared, and her voice betrayed her panic. "Hurry!"

"I'm here." A man's voice rose over the chaos, sounding calm and confident amid the nervous nurses and screeching alarms, but Rosie's panic didn't ease. "This is impossible."

A warm sensation ran through Rosie's arm, and everything went dark.

THE NEXT TIME Rosie woke up, it felt like she was wrapped in a blanket of peace. She could breathe on her own. The blaring machines were silenced. That horrible tube was gone from her mouth. Her eyes roamed over the hospital room and landed on her grandma.

Clara smiled at Rosie wearily. Something was off about her. She looked really tired. When she squeezed Rosie's hand, Rosie squeezed back.

"There you are," Clara said.

She continued to hold Rosie's hand, and Rosie realized her grandmother was using her energy to calm her. The lightning flashes came back, and she remembered.

"My father? Lucas?" Rosie's voice rasped.

"Lucas is fine. He had a gunshot wound in his shoulder, but it healed."

Clara didn't say anything about Rosie's father, but she already knew why. Still, she needed her grandma to confirm it. She needed to shut down any lingering hopes she had before they grew too big.

"My father?"

Clara bit her lip and looked down. "I'm sorry, honey."

Rosie closed her eyes tightly, tears spilling down her cheeks despite the calm energy her grandma passed to her.

Heavy footsteps entered the room, and she opened her eyes. A tall man with graying hair stood by the bed. His hands were tucked into the pockets of his long lab coat.

"Ms. Hart, I'm Dr. Newsome."

The doctor's deep baritone made her wonder if he sang in a church choir in his downtime. The random thought struck her as dumb at a time like this, and she frowned.

"I've been practicing for twenty-seven years, and I've never seen anything so remarkable. Your recovery is miraculous, to put it bluntly."

Rosie glanced over at her grandma, and Clara winked.

"Has there been any discussion about—"

"No," Clara said. "Will you give us some time?"

"Of course." He gave Rosie a smile that seemed practiced.

Something wasn't right. "Grandma, what's going on?"

"Rosie..." She started then paused, and tears filled her eyes. "I'm sorry. This is going to be really hard to tell you. I tried. I tried every day for so long. I just couldn't heal you. I even prayed on it. I don't know why it worked now, after all this time. I can only imagine that this is the work of the Goddess."

"What are you talking about?" Her grandmother wasn't making any sense.

The door burst open.

"Rosie?" Sam stood in the doorway, breathless from running. He looked equal parts terrified and relieved.

Rosie's heart sped, indicated by the beeping of the monitor next to the bed. Sam was there, but he'd changed. The person standing in the doorway wasn't the seventeen-year-old goofy brother she remembered. He was a young man.

Rosie looked at her grandma, begging for an answer.

TWO

LUCAS

The Beckett pack house resembled an upscale ski chalet. An enormous redwood A-frame structure sat atop a stone foundation with large stone pillars. Embedded deep in the woods outside town, the house was nestled in a clearing about a quarter mile from the river.

The splash of water crashing over rocks mingled with the sounds of the forest. Lucas's sensitive hearing took it all in as he stepped across the gravel driveway, his backpack slung over his shoulder.

Roger grabbed one of the bags from the trunk of the car, moved to Lucas's side, and placed a hand on his back. His father's smile was wider than Lucas had ever seen. "We're home, son."

Home. He'd just left the only home he'd ever known. Yet somehow this place called to him. Something deep inside him ached to shift and run, to touch his bare paws to the earth where his ancestors had roamed.

The front door flew open, and Roger's cousin Travis emerged. In his midtwenties with a stalky form, a full red beard, and ginger hair, he was a stark contrast to the other tall, lean, brunette Becketts. A grin split his face before he turned and shouted into the house. "They're here!"

With a loud whoop, Travis leaped from the porch and bounded toward them. Lucas barely had time to brace himself before Travis grabbed him around the middle and lifted him, spinning him in a circle. After dropping Lucas to the ground, he turned and grabbed Roger in a tight embrace. "About time!" The words were muffled as Travis smooshed his face into Roger's shoulder.

Travis's father, Christopher, appeared at the front door, followed by Roger's brother—the pack alpha—Shawn. Their forms filled the doorframe.

"Come in here, you two!" Shawn's blue eyes were bright with excitement. He wore a T-shirt advertising some Milwaukee bar. Lucas envied his uncle's lifestyle—traveling around Wisconsin cities to sample and learn more about craft beer and advertise the family business. For years, Lucas had loved to hear about new local bands his uncle heard play or cool new microbreweries that were popping up. Shawn had grown accustomed to a nomadic lifestyle that served the family business well. The last thing he wanted was to be forced to stay in Beckett Falls as alpha.

So he was begging Lucas to come in and take his place.

"We've been waiting all morning," Shawn said, waving them into the house.

"Come on!" Roger pulled Lucas along as he jogged toward the front door like a kid rushing to see Santa, a vigor in his step that Lucas had never seen before. He couldn't help the smile that curled his lips as he followed his father into the house.

Inside, the A-frame was lit with an enormous

branch chandelier that cast a slight glow over the red-wood beams, but the natural light from the abundance of windows made the light bulbs in the chandelier unnecessary. Floor-to-ceiling windows on every wall gave a three-hundred-sixty-degree view of the forest. Snippets of the river could be seen through the trees.

A deck wrapped around the entire length of the house. A fire pit, a grill, and several seating areas looked like they got plenty of use.

Inside was an enormous open-concept area with hardwood floors. A stone fireplace stood in the center of the space, separating the kitchen and dining area from the living area. An open staircase wrapped around the side of the fireplace and up to a loft.

In one corner of the living area, a big-screen TV was mounted between two windows. Beer cans, half-empty bags of chips, and video game controllers littered a polished wood coffee table in front of a worn leather couch. A matching chair sat off to the side.

On the other side of the open space, a pool table, a dart board, and a foosball table made up a nice little rec room. Next to it, a staircase led down to what looked like a finished basement.

Lucas prayed he would have his own bedroom. He'd never had to share before.

"What first?" Shawn clapped his hands. "Tour or unpack?"

"What's to tour?" Travis groused as he hauled two bags through the front door. Lucas hadn't even seen him grab them from the car. "It's all pretty self-explanatory." Travis pointed around the space. "Kitchen, where we eat. Living room, where we eat and watch TV. Game room, where we eat and play games. Upstairs, where

Shawn does his office stuff. Downstairs, where we sleep. Now, let's go unload." He made a show of dragging the bags toward the stairs. "These are getting heavy."

Shawn rolled his eyes and waved a hand toward the basement. "After you."

As they descended the stairs, the basement came into view. The huge open space had a concrete floor littered with hockey sticks, goal posts, and soccer balls. A large patio door led to the backyard, and doors lined the outside of the room. No creepy cobwebs, no prison cells—it was nothing like the Harts' basement.

Lucas's mind immediately went to Rosie, and he felt a weight settle onto his shoulders.

"Would you like to see your rooms?" Shawn's voice cut through his thoughts before they began to spiral.

"Huh?" Lucas turned toward his uncle.

"Your rooms?" Shawn gestured toward the doors. "Christopher, why don't you show Roger to his room. I'll take Lucas to his. Travis, go get more of the bags from the car."

Nodding, Lucas followed Shawn to one of the doorways while Roger went with Christopher to another doorway a few feet from his. Shawn opened the door and stepped inside. Lucas sighed in relief when he saw only one bed. The queen-sized frame and mattress pressed against one wall, and a dresser sat against the other. Windows lined the upper part of the outer wall, and a small closet stood next to the door.

"It's not much, but none of us spend a whole lot of time in our bedrooms, to be honest." Shawn shrugged. "You're welcome to put a TV in here. I'll give you a credit card to use. Buy whatever you want to spruce the place up."

Lucas nodded as he stepped into the room and set his backpack on the bed, his mind already drifting back to Hanks Hollow. Back to Rosie. What if this was a mistake?

"Lucas..." Shawn took a step forward. "I know you're leaving a lot behind, and you're coming into a new world. But I want you to understand something. This is *your* world. We are your people. We've been waiting for you for a long, long time. Welcome home, buddy."

Something inside him—the wolf that had spent his whole life in search of his home—cried in relief.

~

AFTER SPENDING a couple of hours lugging bags into the house and unpacking, Lucas couldn't ignore the rumble in his stomach any longer. He made his way upstairs, hoping to find something in the kitchen. Shawn and Roger sat at a large oak kitchen table, deep in conversation, and Travis and Christopher were in the living room, watching television. All attention turned to him as he emerged from the basement.

"All unpacked?" Roger smiled. "I haven't even started yet. Feel free to unpack for me."

"Nah." Travis turned his attention back to the television. "He's probably hungry. You guys forgot to feed him."

"I'm not a baby." Lucas narrowed his eyes, but his stomach chose that moment to growl, and a chorus of laughter erupted. His cheeks heated. "But yeah. I guess I could use something to eat. Got anything I can fix in the kitchen?"

Travis barked out a laugh. "The only things in that fridge are beer, cheese, and stale pizza."

"Seriously?" Lucas raised an eyebrow. "What do you eat?"

"Normally, we're at the brewery during the day and eat in town," Shawn said. "Nights and weekends, we eat out or get delivery."

"Delivery comes here?" Lucas inhaled. The Harts never allowed outsiders near their property. "Don't you worry about being seen in wolf form?"

"We don't do anything stupid like order delivery then wolf out," Travis said. "Duh."

"Travis," Shawn scolded him. "Knock it off."

"I'm pretty hungry." Christopher spoke as he yawned, stretching his arms over his head. "I can take the pup to town."

Lucas cringed. *Pup?*

"We'll all go," Shawn said, glaring at Christopher. "Lunch, then we can stop by the brewery."

Excitement bubbled in Lucas's stomach, and he forgot his embarrassment. He couldn't wait to see the brewery. It took all his restraint not to run for the door, and it seemed like everyone moved more slowly than he could take. As they finally drifted outside, Lucas made his way toward his father's car.

"Ride with me, Lucas," Shawn called. "Your dad can ride with Christopher and Travis."

Lucas nodded and followed Shawn to a black Subaru Outback. He climbed in and buckled the seat belt, dreading an awkward car ride. He knew his uncle well, but they weren't close enough for that comfortable-silence thing yet, and Lucas wasn't much for talking.

Fortunately, Shawn didn't seem to have any

trouble filling the silence. The man didn't shut up the entire car ride.

"Right over there..." Shawn pointed at an open space in the trees. "That leads to the highest point of the bluffs between here and town. Great spot for a run. We go through there a lot. Your dad and I used to have races up and down the river all the time. He used to beat me when we were younger, but your old man can't keep up with me now." Shawn laughed and gave Lucas's arm a light punch. "Up ahead, where the forest thins out, you can see town a lot better. Some great trails are on the other side, but we don't run out there much. Obviously, we like to stay closer to the pack house when we shift, but there are some nice hiking trails when you're on two legs. Your dad said you like to jog. You'll have lots of places to do that."

Everything Lucas knew about Beckett Falls, he'd read online and heard secondhand from his family. He'd been too young to remember his time there as a kid. Nothing prepared him for what he saw when Shawn's car emerged from the crop of trees and the small village came into view. His eyes were immediately drawn to the enormous waterfall in the distance that fed the river that ran through town. A bridge stretched across the gorge—a perfect spot to view the beauty of the falls on one side and the town on the other. Lucas couldn't wait to hike the series of trails that led to the overlook.

The river thinned as it neared the village, and it trailed right through the middle of town. A stone bridge crossed over the river and connected the two parts of what looked to be a bustling main street. The Bavarian architecture coupled with the cobblestone streets made it look like something from a European postcard. In the distance, a huge building with a large parking lot packed with cars appeared to be the center of activity. The brewery employed most of the town.

"Wait until you taste Mac Jenson's pizza." Shawn groaned in pleasure. "You'll never want to eat anything else again."

Shawn pulled the car into a streetside parking space in front of one of the many buildings that lined Main Street. A windowed storefront read Mac's Pizza. The smell hit Lucas like a freight train, and his stomach growled in anticipation.

A car pulled into the spot next to them, and Lucas's father got out of the front passenger seat. They all made their way inside, and a chorus of friendly greetings met them as they entered. Customers sitting at the tables and employees behind the counter all stopped what they were doing to say hello. Whether they did that for everyone or just the Becketts, Lucas wasn't sure.

"Mac!" Shawn called out to a large man behind the counter. "How you doing?"

"Can't complain!" Mac's eyes widened as they made their way toward the front of the restaurant. "Is that Roger Beckett I see?"

"How are you, Mac? Long time, no see!" Roger reached across the counter to shake Mac's hand.

"Long time!" Mac laughed. "How long has it been? Ten years?"

"More like twelve." Roger frowned.

"Don't tell me this is little Lucas. He's all grown up, Roger! He's almost as tall as Shawn!"

"He really did some growing, didn't he?" Roger ruffled Lucas's hair, and Lucas pushed his father's hand away. "How's business?"

"Great! Your family keeps me busy!"

"I'll bet. Still ordering the Mac special every night?"

"Just about every night!"

"Make it three today," Shawn said. "That should be enough for five hungry Becketts. And three pitchers of lager with five mugs."

"Comin' right up!"

Shawn clapped Lucas on the back and steered him toward one of the tables. Once they were all seated, the buzz of conversation in the restaurant continued around them. Lucas glanced around and noticed the looks that turned his way and the whispered words that followed.

"Small town," Shawn said. "You'll be the topic of conversation for a while."

Lucas scowled. "Terrific."

"Hey, soak it in." Travis gave a predatory smile. "The girls will be after you like a wolf after red meat."

A painful jolt ran through him. He studied his fingernails, trying to avoid eye contact.

"Don't listen to him," Roger said. "He's just jealous."

"Your lager, fellas." Mac put the pitchers and mugs on the table then nudged Lucas. "If the sheriff comes in here, you make sure you tell him you're here with your father, you hear? No way that baby face can pass for twenty-one."

"Yes, sir." Lucas grinned.

"The sheriff won't give you any trouble." Shawn winked. "Tell him it's business related. You need to learn the trade."

"He's been learning the trade for years." Roger rolled his eyes. "If I were a better father, I might be worried about that."

"I heard you've been tending bar and expanding

the inventory in Hanks Hollow." Christopher took a sip of his beer.

"Yeah, at Miller's. Charlie gets a mix of locals and vacationers. The locals like to stick to the same old stuff, but the vacationers are always looking for what's trending in craft brew. I've been keeping him stocked. He's been doing great business."

Shawn clinked his glass against Lucas's. "Cheers. I'm proud of you, kid. We've taught you well." He took a sip of his beer then set it down. "I trust you've included the full array of Beckett's in his inventory?"

"Of course," Lucas said. "It's the best in Wisconsin."

"Hear! Hear!"

Lucas ducked his head in surprise when it seemed every person in the entire restaurant raised their glass. A small laugh erupted as he scanned the smiling faces. The jovial atmosphere was infectious.

THREE

LUCAS

FULL DIDN'T BEGIN TO DESCRIBE HOW LUCAS felt. Shawn hadn't been exaggerating about the pizza. Lucas had polished off three enormous slices. After Shawn paid the tab, they had left the restaurant to head across town to the brewery.

The parking lot was nearly full, but there were reserved spaces for the Beckett vehicles at the head of the lot. As they walked through the doors, Lucas was taken aback by how large the space was.

The main entrance had a bar where tourists could sample beer. Happy visitors sat on the barstools and sipped brews while they made small talk with the bartenders. The ease and content of vacationers was something Lucas was familiar with. In Hanks Hollow, their carefree body language made them easy to spot among a sea of overworked warehouse employees looking to wind down after a hard day. He felt a small pang of remorse for leaving his job at Miller's.

Lucas shoved his hands into his pockets as he studied the plaques and photographs that lined the walls. Other people milled around him, reading about how the Beckett family had settled the area in the 1800s and built the town and the brewery.

A lot of history about the Beckett family, the tourists *wouldn't* find posted on the walls.

He followed his family through the main area, into the back. Christopher and Travis went off to check on the workers, and Shawn gave Roger and Lucas the tour. He started in the room where grain was mixed with hot water to bring out the sugar that turned into alcohol.

"Is this grain from the fields the Becketts own?" Lucas pointed at the bags that lined the walls.

The Becketts owned farmland south of their territory, where they hired farmers to work the fields and harvest the crops used in their brews. Lucas had met many of those farmers during his trips to the The Wild Boar, a small farm-town tavern where he and his father had met with the rest of the Beckett pack, minus Marcus and Brody, once a month for as long as he could remember.

"Yep, all grown on Beckett land," Shawn said proudly. "Both the grain we use here and the hops we use to flavor the beer downstairs. We get our other ingredient flavors from local farmers. Berries, honey, citrus... it all comes from Wisconsin."

Lucas knew all that. He'd been learning about the Beckett brew business for years. Still, it was cool to hear it all while standing in the brewery.

After they visited the flavoring and fermentation areas, they entered the bottling area. A metal staircase led down to the main floor, where the bottling took place. They had a view of the factory floor, where the workers manned machines that filled bottles and cans and packaged them in boxes for shipping. The whir of machinery and the clang of bottles and cans filled the air, and Lucas found it nearly impossible to hear his uncle talk.

Shawn pointed at the floor by one of the pieces of machinery before turning to Lucas and Roger and rolling his eyes. At first, Lucas didn't see what he was pointing at, but then he saw it and laughed. Travis had leaned in closely to one of the workers, openly flirting. He played with her long blond hair and smiled adoringly at her.

Lucas cringed as he made his way down the stairs behind his father and Shawn. That was a sexual-harassment suit waiting to happen.

"They're dating!" Shawn yelled. "But he's not supposed to be flirting with her on the floor! This place is dangerous. It's not for goofing arou—"

Before Shawn could finish his sentence, he lost his footing on the stairs, tumbled to the bottom, and landed hard on the concrete floor.

"Shawn!" Roger ran down the stairs after him. "Are you okay?"

Lucas followed closely behind and helped Roger try to hoist Shawn up from the ground.

"Ah! Stop!" Shawn held out his hands. "My shoulder."

"What the hell happened here?" Travis approached, his brow creased in concern. "Shawn? Did you fall down the stairs again? Seriously, you need to get out of this factory and back on the road, dude. You're going to put yourself in the hospital."

"This has happened before?" Roger scowled.

Travis shrugged. "It's Shawn. Have you seen those clown feet? He trips over them all the time."

"I think we need to get him to a doctor," Lucas said. "He looks pretty banged up. He might have dislocated his shoulder."

"No!" Shawn barked, his cheeks reddening. "No doctor. I'll be fine."

The young woman Travis had been flirting with slowly walked toward Shawn, her hand out as though she was about to touch him.

"Let me look," she said.

"Sophie!" a woman who looked almost identical to Travis's girlfriend shouted. Her blue eyes narrowed in anger as she watched. "Come on! The line is backing up."

Sophie snatched her hand away from Shawn and turned to the other woman. She ducked her head as though she'd been caught stealing a cookie.

"Go on, Sophie. We can take care of him." Travis winked at her as she turned to leave.

Lucas frowned in confusion when he caught Travis's gaze.

Travis laughed. "They're sisters."

Nodding, Lucas turned his attention back to Shawn. He helped to haul the tall man up from the floor and tried not to let his disappointment show. The tour was over.

THE BECKETTS RETURNED to the pack house early afternoon. Though Lucas was disappointed they had to leave, he still rode a high of excitement at what he had seen. The brewery was so cool.

He'd driven Shawn's car home while Shawn nursed his injured shoulder. Lucas had tried repeatedly to get him to agree to go to the doctor, but Shawn refused.

As they filed into the house, Lucas headed toward the stairs—he had more unpacking to do.

"Lucas." Shawn nodded toward the door. "Come

with me. I want you to meet Brody. He should be home from school now."

Lucas had almost forgotten about Marcus's son. Brody was only twelve years old. He didn't live in the pack house with the rest of the Becketts. Marcus had built them another house closer to the river.

Lucas followed Shawn out of the house, down the porch steps, and onto a well-traveled trail that snaked through the woods.

"He's not there alone, is he?"

"God no." Shawn laughed. "He and his nanny, Ginny, are close. She takes good care of him. I've been staying there since Marcus got sick. Brody needs some guidance. He's been through a lot."

"Right." Lucas winced. "He found Marcus, didn't he?"

"Yeah, and it wasn't the first time he found his dad passed out drunk. Poor kid was cleaning up after the jerk all the time. I tried to help the best I could, but Marcus kept us all at arm's length. He didn't trust anyone."

"Was Brody from a surrogate?"

Shawn nodded. "Yeah, although Marcus would have preferred the old-fashioned way. He's into that traditional crap. I think he knew it wouldn't work. We don't have creepy basements and prison cells. That's just insane."

Shawn's attitude was refreshing. Nothing about the Beckett pack screamed stuffy old tradition. Although Simon had worked hard to get the Harts past it, the feeling of the old ways still lingered in the air at Hart House.

The sound of the river grew louder, and they stepped into a clearing along the riverbank. Ahead, a giant house sat to one side. Lucas paused his steps and gaped. He'd imagined that Marcus had built a small cabin for him and Brody, not a house large enough for an entire pack.

Shawn laughed. "Yeah, Marcus didn't do anything halfway. Part of me wonders if he had plans to grow a whole second pack to live here. Wouldn't that be something. A whole house of little Marcus clones." Shawn shivered.

The two-story house had a large second-story deck on the back that overlooked the river. Must have been some great views from up there. Like the pack house, it had windows all around, and Lucas could see some of the layout within. An old woman stood in the kitchen, preparing food, and a kid sat on a couch, reading a book.

Shawn led Lucas up the stone walkway to the front door then turned the doorknob and stepped inside. As he poked his head in, he called out, "Knock, knock. Who's home?"

Lucas's gaze travelled around the main area. An enormous living room lay out before him with a kitchen beyond it. To the right of the kitchen was a dining area with a big oak table. Past the kitchen and dining area, a doorway led to another area of the house. To the left of the kitchen, an open staircase led to the second floor.

The smell of browning meat hung heavily in the air. The tiny woman looked to be in her midsixties. She had short, carefully styled gray hair and manicured nails, and she wore a nice outfit with clean lines. The woman looked much different from the nanny he'd grown up with.

The woman was cutting a tomato and didn't look up as she spoke. "Supper will be ready soon. We're having spaghetti."

"Sounds great, Ginny. Thanks," Shawn said. "We'll have another mouth to feed tonight."

Ginny looked up. When she saw Lucas, a bright smile lit her face, and she winked. "The more, the merrier."

When her gaze trailed over to Shawn, her jaw dropped, and she set her knife down on the counter. "Shawn Beckett, did you fall down the stairs again?"

Shawn, scratched and bruised, was holding his shoulder. He pressed his lips into a thin line and huffed a breath out through his nose. "Yes."

Ginny shook her head before she picked up the knife again and resumed slicing. "I swear you are the clumsiest man I've ever met."

In the living room, the kid Lucas had seen through the window looked at Shawn with a small smile before his gaze shifted to Lucas. His smile dropped, and uncertainty crossed his features.

"Hey, Brody." Shawn stepped forward. "Do you remember me telling you about Roger and Lucas?"

Brody nodded, glancing back and forth between Lucas and Shawn.

"This is Lucas." Shawn nodded toward him. "Lucas, this is Brody."

When Brody met Lucas's eyes, Lucas felt a tug at his heart. There was something about the boy. He was young, but his eyes carried a wisdom that a kid his age shouldn't possess. More than smart. Experienced. Like he'd seen more than a kid should see.

Shaggy brown hair hung low on his forehead, his gangly limbs had sharp elbows, and he wore oversized clothes and dirty sneakers. This kid could have been Lucas a few years ago.

"Hi, Brody." Lucas stepped forward. "It's good to

meet you." He nodded toward the book. "What are you reading?"

Brody held it up. "Stephen King. *Pet Sematary*."

"That's a good one." Lucas sat down next to him. "One of my favorites, actually. You know, I've read every Stephen King book ever written. I have them all, if you ever want to borrow them."

Brody's eyes widened. "Really?"

Lucas smiled at him. "Really."

An overwhelming sense of protectiveness came over Lucas. A need to guide the kid in the right direction. He'd never felt something so strong.

Brody was part of his pack. And it was his job to protect him.

FOUR

SAM

Sam stepped into the darkened house and shut the door behind him. He leaned against the frame and sighed, wearily running a hand over his face. They had finally gotten Rosie to sleep when he left the hospital. It had taken a long time to get her calmed down. Even her grandmother's special touch didn't seem to do the trick. She fired off question after question.

How do you tell someone they've lost a year and a half of their life?

He raised his head and stood straight as he heard the pounding of footsteps on the stairs. Michael and Daniel approached, anxiety written all over their faces.

"Well?" Daniel's eyes widened as he examined Sam. "How is she?"

"She's got a lot to deal with, and she's freaked out," Sam whispered. "For her, it's like Dad just died. She hasn't had time to deal with it like we have. But she's healthy. The doctor couldn't believe it. Said it was a miracle."

Sam closed his eyes and said a small prayer of

thanks. How many times had he wished for this? They had Rosie back.

"A miracle?" Michael raised an eyebrow. "Or her grandmother?"

"I don't know, to be honest." Sam furrowed his brow. "Clara has been trying to heal her for the last year and a half. Why did it suddenly work now?"

"I don't care," Daniel said. "She's alive, and she's healthy. It doesn't matter how."

Sam put a hand on Daniel's shoulder. "You're right."

"Can we see her?" Hope was shining in Michael's eyes.

"The doctor said in a day or two, he'll allow visitors. I'll let you know. She's been asking for Lucas, though, so I'm hoping the doctor will let him in tomorrow—"

Sam paused when Michael and Daniel exchanged glances.

"What is it?"

"Roger and Lucas are gone." Michael frowned.

"Gone?" Sam narrowed his eyes. "What do you mean, 'gone'?"

"Their stuff is gone," Daniel said. "Their rooms have been cleared out."

"What?" Sam shook his head, shouldering past Daniel. He headed for the stairs then took them two at a time until he reached the top. After barreling across the hall and into Lucas's room, he froze. The bed was made, the room pristine. It looked as though no one had ever lived there.

Sam took another step into the room, his mind racing. What the hell? He reached for his phone, ready to send a message, when his gaze landed on the phone sitting on the dresser—Lucas's phone. He stepped forward and picked up the device, inspecting it. Nothing was wrong with it. It had just been left there.

"Lucas's truck is still in the garage," Michael said. "So is Roger's car."

Confusion muddied Sam's brain. "When was the last time either of you saw them?"

"Grandpa's funeral," Daniel whispered.

~

THE HOT WATER that hit Sam's face couldn't wipe away his exhaustion. He scrubbed his hands through his hair, rinsing the shampoo out, then turned the water off and stepped out of the shower, grabbing his towel. After rubbing it over his head, he tied it around his waist and stepped out of the bathroom and into his bedroom. After throwing himself onto his bed, he stared up at the ceiling.

In the last week, they'd lost Stuart, Becca had nearly been killed by Amos, Sam had become alpha, Rosie had woken from a coma, and Lucas and Roger had disappeared. Enough already. He couldn't take anything more.

When his phone buzzed on the nightstand, he grabbed it. Smiling at Becca's name on the caller ID, he hurried to answer the call. "I really need to hear your voice right now."

"Is everything okay?"

Sam kicked himself at Becca's worried tone. She was waiting for word on Rosie.

"Rosie is good. Really good. The doctor said she's very healthy."

"Sam, that's amazing. I can't believe it." She

paused, and a sniffle came through the line. "I really want to see her."

"The doctor said she can have visitors in a day or two."

"So this seems great. Why do you sound so stressed?"

"Rosie is healthy, but she's upset. It was hard to explain to her that she's been in a coma for a year and a half."

"Oh God. Sam, I'm sorry. That must have been awful."

"That's not the worst part." Sam closed his eyes.

"What? What is it?"

"Lucas and Roger are gone."

"Gone? What do you mean, 'gone'?"

"I mean gone. As in they aren't here anymore. I don't know where they went." Sam fought the sting of tears. Did they decide to go rogue? That didn't seem likely. Things were bad under Amos but not that bad. Marcus wouldn't take them back into the Beckett pack. Where could they have gone?

"How could they just leave? Can't you call them?"

"They left their phones."

Becca sighed. "I guess that means Lucas isn't coming to work tomorrow."

Sam snorted. "I think I would recommend finding someone to cover his shift."

"What are you going to tell Rosie?"

Sam sighed. "Nothing yet. I don't want to stress her out more."

"She's going to find out eventually. She'll want to see him."

"I know." Sam rubbed his palm into his eye. "I'll cross that bridge when I come to it."

Becca was quiet for a moment. "What about us?"

Sam flinched. "What about us? What do you mean? I thought we were good."

"Sam, we're good." Becca laughed. "I mean what about telling Rosie about us."

"Oh." He hadn't thought about that. "I don't know. Maybe we should wait a little while on that too. I mean, she's got a lot to deal with right now."

Becca sighed. "You want to come over?"

Sam groaned. "You have no idea how much I would love to. But I think I need to stay here. I need to keep an eye on things."

"Because you're the alpha." Becca said it like she was testing it out. Trying to make it sound casual and normal. "Does this mean you won't be able to come over as much?"

"I guess it kind of does." Sam frowned. "But maybe you could come here."

He frowned when he heard her breath hitch. A long, silent pause followed. She sniffled again, and Sam wished he could hold her.

In a soft, watery voice, she said, "I don't think I can."

"You'll be safe here, Becca. I swear."

"Wouldn't that be breaking more rules?"

"No more than I'm already breaking."

"I don't know..."

"Do you work this weekend?"

"No."

"Okay. How about you spend the weekend with me. Here. If it feels weird, I'll take you home."

Silence stretched on the other end of the line for a few moments before Becca answered quietly, "Okay."

FIVE

ROSIE

A STRANGER STARED AT ROSIE IN THE MIRROR. She had the same pale skin and freckles Rosie had seen her whole life, but the person staring back at her was older. The lines on her face longer and more defined. She was taller and had curves. Under the less than flattering hospital gown, Rosie could see the outline of breasts that weren't hers. Puberty must have finally hit at some point.

"Rosie?" Her grandma called to her from outside the small bathroom. "Are you all right in there? Do you need help?"

"I'll be right out."

Rosie washed her hands slowly and dried them with a paper towel. It was the first time she had been able to use the bathroom on her own since she woke up two days ago. They had finally removed all the tubes and wires and allowed her to get up and start moving around. The doctor marveled at her miraculous recovery. He said people didn't typically wake up from such a long coma, and if they did, they certainly didn't start walking and talking as though they'd just woken up from a nap. Months of physical therapy should have been involved before she was able to get out of bed. But as soon as he started talking about a barrage of tests and consulting other physicians in the area to document Rosie's case, her grandma shooed him out of the room.

Taking a deep breath, Rosie opened the door. Her grandma sat in the chair next to the bed, playing with a piece of loose string on her dress. Sam stood in the corner, staring out the window. With his sleeves rolled up to his elbows and his hands in his pockets, he stood tall like a man instead of slouching like a petulant teen. Not like her Sam.

The two of them had spent the past two days slowly filling Rosie in on things she had missed while she "slept." Her father died the night she fell. Stuart died a week ago. Amos took over as alpha until Sam challenged him then killed him a few days ago. Rosie tried to take it all in, but she felt like there was more they weren't telling her. A year and a half was a long time. A lot must have happened.

Daniel and Michael had come by to visit the day before. It was good to see them, but it felt strange too. They looked older. More mature. Rosie had wanted so badly to ask why Lucas wasn't with them. She missed him so much that it hurt.

Rosie's grandma stood up to help her back to the bed, but she brushed her off.

"I'm okay," Rosie said. "I can do it."

Rosie unsteadily made her way across the room, acutely aware of both her grandma and Sam holding their hands out in case she fell. With an exhausted sigh, she sat down.

Sam cleared his throat before he spoke. "The doctor said you can be discharged in a day or two. They just want to run a few more tests to make sure you're okay."

As much as she wanted out of that hospital room, the fear of what waited for her outside left a burning feeling in her stomach.

"Why don't you stay with me for a while," Clara said. She must have sensed Rosie's unease. "Let you get your bearings a little."

Rosie looked at Sam, and he smiled at her reassuringly. "Whatever you want, sis."

Rosie nodded slowly and looked down at her hands. She started picking at her nails. They were trimmed and painted purple, and she wondered who'd done that. Had to be Becca. She focused on the polish. The other stuff was too big. Too much. Where did she fit in to this life that had gone on without her?

"Hey." Sam's voice snapped Rosie out of her spiraling thoughts. He squatted so that he could look her in the eye, and he placed a warm hand on hers and squeezed. "It's going to be okay, Rosie. We'll get through this together. I promise."

Rosie gasped as she remembered the same reassuring words from her father. Then it hit her. Those words had been uttered two years ago.

Nothing was okay.

Cold fingers. She couldn't warm them. The temperature in the room was fine. Balmy even. But her fingertips and toes were like ice. The mate bond within her still fizzled low. The embers barely burned. Their glow didn't warm her. The roaring fire lacked kindling.

Where was Lucas?

Tightness in her chest remained. The constant

reminder that not all was well. He was still missing. All would not be well until they were together again.

A soft knock came at the door. Rosie tore her gaze away from the window to look at the nurse who peeked her head into the room. "I have fresh bedding. How would you like a shower, sweetie?"

A shower sounded amazing. But only if...

"Can I take it by myself?" The thought of being bathed by the nurse didn't sit well with her. Every last ounce of her dignity had been slowly stripped away over the last few days. Please let her hold on to something.

"Of course." The nurse's smile brightened. "The doctor cleared it this afternoon."

Thank God.

The nurse stepped forward and set the sheets on the chair. She held a fresh gown and a towel out for Rosie to take as she climbed out of bed. Rosie took the offerings and shuffled across the room to the small bathroom. She stepped inside and closed the door behind her.

Reaching into the tiny shower, she turned the water on all the way to the hot side, but she grumbled when it only turned warm. She slipped the gown off and stepped into the spray, suppressing a moan when the water hit her face. Tiny shampoo and conditioner bottles sat on the ledge, and she took her time washing her hair.

When she stepped out of the shower, she felt like a new person, the stale hospital smells and grime finally replaced by a fresh, clean aroma.

Not finding a brush, she combed her fingers through her long locks. The curls were already a tangled mess. Some things never changed.

She dried herself off with the towel and slipped

the new hospital gown on. When she stepped out of the bathroom, the nurse was finishing making her bed.

"Feel better?" Her chipper voice didn't even grate on Rosie's nerves.

"You have no idea." Rosie stepped forward and sat in the chair next to the bed. "Did anyone visit while I napped earlier?"

"Yes, Martha stopped by." The fact that the nurse knew Rosie's friends and family by name unnerved her a little. "She said she'll see you when you get home. She left you the potted plant by the window over there."

Rosie glanced at the window, where a small houseplant sat in the sun. It needed some love. She would touch it up after the nurse left.

"What about Lucas?" Rosie tried not to sound too hopeful. "Did he come?"

"Who?"

Rosie scowled. The woman seemed to know every person in Rosie's life. How did she not know Lucas? She held her hand above her head. "Tall. Brown hair. My age."

"I'm sorry, sweetie." The nurse looked confused. "I don't know anyone by that description. The only boy your age who came to see you was your brother."

What? That couldn't be right. Rosie averted her gaze, finding the window again. She studied the clouds, her mind working. Her grandmother said Lucas had healed. He'd been injured, but he was fine. Now that she thought more about it, Sam didn't say much about him. Was he okay?

"Oh, there was one other boy your age who came a few times. Cute, shy thing. Blond hair, green eyes."

Calvin. Rosie was touched he'd come to see her, but she really wished it had been Lucas.

"All set." The nurse stood and faced Rosie. "Do you need help getting back into bed?"

Rosie shook her head. "I can handle it."

"Okay, then. Ring if you need anything."

"Thank you," Rosie whispered as she watched her leave.

Rubbing her fingers together, Rosie felt them getting colder.

SIX

ROSIE

Rosie stood and stretched before she climbed back into bed. She had just settled in when another knock came at the door. The head that poked in lifted her spirits to the sky. She fought the urge to jump from the bed and run across the room.

"Becca!"

"Rosie!" Becca ran forward, threw herself on Rosie, and squeezed her. Rosie squeezed back so tightly that she thought she might crack a rib. She didn't care. She just didn't want to let Becca go.

"I don't even know where to begin," Becca said as she pulled away. She was crying so hard, snot dribbled over her upper lip. Wiping her arm across her nose, she sat next to Rosie on the bed, grasping her hand. "I just can't believe it. I never thought I would see you awake again."

"You have no idea how good it is to see you," Rosie said. "Nothing is right. Everything is different. I just can't..."

Rosie stopped talking and stared at Becca. She felt a tremendous amount of guilt in Becca's energy, but it was mixed with anger.

"What is it?" Rosie asked, not really wanting to

know. She didn't think she could take another piece of
bad news.

Fresh tears leaked from Becca's eyes. "Why didn't
you tell me? All these years."

"What?"

"So much for easing into it slowly." Becca rolled
her eyes. "We talked about how to tell you, but I don't
think we really agreed, you know? He wanted to wait
and take it slow. I said we should just rip off the Band-
Aid and tell you quick."

"Becca! What the hell are you talking about?"

"Rosie." She paused, staring straight into Rosie's
eyes. "It just happened, okay? It happened so fast.
One minute, we were just friends... Then I was in
love, you know?"

"No," Rosie said. "I don't know. When are you
going to tell me?"

"Me and Sam," she said. "We're... together."

"Sam?" Rosie was slowly connecting dots that
shouldn't have taken so long to connect. "My Sam?"

"I'm sorry, Rosie!" Becca gushed. "Please don't be
mad! I love you, and your friendship means the world
to me, but I really love him, okay?"

"I'm not... mad," Rosie said slowly. "Just confused, I think."

Rosie looked out the window, trying to compre-
hend what this meant. Sam and Becca... in love.

"I know."

Rosie flinched.

"He told me. I know it's supposed to be, like, this
big secret you're not supposed to tell, but we were getting pretty serious, and I knew something was up."

Guilt flooded through Rosie, and she averted her
gaze.

Becca took Rosie's hand. "I know why you never

told me, but jeez. I really wish you would have. I wouldn't have told anyone."

"I know," Rosie said. "I wanted to. So many times."

Becca nodded. "That's what Sam said."

Rosie looked at Becca carefully. "You don't seem freaked out. I really pictured you freaking out a lot."

"Oh, I did! I totally did. But then I was kidnapped by Amos, and that sort of forced me to come to terms with things faster, you know?"

"Wait." Rosie shook her head. "What?"

Becca's eyes rounded. "Oh, you don't know! Rosie, it was so scary. Somehow, he figured out that Sam told me about the whole werewolf thing. He knocked me out and put me in your basement. He was totally going to eat me."

Rosie closed her eyes. "Oh, Becca. I'm so sorry."

"Sam was so brave." Becca smiled. She looked like a starstruck teenager. "He challenged Amos and be-came... *alpha*." Becca made a show of shivering. "I'm not going to lie. It's sexy as hell."

"Oh my God." Rosie covered her face with her hands. "We'll need to set some ground rules for these conversations. No details, I beg you."

Becca giggled. "I'll keep it PG. I promise."

"So, you know everything?" Rosie asked.

"I know it all," Becca said. "I know you're the only female and that you and your grandma are"—she cupped her hand next to her mouth and whispered—"witches."

Rosie bit back a laugh.

"He told me about your powers. Your healing and the feelings thing. I know that part wasn't really his secret to tell." Becca winced. "But don't be mad. We didn't think you were ever coming back to us."

Rosie smiled. "I'm not mad. I'm kind of relieved, actually. You have no idea how many times I wanted to tell you."

"It explains so many things." Becca shook her head. "You always made me feel better. Always. No matter how freaked out I was—and I freak out a lot—I always felt better with you."

"Yeah, well, you gave me lots of practice when I was learning to use my magic. That's for sure."

Becca pulled Rosie in for another hug.

"I love you," Becca said. "You know that, right?"

Rosie squeezed her tighter, feeling so much better than she had in days.

"I love you too."

~

THEY SPENT the rest of the afternoon sitting on Rosie's bed, talking. Becca told Rosie about how she and Sam had gotten together and about how things were going at her father's restaurant, and of course, she shared more gossip than Rosie really cared to know about.

"So, Patty Johnson is now Patty Hebl, and she's popping out kids. I'm like, jeez, slow down, you know?"

Becca braided Rosie's hair, and Rosie was starting to feel like her old self again. Just like old times, Becca kept Rosie anchored to the real world. She wasn't listening very closely to what Becca was saying, but her voice comforted Rosie in a way nothing else could.

"And I don't know what the deal is with Cassie Barnes. Her skirts keep getting shorter, and she flirts with every man in town." She rolled her eyes. "I mean, she was hanging on Lucas all the time."

Rosie tensed, and Becca stopped braiding her hair.

"Lucas?"

"Crap," Becca whispered. "My big, fat, stupid mouth."

Rosie turned to look at her.

Becca's face froze in a look of horror. She hesitated for a few moments before she spoke. "He was working at my dad's restaurant," she said carefully.

"Okay." Rosie nodded. "Bussing?"

"Bartending." Becca smiled. "He really liked it. He started smiling again. He was messed up for a long time, Rosie. He wasn't the same after you fell."

"I can see him enjoying that." Rosie couldn't keep the tears at bay. They welled in her eyes and spilled onto her cheeks. "Why hasn't he come to see me, Becca? Is there someone else? Is it Cassie—"

"No." Becca shook her head vigorously. "That's not it."

"Then why? He knows I'm awake, right?"

Becca sighed. "I'm going to get into so much trouble for this." She closed her eyes. "Sam said Roger and Lucas disappeared right before you woke up."

"What?" Rosie's heart dropped to her stomach. "Where..."

"No one knows where they went." Becca shrugged. "I'm sorry." After a moment of silence, Becca pulled at her hair, resuming the braid. Rosie waved her away, running her hand through her curls and undoing Becca's work.

"I'm kind of tired." Rosie avoided Becca's gaze as she spoke. "I think I need a nap."

"Are you sure?" When Becca reached for Rosie's shoulder, she shied away from her touch.

Becca snapped her hand back as though she'd

been burned, but Rosie couldn't bring herself to apologize for being rude. She just needed to be alone. Becca sniffled and whispered an apology, but Rosie couldn't bear to look at her.

"It's okay." Rosie scooted under the covers, turning her back to Becca. "I'm just tired. Could we maybe get lunch next week?"

"Yes!" Becca sniffled again. "That would be great! I'll text you."

Rosie nodded and listened as Becca collected her things.

"I'm really, really sorry, Rosie." A hand brushed lightly over the top of Rosie's head before Becca turned and rushed out the door.

As soon as the door clicked shut behind Becca, Rosie buried her head in her pillow and sobbed.

A NOISE WOKE Rosie from a dreamless sleep. Her eyes flitted around the darkened room. Still in the hospital. It took a bit to get her bearings. She could just make out the outline of the couch in the corner, where her grandmother had slept the last two nights. Rosie had insisted she go home and get some rest in her own bed.

An unsettling feeling came over her, like she wasn't alone. She sat up slowly, turning on her bedside lamp. The room was empty, but the feeling lingered. Something was off. She sat back in bed and stared at the ceiling tiles. Closing her eyes, she tried to calm herself. Nothing was there. It was in her head.

She took a few deep breaths and tried to get herself to go back to sleep, but her mind wandered to the conversation she'd had with Becca earlier. The uneasy feeling subsided, replaced by a growing ache in her chest. Where did Lucas go? Would he be back? A shiver ran through her as the embers of her mate bond flickered weakly.

When she opened her eyes, the ceiling tiles came back into view. She'd counted them a dozen times. A tear slipped from Rosie's eye and trailed down the side of her face, into her hair.

She closed her eyes again, rolled onto to her side, and opened them once more. A vase was sitting on her bedside table. She had lots of flower arrangements in her room, but this one was new. Blackened petals. Wilted leaves. The smell of rotten stems and stale water hit her, and she wrinkled her nose. She sat up and stared at them. They hadn't been there when she had gone to bed.

Who would leave dead roses in her room?

SEVEN

SAM

Sam took a deep breath, trying to calm the gerbil making the wheel in his stomach spin. He was about to have his first video conference with the Council since he announced he'd challenged Amos and killed him. He rocked back in the office chair, tapping his fingers against the large mahogany desk. The spacious office felt claustrophobic. What he wouldn't give for Rosie's calming energy right now.

The computer gave a strange chirp, and Sam clicked the icon to join the call. The three United States Werewolf Council members filled his screen, their presence no less intimidating than if they were standing in the office with him.

"Sam." Jagger greeted him with a tight smile. "How is your pack acclimating to the shift in leadership?"

Right down to business, then. Okay. "They're doing well." Sam cleared his throat. "We've had an eventful week."

"So we've heard." Garrett raised an eyebrow. "We talked to Shawn Beckett."

Sam swallowed, trying to keep the confusion from showing on his face. Why would they speak to Shawn

Beckett? The Council only spoke to alphas. Marcus was alpha to the Beckett pack. Sam chose to stay silent, waiting for Garrett to continue. His father's words rang in his head. *Keep a straight face, and stay silent. Let them do the talking.*

"Shawn told us that Roger and Lucas have rejoined the Beckett pack."

"What?" Sam sat up straighter.

Roland smirked. "He had no idea."

So much for keeping a straight face. "They didn't tell anyone they were leaving. I didn't know that Shawn..." Sam gave up trying to hide his confusion. "What about Marcus?"

The Council members exchanged glances.

"Marcus Beckett is in a hospital, on life support." Garrett steepled his fingers. "I take it you didn't know that Shawn Beckett is now the Beckett pack alpha."

"Amos didn't share much pack business with us."

"I see." Garrett glanced at the other Council members.

Sam squirmed. Great. The meeting was off to a wonderful start. Damn Amos.

"The rogue has been causing a lot of trouble." Roland narrowed his eyes. "We've heard multiple reports that it smells of your pack."

"I can't explain that." Sam averted his gaze. "None of the Harts have left our territory. The Cramers are convinced it's us, and they've hit back by attacking livestock and pets in our area—"

"If this situation isn't brought under control, we'll be forced to step in," Jagger said tersely. "It's getting out of hand."

"I understand." Sam took a breath. "I'll arrange a meeting with the other alphas."

"That would be best," Garrett replied. "Now that

there is new leadership, maybe this rogue situation can finally be brought under control."

Sam took a deep breath. "There's something else." He eyed the Council members. "My sister, Rosie, is awake."

Their reactions would have been funny if the situation weren't so serious. All three dropped their jaws.

"When did this happen?" Jagger asked. "How is she?"

"Just a few days ago." Sam swallowed. "She's doing well. She's being released from the hospital today."

"Already?" Garrett's eyes rounded. "That's incredible. How is that possible?"

"I think you already know the answer to that." Roland's voice was barely audible. "The rumors are true."

The Council members exchanged glances again, and Sam's stomach flipped.

"We need to speak with the World Council about this." Jagger's words were clipped, and he barely glanced at Sam. "We'll be in touch."

The Council members disappeared from the screen in a blink.

Did they just hang up on him?

Sam sat back and exhaled a long, slow breath. What did Roland mean about the rumors? Sam recalled William Cramer's threat when Rosie had been attacked by Bruce. He'd witnessed Rosie using witchcraft. William had promised to keep it quiet if they spared Bruce. Did he go to the Council anyway?

He turned to stare out the window. Lucas and Roger were back with the Becketts. Lucas had never felt completely at home at Hart House. Sam should be happy for his friend.

He slammed a fist down on his desk. Was it selfish of him to be pissed that Lucas couldn't even be bothered to tell him goodbye? Lucas was his brother. Maybe not in blood, but in every way that counted.

Sam sighed and ran a hand through his hair. His first week as alpha was off to a really rocky start.

EIGHT

SAM

SAM SHUFFLED THE PILLOWS AROUND ON HIS BED
for the fourth time. He sniffed, making sure any lingering body odor or dirty-sock smells were gone.
Martha did a good job of keeping the place clean, but
it was hard to keep up with a house full of
filthy men.

He rushed to the bathroom and checked again to
make sure the toilet was clean and the seat was down.
On the counter, a new toothbrush sat, still in its packaging. Pink. Becca liked pink. She would probably
bring her own, but no harm in having an extra, just in
case.

After returning to the bedroom, he peered out the
window. He'd left the gate open at the end of the driveway. She should be arriving any moment. Talking
her into coming had been a monumental feat. She'd
tried backing out at least three or four times. He'd
been as patient as he could, trying to remember he
was asking her to spend the weekend in a house full
of werewolves.

In the house where she'd almost been killed by a
werewolf.

Sam clenched his jaw as he recalled the image of

Becca huddled inside that cell. If he could go back in time and kill Amos all over again, he would.

At the soft hum of an engine in the distance, Sam dialed up his hearing. Definitely Becca's Bug. He turned and shot through his room, down the hall, and nearly tripped over his feet on the stairs. He opened the door, and sunlight hit his face as he stepped onto the veranda.

He held his breath as he watched her car slowly make its way up the driveway and around the circle in front of the house. She parked in front of the sidewalk and cut the engine. He stood waiting for her to get out of the car, but she didn't move. Then the sound hit him. Crying. Sobbing.

Sam was down the porch stairs before he realized he was moving. He found himself next to the driver's-side door, ready to rip it off the frame. He took a breath to control himself and slowly opened the door. Becca's hiccupped sobs hit him, and his stomach clenched. He crouched next to her, running a hand up and down her arm.

"What is it?" He tried to keep his voice even. "What's wrong?"

"I... I..." Becca tried speaking between sobs. "I... t-t-told... R-Rosie..."

"You told Rosie what?" Sam continued rubbing her arm, trying to make sense of the spluttered words.

Becca took a deep, stuttering breath. "Yesterday, I told Rosie a-about Lucas. I'm s-s-so sorry, Sam. You were r-r-right. We should have w-w-waited. She was s-s-s-so upset!" Becca wailed and covered her face with her hands.

Crap. Sam clenched his jaw and tried not to let his frustration show. "It's okay, Becca. She was going to find out eventually."

"She probably hates me now!"

"She doesn't hate you."

"You didn't see her, Sam. She wouldn't look at me."

"She was just upset."

"I know, but she usually talks to me when she's upset."

Sam pulled Becca toward him and hugged her, running his hand up and down her back. "She'll come around." Silently, he hoped he was right. His sister had been through so much. He wished he could spare her this additional heartache.

What should he tell Rosie? If he told her Lucas was with the Becketts, she would want to go to him. If Lucas chose his pack over Rosie, Sam wasn't sure she could survive that.

No. He couldn't put her through that. He would ask Shawn to give Lucas the message that Rosie was well. If Lucas didn't come back to Rosie, then they had their answer. Sam could try to break the news to his sister gently once he knew where Lucas stood.

Until then, Sam would keep the news of Lucas's whereabouts to himself.

～

Next to Sam, Becca exhaled a deep sigh that sounded content. He pulled her closer against him and kissed her forehead. Her bare skin against his chest was soft. Her long blond hair fell over her back, and he ran his hands through the silky locks.

The day had been a success. After her initial meltdown, she'd calmed, and they spent the rest of the day wandering the grounds. Sam showed her the gardens and explained how much more beautiful they would be when Rosie was home to give the plants life again.

They toured the entire house. Becca said she'd only ever seen the kitchen, Rosie's room, and the basement. At dinner, Daniel made small talk, and Michael stayed silent, for the most part. That had been at Sam's request. The last thing he wanted was for Becca to hear an inappropriate joke or for Michael to ask Becca to pull his finger.

Not that Becca wasn't already familiar with Daniel and Michael. She knew them well enough. They'd spent plenty of time at Miller's over the years. Still, he wanted the weekend to go perfectly, and fart jokes didn't fit the agenda.

"I'm going to take some clothes to Rosie tomorrow," Becca said softly. "Something for her to wear home from the hospital."

Sam nodded. "I think she'd like that."

"She probably hasn't even thought about it." Becca rolled her eyes. "Girl needs a whole new wardrobe. I'd be dreaming about it for weeks, but you know Rosie. She'll be cringing at the thought of going shopping. Doesn't mean I'm not going to drag her into every store on Main Street."

"Yeah, she never really liked shopping much." Sam traced a finger down Becca's arm. "I have a credit card for her. I'll make sure she gets it before you take her. I have a phone for her too. Even managed to get her the same phone number she had before."

Becca smiled at him. "You're such a good brother."

"I'm trying to think of what she'll need." Sam scowled. "I want to try to give her some kind of normal."

"You're doing great."

Sam looked into Becca's eyes. "Today was good. Hart House isn't so bad, right?"

"As long as we stay away from the basement, it's great."

"Yeah." Sam frowned. "I wish I could get rid of the basement."

Becca raised an eyebrow. "You can."

"What?"

"You're alpha." She smiled shyly.

"Yeah." Sam rolled his eyes. "I'll just rebuild Hart House and gut the basement. No sweat."

"I would if I were you," Becca said. "I don't know how you manage to live above that creepy place all the time. Knowing what happened down there."

Sam furrowed his brow. He hadn't really thought about it, but she was right. Amos wasn't the last thing that remained of the horrors of the Hart family past. The basement was a constant reminder of all that was evil about the old traditions. Would he ever be able to go down there again without the image of Becca cringing in that cell resurfacing in his mind? Something cold and uncomfortable settled in his bones, and the Hart House he'd always known and loved suddenly felt different. It tainted the good memories he had and left him feeling disgusted and angry.

NINE

ROSIE

Daytime television hadn't changed in the last year and a half. It still sucked. Rosie clicked through the channels on autopilot. She had no desire to watch the news. Soaps—uh-uh. Talks shows—pass. Rosie tossed the remote onto the bed and stared up at the ceiling, hoping she wouldn't die of boredom before noon. She'd been counting down the minutes to her checkout time. Too much time alone with her thoughts hadn't been going well. After crying herself to sleep, she'd woken the next morning and cried into her breakfast. When the tears dried up, an emptiness took hold.

The fading embers of the mate bond left her cold and hollow. She shoved it to the back corner of her brain. Too much. The ache. The loss. It was too much to bear. Shove it down. Swallow it. Don't think about it.

Her grandmother should have arrived already. Without Clara's company, Rosie resorted to counting ceiling tiles again. She was on number sixteen when the door clicked open, and she shot up in bed. Her jaw dropped when she saw the blond-haired boy standing in the doorway.

"Rosie?" Calvin's green eyes held more sadness and tension than she remembered. He studied her before he looked away bashfully. "I hope it's okay that I came."

Rosie snapped herself out of her shock. "Of course! Calvin, come in."

A small smile twitched at his lips as he crossed the room. Rosie stretched her arms out, inviting him into a hug. He sat on the edge of the bed and embraced her. She wrapped her arms around him and laid her head on his shoulder, closing her eyes.

For a moment, she pretended he was Lucas, and she tightened her hold on him. Guilt tugged at her, and her eyes popped open. She pulled away and forced a smile.

"I'm really happy to see you awake," Calvin said. "I never thought I would talk to you again."

"Thank you for coming to visit me," Rosie said. "It means a lot."

"I wanted to see you."

Rosie bit her lip then asked, "Are things going better for you at home?"

Calvin looked away, and his Adam's apple bobbed as he swallowed. "No."

"I'm sorry."

"It isn't your fault." Calvin turned back to her. Tears misted in his eyes, but he smiled. "You made things better. Even if it was just for a little while."

Rosie nudged him. "You'll make everything right when you're alpha."

"I'm not going to be alpha." Calvin lowered his head. "My dad all but banished me. He named Ethan as next in line. Bruce will take over if Dad steps down or dies before Ethan is of age."

"You're kidding!" Rosie's stomach dropped.

Calvin shrugged. "It's better this way. He doesn't try to push me and leaves me alone. Just pretends I don't exist."

"But, Calvin, the Cramer pack will be so much better with you. You can change things—"

"No, Rosie. It's done."

"So you're just going to let your family keep doing what they do? Hurting people? Spreading hate? Calvin, you could make real change."

Calvin shook his head. "The Cramer pack will never change. My family is set in its ways. I'm more worried about..."

"Worried about what?" Rosie tried to meet Calvin's eyes, but he looked away again.

"Nothing." Calvin cleared his throat. When he turned back to her, he smiled. "Let's talk about something else. How are things with you?"

Rosie sighed. She filled Calvin in on her last few days at the hospital but left out the details about Lucas. It dawned on her that Calvin had visited on more than one occasion, and she wrinkled her nose in confusion.

"How did you get here? I didn't think you had a car. And I doubt your dad was cool with you coming to see me."

Calvin shrugged. "Like I said, I've pretty much become invisible to him. I have my own car. Bruce questioned me once when I disappeared for a day, but when I told him I went to a few different hiking spots, he got bored and didn't ask me about it again."

"Well, I'm glad you were able to get away long enough to come," Rosie said. "It really is good to see your face."

Calvin's smile brightened his features, and some of the sadness left his eyes.

After they talked for another half hour, he stood. Before he turned to leave, he looked her over as though contemplating something. Then he took a breath, leaned down, and kissed her. The kiss was soft and sweet, but Rosie could feel the urges pulsing through him. The internal struggle to contain himself came through in his touch, like a dog fighting the urge to go for the treat he'd been told not to touch.

When he pulled away, he stayed close, his face inches from hers. He stared into her eyes as he whispered softly, "You once told me not to be afraid to do that with other girls, but there will never be another girl like you.".

~

Rosie stared at the television but paid no attention to what was on. She touched her lips as she thought again about Calvin's bold move. A huge part of her wished it had made her feel something for him. But it just made her miss Lucas even more.

A knock on the door made her pulse race with excitement. Her grandma was finally going to take her home.

The door opened. Instead of her grandmother, Becca poked her head in. The worry etched on her best friend's face tugged at her heart, and Rosie's guilt made her frown. She forced a smile and waved Becca in.

Becca stepped into the room, carrying a large department store bag. "Rosie, I'm so, so—"

"Please don't apologize, Becca." Rosie sighed. "I owe *you* an apology. I shot the messenger. I didn't mean to do that."

"You were upset." Becca bit her lip. "I hate that I'm the one who made you that way."

"Not your fault."

Becca shrugged. "I know." She gestured to the bag. "Anyway. Thought you might need something to wear home from the hospital. I'm betting your grandmother will bring something for you, but let's face it, I have much better taste."

Rosie hadn't even thought about that. How had she not thought about what she would wear? None of her clothes from before would fit her now.

"Don't worry." Becca smiled, gesturing to the bag again. "It's nothing too out there. I thought you and I could go shopping eventually. Get you some clothes."

Rosie frowned. "You know I hate shopping."

"Yes, I do." Becca laughed. "Believe me. But you don't have much of an excuse to say no this time. You need clothes. And who better to guide you in getting a whole new wardrobe than me?"

God help her. Becca would have Rosie in dresses and high heels. Rosie tried her best to make her smile look genuine. "How can I say no to that?"

"You can't." Becca sat down on Rosie's bed and pulled the clothes out of the bag. A plain white tee and a pair of black yoga pants. Simple enough. Rosie could wear them. Maybe she was being harsh. As much as Becca tried to pull Rosie out of her comfort zone, she knew Rosie like no one else.

"Thank you, Becca." Rosie placed a hand on hers. "Really."

Becca waved her off. "Go put this stuff on so that we can leave as soon as your grandmother gets here. I don't know about you, but I've had enough of this place."

"Ha!" Rosie grabbed the clothes and shuffled to

the bathroom. She shouted over her shoulder as she closed the bathroom door behind her, "Preaching to the choir!"

~

WHEN CLARA finally made her way into Rosie's hospital room, Becca and Rosie were tucked together under the covers, watching an episode of *Judge Judy*.

"Oh God." Clara rolled her eyes. "How can you watch this nonsense?"

"Please tell me we can go home now," Rosie said.

"You have a couple of forms to sign at the front desk, then we can go." Clara smiled and held up a bag of clothes. "I see you don't need these."

After pouting all the way down to the car because hospital policy required that she ride in a wheelchair, Rosie bolted out of the chair and leaped through the sliding glass doors at the exit. When she finally inhaled a deep breath of fresh outdoor air, every cell in her body came alive.

"Are you going to hang your head out the window on the way home too?" Becca laughed at Rosie as she continued sucking fresh air in through her nose.

"If Grandma will let me, I might."

Becca laughed again. "Will you call me later?"

Rosie nodded then paused. "I don't have a phone."

"Sam has one for you." Becca patted her arm. "He's been meticulous about getting everything you might need. I'm sure he'll bring it over tomorrow. I know he's planning to drop by."

When Clara brought the car around to the front of the hospital, Becca waited for Rosie to climb in before she said goodbye and headed off toward her own vehicle. Rosie watched her go before she shifted her gaze to her grandmother. Clara focused her attention on the task of driving, so Rosie stayed silent. Her grandmother drove like the stereotypical old woman—radio down, two hands on the wheel, and her face practically plastered to the windshield as she watched for other cars.

Despite Clara's old-lady, snail-paced driving, the trip didn't take long. As they exited the highway and made their way down the long stretches of road that cut through the forest, Rosie felt comforted by the towering trees.

When they arrived in Hanks Hollow, Rosie studied the buildings. Everything seemed the same. She could almost pretend she hadn't been gone more than a year. A few familiar faces passed by on the sidewalk as they drove down Main Street.

They ventured out the other side of town to her grandmother's lakeside cottage. As the car slowly crunched over the gravel driveway, the little house came into view. The familiar porch with flowers blossoming all around it. The trellis over the walkway. The crab apple trees. The beach in the distance. For the first time since Rosie had woken, she felt herself relax.

TEN

ROSIE

Early September meant many of the flowers had gone to sleep for the season, but as Rosie walked through the garden with her grandmother, she concentrated her energy on those that still held on before the chill of fall set in. Drooping leaves perked, and new flowers blossomed.

"Rosie." Clara smiled. "Your power has grown. I can feel your energy."

Rosie felt the presence of a doe in the woods, and she called to it. The deer jogged out of the trees toward them and paused. Clara's breath hitched, but Rosie just smiled. It ducked its head and inched toward Rosie's outstretched hand. Rosie patted its head then silently shooed her away. The doe took off for the woods again, leaping in a practiced pattern and expertly dodging trees and roots.

"Amazing," Clara said.

They headed toward the front of the house. Clara groaned as she lowered herself onto the top step of the porch, and Rosie followed, easing onto the step below her.

"How are you doing, honey?" Clara looked up at

the darkening sky. "You must have a lot going through that pretty little noggin' of yours."

Slowly, snippets of her time away crawled into Rosie's mind. They'd been creeping in over the last few days. It started as flashes of images. Then the memories started to take hold. The dreams. The gods. Her father, her mother. Stuart...

"Penny for your thoughts?" Clara nudged her shoulder, bringing her to the present. How much should Rosie tell her? She was the least likely to think Rosie was crazy or to explain it all away as a weird endorphin rush. Yet something felt private about it. Too private for her grandmother, even.

"Just... Just thinking about what's next."

"What do you *want* to do next?" Clara pulled on one of Rosie's curls. "The world is at your feet. Your choices are endless."

"Maybe I'll start with my GED." Rosie sighed. "I need something attainable to focus on."

"That's as good a place to start as any." Clara laughed. "Have you given any thought to what lies beyond that?"

"I used to think about it a lot." Rosie tilted her head. "About how I would use my gifts for good. The way you do."

Clara nodded, urging her to continue.

"I was thinking about massage." Rosie glanced at her grandmother bashfully. "It would be a way to heal and share my energy. What do you think?"

"I think it's a fabulous idea." Clara beamed.

Heat flooded Rosie's cheeks. "Thanks, Grandma."

They sat in silence. In the distance, lake water lapped against the shore. Crickets and frogs sang in the forest. Rosie's mind went to Lucas, and she fought against tears when she felt the sting in her sinuses.

"What is it?" Clara's voice was gentle. "What has you so sad?"

"Lucas is gone." Rosie focused her gaze on the woods. "He and his father disappeared before I woke up. No one knows where they went."

Clara was silent for a few moments before she spoke quietly. "That boy loves you. I felt it pour out of him in a way I've felt only one other time in my long, long life. There's a bond between you, isn't there? Something strong."

Tears dripped down Rosie's cheeks as she scrunched her face in agony. She choked out her answer. "Yes."

"It's stronger than love."

"Yes." Rosie's voice wavered. "A mate bond."

"Then you'll be together again, dear." Clara rubbed Rosie's back soothingly. "Something like that is bigger than you. Bigger than all of us. The gods have a plan. You'll find your way back together."

~

THE AROMA of lavender incense filled the air, and soft bubbles trailed over Rosie's skin. If the bath water hadn't started to go tepid, she could have stayed in the tub all night. A song she didn't recognize played softly from her grandmother's old radio on the bathroom counter. She hummed with the catchy tune as she rinsed the last of the conditioner from her hair.

The station switched to a commercial, but the song continued to buzz in her brain. She would need to catch up on what she'd missed over the last year. Maybe she could get Lucas to make her a playlist.

Rosie froze, realizing she'd made herself forget

again. Easier that way. When she blocked it all out, the pain eased. She swallowed, pushing it all to the back of her mind. She could make her own playlist. Tears pricked her eyes, and she cursed under her breath as she ground her palms into her eyelids, stemming the flow. After a few deep breaths, she steadied her shaking limbs.

Water puddled on the floor as she stepped from the tub and reached for the towels her grandmother had left for her on the bathroom counter. After she wrapped one snugly around her body, she used the other to squeeze water from her hair.

Humming the tune, which was now stuck in her head, she padded out of the bathroom and into the living room. Clara snored softly in the recliner, and Rosie smiled as she made her way across the room toward her. She pulled the throw blanket up to cover her grandmother's shoulders.

Then she turned and headed back to her bedroom. As she crossed the threshold into the room, a chill ran over her. Something was off. An energy left her feeling uneasy. Her stomach clenched as she stepped quickly across the room to the closet. Clara had left her some sweats and T-shirts to get her by until she had the chance to go shopping. Rosie let the towels drop to the floor then grabbed an oversized tee and pulled it over her head. She chose a pair of sweatpants and slid them on, tightening the drawstring around her waist. The too-long legs bunched over her feet, but they would do. The uneasy feeling didn't subside, and she felt the urge to leave the room quickly.

It was when she bent down to pick the towels up off the floor that she saw it. She froze, her breath caught in her throat. Spread across the bed were a dozen dead roses bathed in a pool of red. The metallic smell hit her like a tidal wave. It was blood.

Rosie screamed.

"You're sure you didn't hear anyone?" Sheriff Hill repeated for what seemed like the hundredth time.

"I didn't hear anything," Rosie insisted. "When I left my room to go take a bath, nothing was on the bed. When I came back, there they were."

Rosie glanced toward the bedroom and shuddered. She and her grandma sat at the kitchen table, giving the sheriff as much detail as they could muster. After Clara had heard Rosie screaming, she came running. When she saw the bed, she shoved Rosie out to the kitchen and called the sheriff immediately.

"And you were sleeping?" the sheriff asked Clara again.

"Yes," she said. "I had my after-dinner tea, just like I do every night. I got drowsy, so I sat in the recliner and fell asleep."

"And this is the tea you drank?" He lifted the cup from the table with a gloved hand and sniffed the contents.

"Yes," Clara said. "It's just chamomile."

"Get some prints off this, and send the contents

out for testing." He handed the cup to one of his deputies.

The deputy nodded and headed toward the front door.

"Wait." Horrified, Rosie gripped the table. "Do you think my grandma was drugged?"

"It's hard to know for sure until we test it." The sheriff scratched his head. "But she slept through a break-in. It's possible." He eyed Rosie and Clara and sighed. "Is there somewhere you can stay tonight while we finish our investigation?"

Rosie swallowed thickly. It hadn't dawned on her that they would need to sleep somewhere else. The whole situation was so surreal.

"I'll get us a hotel room," Clara said.

The sheriff nodded as he checked over his notes one more time. "We'll be in touch." He put a hand on Clara's arm and smiled at Rosie. "We'll figure this out."

"Thank you, Craig," Clara said.

A loud commotion by the door turned to shouting, and Rosie recognized her brother's voice. "Let me through! She's my sister!"

Rosie started to jump up from the table, but her grandma put a hand on her arm. Clara stood and went to the front of the house. After an exchange of words with the officer guarding the door, she came back to the kitchen with Sam and Becca in tow.

"Are you both okay?" Sam's wide eyes trailed over Rosie before they flitted over to Clara, and Rosie wondered what her grandma had told him when she called.

"We're fine." Clara raised her hands in a calming gesture.

Sam pulled Rosie into a hug. His arms crushed her as they wrapped around her back.

"You can't stay here." A stern voice accompanied his furrowed brow and determined brown eyes as he pulled away, and he suddenly reminded her so much of her father that it took her breath away. "Neither of you. It isn't safe."

Becca pushed past him, taking her turn to give Rosie a hug. Sam and Becca's presence reassured Rosie, and her anxiety melted away. Then she realized after a beat that it was thanks to her grandma. Rosie felt Clara's calming energy enveloping her.

Clara glanced toward the chaotic scene. "We've already discussed getting a hotel room."

"You're both welcome to stay with me," Becca volunteered. "I have a pull-out couch."

Rosie knew her grandma's impulse would be to tell Becca she didn't want to impose, but Rosie wanted to take her friend up on the offer. She didn't want to stay in a hotel room.

"You're such a sweetheart, Becca." Clara put a hand on Becca's cheek. "Rosie, why don't you stay with Becca? I'll get the hotel room. I'm sure they'll let me back home in a day or two."

"Or..." Sam stared at Rosie. "You can come home. It's the safest place for you."

Rosie's mouth twitched. She wanted nothing more than to go home, but the home she wanted to return to didn't exist anymore, and she was terrified to face the one that had taken its place. The home with no father. No Stuart. No Lucas or Roger.

"I'm not sure I'm ready for that, Sam." Rosie bit her lip and pretended not to notice his disappointment.

"Rosie, you can't hide forever." Sam's expression

shifted, and he looked like her father again. "Things are different, and it's going to be difficult to face your new reality. But the longer you put it off, the harder it's going to be."

Tears stung Rosie's eyes. When did Sam become a grown-up?

"Your brother is right." Clara stretched an arm around Rosie's shoulders. "It's time for you to go home."

~

FROM THE OUTSIDE, Hart House looked the same. Under the bright moonlight, the massive house with the giant veranda greeted her like an old friend, inviting her in. She stepped through the front door, and echoes of the past swept over her. Games of hide-and-seek and tag. Good-natured ribbing at the dining-room table. Loud, violent Monopoly nights that got out of hand.

She swallowed the lump in her throat and stepped into the foyer. Nothing had changed. The same paintings hung on the walls. The same knick-knacks were on the entry table. To the right, in the living room, the same leather couches sat by the giant stone fireplace. To the left, in the den, the large ma-hogany desk was still in front of the giant bay window across from the sitting area and the office fireplace. Rosie could see the dining table down the hall. She closed her eyes and pictured her father sitting at the head of the table, watching over the pack, a smile on his face.

"It's late."

Rosie jumped when Sam placed a hand on her shoulder.

"Why don't you head to bed. We'll talk in the morning."

"Is my room..."

"Just the way you left it."

Something about that felt wrong. Her room had sat empty all this time? Rosie turned to the stairs and slowly made her way up toward her bedroom. Halfway up, she turned to Sam, unsure, but he gave her a reassuring smile, and she jogged the rest of the way to the top.

As she opened the door to her room, she held her breath. Sam had been right. The bed had been made with the same sheets. Her plants sat in their same spots. Someone, probably Martha, must have watered them. In the bathroom, her hairbrush still sat on the bathroom counter, red curls still coiled in its bristles.

Fresh toiletries had been laid out. All her favorites. The lavender soap her grandma made for her. Shampoo, conditioner, and lotion. Fresh towels lay neatly folded on the racks.

Rosie stepped out of the bathroom and across her bedroom to the French doors that led to the balcony. She opened the doors, and a rush of cool night air brushed over her. Beyond the immaculate lawn below, the forest lay quiet. It seemed to hold its breath with her. Waiting.

"I'll be there tomorrow," she promised.

TWELVE
SAM

Sleep evaded Sam. Too many thoughts ran through his mind. Lucas... the Council... the rogue... the other alphas... Becca... Rosie.

Who'd broken into Clara's house? Who'd threatened his sister? His fists bunched in the sheets as anger boiled in his veins. She hadn't even been out of the hospital a full day. It had to be someone close. Of course, the entire town talked about that weird Hart girl who'd woken from a coma—everyone knew about her. Some things never changed. Poor Rosie had been called a freak since kindergarten. People were cruel.

The sun still sat below the horizon when Sam dressed and headed down to the garage. Clara's house had been too crowded for him to pick up any kind of scent yesterday, but no one would be there now. Time to do some sniffing.

He made the quick drive through town to Clara's little cottage and parked in the driveway. Sneaking inside was a piece of cake—courtesy of the key he'd taken from Rosie. He stepped quietly through the darkened house, taking deep breaths through his nose. Incense... Clara's old-lady smell... Rosie... aftershave and cologne leftover from the police.

It was no use. Too many people had been through.

Ready to give up, Sam turned toward the door, but as he took a step, he froze. There... one scent out of place. It smelled of their pack. When a werewolf shifted from human form to wolf form, the scent changed with it. A wolf had definitely set foot in the house. Not Rosie... and none of the other pack members had been there. He sniffed again. Not Daniel or Michael... Amos? Yes, it smelled like Amos.

Impossible. Amos was dead. Sam took another long whiff, but the scent was lost among the thousands of herbs, oils, and plants Clara kept on the shelves.

Damn.

After stomping out of the house and back to his SUV, Sam climbed inside. Just as he started the engine, his phone vibrated in his back pocket. He dug it out and looked at the caller ID. Not recognizing the number, he answered with an impatient huff. "Hello?"

"Sam," Jagger rasped, and Sam sat up straighter.

"Jagger. What can I do for you?"

"The Council will be at Hart House next Monday. Two o'clock. Be sure the entire pack is in attendance."

"Of course. Does—"

Sam pulled his phone away from his ear and looked at it. Jagger had hung up. He threw the device onto the passenger seat and ran his hands through his hair, fisting his fingers into the strands and fighting the urge to pull. Being alpha would make him bald if he wasn't careful.

He pulled the truck out to the road and made the drive back to Hart House.

~

"Is she coming down?" Michael spoke with his mouth full, spraying pieces of egg across the table.

"Gross, Michael!" Daniel wiped stray pieces of egg from his shirt. "Swallow first, then talk, you heathen."

When Sam had arrived home from Clara's earlier, he'd found Michael and Daniel camped outside Rosie's room. Worried they would wake her up, he corralled them downstairs for breakfast.

"I don't know," Sam answered. "Yesterday was a lot. Maybe she wants a little extra sleep."

"Isn't a year and a half enough sleep?" Michael barked out a laugh.

"Dude." Daniel said, shaking his head. "Too soon."

Sam scowled. "You're a doofus, Michael."

"Come on." Michael shrugged. "It was a little bit funny."

Sam ignored him and cleared his throat. "I'm going to need you both on high alert."

"Don't worry, Sam." Michael sat up straight. "Whoever left those roses for Rosie isn't getting within a mile of her again. We'll make sure of it."

"You know we'll do our best to keep her safe," Daniel chimed in. "Whatever it takes."

"I know I can count on you guys." Sam smiled at them, but it faded as he continued. "I dropped by Clara's house this morning, and I smelled someone familiar."

"What?" Daniel's eyes rounded. "Who?"

Sam sighed. "I'm pretty sure I smelled Amos."

"Sam..." Michael's face scrunched with confusion. "Amos is dead. I had the pleasure of getting rid of his body."

"I know that," Sam snapped. "But I definitely smelled one of the pack, and I could have sworn it was Amos's greasy scent. You know how he always had that undercurrent of..." Sam gestured with his hand, trying to find the right word.

"Yeah." Daniel and Michael spoke together, both wrinkling their noses like they smelled the stench.

"Has he ever been there before? Maybe it was left over from some other time," Daniel reasoned.

"I don't know." Sam shook his head. "It's weird. Just keep alert." Checking his watch, Sam scooted away from the table. He had a video call scheduled with the other alphas at nine, and he didn't want to be late. "I'll catch you guys later."

Sam made his way down the hall and around the corner to the office then slid the pocket door closed. After taking a deep breath, he went to the desk, took a seat, and booted up the laptop. He barely had the video-conference app open when the call came in. He clicked on the icon to join the call. Shawn Beckett appeared in one box on the screen, and William Cramer appeared in another.

"Sam Hart." William spoke first. "The new Hart alpha. How is that going?"

"We've got a lot going on here, but things are going well. Thank you for asking, William. How is your pack?"

"My pack is well. Strong as ever." William smiled. "Shawn, I hear your pack has grown."

Shawn cleared his throat, and something that looked like anxiety crossed his face. "Yes. Roger and Lucas have rejoined our pack, and we're happy to have them back."

A rock settled in Sam's stomach. He tried to keep his face neutral. "I'm happy for them. I know they missed their family very much. We miss them, but I want them to be happy."

"Thank you, Sam." Shawn dipped his head. "That's very gracious."

"I have news that I'm hoping you'll pass along to them." Sam cleared his throat. "They left their phones behind, or I would have contacted them sooner."

"Of course." Shawn nodded. "What is it?"

"My sister, Rosie, is awake."

Shawn's eyes rounded for a moment before his lips pressed into a thin line, worry etched across his forehead. The expression vanished quickly, and he smiled. "Of course. I'll pass that message to them. They'll be happy to hear it."

"I'm surprised to hear this," William said. "I thought it was certain she wouldn't come out of her coma."

"She's awake and doing well," Sam said. "She's home."

William's jaw dropped. "Home? Already?"

"The doctors called it a miracle," Sam said carefully.

"A miracle?" William raised an eyebrow. "Or something else?"

"Does it matter?" Sam gave a tight smile. "She's doing well. *That's* all that matters."

"Of course." William gave one of his artificial smiles that made Sam's skin crawl. "You all must be thrilled."

"I am. We all are. Now, about the rogue." Sam took a breath, ready to change the subject. "I have heard the reports that it smells of our pack, and I want to assure you that I'm as confused about that as any-one. I would like very much to find out who the rogue is. I'm willing to work with you to figure it all out if we can agree to move forward peacefully."

"You have full cooperation from the Beckett pack, Sam," Shawn said. "We're ready to find out who it is and turn him over to the Council so that they can deal with him once and for all. Your support is appreciated."

Silence stretched as William stayed quiet. Finally, the trademark smug smile stretched across his face again. "Of course, Sam. I'm glad to hear the Hart pack is finally willing to admit their wrongs and do what they can to correct them."

William was baiting Sam, trying to get him to argue that the Hart pack had done nothing wrong. It took every ounce of Sam's strength not to bite. His father's warnings rang in his head. The old lectures about William's tricks came back to him.

"Wonderful. I'm glad the Cramers understand this was all a misunderstanding and will stand down on the attacks on Hart territory." Sam smiled. "It's really great how we all work so well together."

After a pause, William nodded. "It is, isn't it. I'll tell Adam and George to back off."

THIRTEEN
ROSIE

When Rosie peeled her eyes open, she stared at a familiar ceiling. Her ceiling. For a blissful moment, she pretended the past few days had all been a dream. Any moment now, her father would pound on her door, demanding she wake up and get ready for school. Downstairs, she and Lucas would steal glances at each other across the breakfast table as they spoke to each other telepathically. His eyes like turquoise water in the Caribbean Sea....

She pressed her head into her pillow and pulled her covers up to her chin as she rolled toward the window. A bright, cloudless sky with the sun high overhead told her she'd slept late. Really late. The desire to stay in bed longer was trumped by an obnoxious growl in her stomach.

With a frustrated groan, she pushed her covers back and rolled out of bed. After she padded across the room, she rummaged through her duffel bag on the floor by the door. Sam must have brought it up for her at some point. She hadn't had much to pack when she left her grandmother's, but at least she had a couple pairs of sweats.

After choosing a gray T-shirt and a pair of black

sweatpants, she shuffled off to the bathroom. She took a quick shower, dressed, and pulled her hair into a loose bun. Opening the bedroom door, she peeked her head into the hallway. No one was there. With a little sigh of relief, she crept down the stairs. In the foyer, she stood for a moment, not sure where to go or what to do.

Food. She needed food.

She made her way down the hall and through the dining room to the main kitchen and poked her head inside. Martha stood by one of the counters, cutting some onion. She looked a little grayer but, otherwise, the same old Martha. Rosie had planned to make herself a peanut-butter-and-jelly sandwich, but maybe Martha would give her something better.

Rosie cleared her throat. "What does a girl have to do to get something to eat around here?"

Martha looked up, and her jaw dropped. "Rosie?" She put down her knife and walked toward her, looking her up and down. "Rosie!" She gathered her up in a squishy hug.

Rosie buried her face in her shoulder, trying not to cry. Martha smelled of onions and dryer sheets. Just like old times.

"Oh, dear girl, I have missed you so much." Tears glittered in Martha's eyes as she pulled back and placed her hands on Rosie's cheeks. Rosie placed her own hands over Martha's and squeezed.

"It's really good to see you," Rosie said. "You look great."

"Oh, you're as sweet as ever." Martha grabbed Rosie's hand. "Come and get something to eat."

She pushed Rosie down onto a chair next to the table as she went to the refrigerator.

"I just got some fresh eggs this morning." She

cracked them over the skillet on the stove and turned on the burner. "You'll never guess who I ran into at the store. Do you remember Sheila Marsden? Well, she was trying to hide it, but she was *definitely* pregnant." Martha put some bread into the toaster as she fake-whispered and mimed a round tummy. "She runs around town so much that I wouldn't be at all surprised to learn she has no idea who the father is."

"Martha!" Rosie barked out a laugh. So many times, she had sat and listened to Martha's gossip.

After a long story about some woman having an affair with a mail carrier, Martha took a plate to Rosie and set it down. Eggs over easy with a stack of toast—just how she liked them. The old woman had remembered. It seemed silly how something like that could feel so comforting. Martha went back to the stove and threw a few pieces of bacon onto the skillet as Rosie devoured what was on her plate.

After about an hour of catching up, three plates of eggs, and about a dozen pieces of bacon, Martha shooed Rosie out of the kitchen, telling her she needed to get lunch going. Rosie ventured outside, her legs taking her straight to the backyard.

The garden at Hart House had always flourished with beautiful flowers from late spring to early fall, a paradise of bright blossoms and rich green shrubs. As Rosie stood in the middle of the garden and stared at the drooping leaves and shriveled buds, she frowned in disappointment.

"I tried."

Daniel's voice startled her, and she turned to see him watching her closely as he approached. He had a guilty look on his face, like a child who brought home a bad grade.

"I tried really hard at first. After a while, I knew it

was hopeless, but I still tried." He squinted his face in frustration. "They weren't happy without you here."

Rosie thought about him working to keep the weeds away and the plants pruned just right. He worked tirelessly to keep everything looking beautiful and seemed to really enjoy it. And he was good at it.

She gave him a small smile before she closed her eyes and reached out. The dismal fog that greeted her was like a gray, cloudy day. Energy within her seeped out her pores and swept away the fog. She absorbed the aura surrounding the plants and animals as they became one. Picturing a sunny day that drove away the clouds, she let that feeling spring from her fingertips.

When she opened her eyes, she looked into Daniel's astonished face. She smiled, feeling the life around her. Flowers blossomed, and lush green plants had perked up like magic. Birds chirped.

Tears glittered in Daniel's eyes as he turned in a circle, taking in the sights. He walked through the garden, touching the blossoms. "Words can't explain how good it feels to have you back here."

"You do such an amazing job of keeping it all looking beautiful, Danny."

"It wasn't enough."

At his sad frown, Rosie stepped forward and placed a hand on his cheek, letting her energy pour into him. He closed his eyes and smiled, his shoulders relaxing.

"I really missed that." He took one last look around and gave Rosie another smile before he stepped out of the garden and made his way across the lawn to the house.

She watched him go then turned toward the back

of the yard, ready to go sit in her spot and feel the reassuring presence of her old oak friend.

Ahead, the forest called to her, and she skipped through the grass, excitement putting a bounce in her step. As she drew closer, something looked off about the tree line. A throbbing pain started at the base of her skull when she realized what was missing.

"No," she whispered, breaking into a run.

As she approached her spot, where the yard met the forest, she choked out a sob. Every cell in her body screamed when she saw the mangled tree stump where a tall, proud oak had once stood. Cut down. They cut it down. She cried out in agony as she fell to the ground next to the place where she had spent so much of her childhood.

The strong, reassuring presence forever gone.

She leaned against the stump and pressed her face against the rough bark. Closing her eyes, she concentrated, trying to feel its energy. Nothing. Coldness spread through her, and it all came crashing down on her at once.

All gone. Her tree... her childhood... her love... her father. She sobbed at the loss of everything that was solid and strong in the life she'd once known.

FOURTEEN
ROSIE

Rosie's eyes opened slowly, and she turned her head, taking in her surroundings. She had fallen asleep on the ground next to her oak. As she stared at it, fresh tears filled her eyes, and she sniffed.

She knew what she needed to do next.

When she reached the cemetery, she found her father's plot and ran a hand over the top of the gravestone. She kneeled in the grass and closed her eyes, taking a deep breath. Tears burned her eyes, and a whimper escaped her lips. "Daddy. I miss you so much."

She opened herself up to the energy around her, but she couldn't feel anything. The air felt as cold and empty as the oak's dead stump.

Sighing, she stood, then she made her way over to Stuart's plot. She crouched in front of the gravestone and gently ran her fingers over the inscription. "Thank you for all your stories."

She stood and took one final look at each plot before she turned and headed back toward Hart House. The long walk wore her out, and when she got home, she went straight to her room and slid under the covers, wallowing in her sorrow.

It was early evening when someone knocked on Rosie's door. Sam peeked in, frowning when he saw her. She probably had puffy eyes and a red nose. Used tissues were scattered over her bed and the floor.

He sat on the edge of her bed and took her hand, silently waiting until she was ready to talk.

"The oak," she said finally, sniffling. "When was it cut down?"

He tensed, letting go of her hand.

"Oh no." He muttered a curse, pinching the bridge of his nose as he squeezed his eyes shut. "I'm so sorry, Rosie. I forgot." He sighed, seeming to debate whether to go on. "Amos had it cut down shortly after you fell. He claimed it was diseased. I wanted to kill him for it. Lucas almost did."

She flinched at the mention of Lucas.

"Yeah." He caught her eye. "As soon as we saw the tree, Lucas shifted, and I had to tackle him to keep him from finding Amos and tearing his throat out. Maybe I should have just let him."

Rosie looked out the window. Birds perched on the balcony railing, chirping happily. The last remnants of the sun painted the sky in beautiful swirls of pink, yellow, and orange. None of it fit her mood. Rain seemed much more appropriate.

Sam took a deep breath then let it out. "I need to tell you something." Rosie frowned. She couldn't take any more bad news.

"The Council is coming to Hart House. Next Monday."

Blinking, Rosie watched Sam closely. "Why?"

"They want to see you." Sam furrowed his brow. "I think they've heard whispers about witchcraft." He set his jaw. "I won't let them hurt you."

"I don't think you'll have much of a choice."

A flicker of anger passed over Sam's face. "We'll figure this out, okay? Just let me do the talking."

Rosie nodded, having no energy to argue. Her gaze slid to the window again.

"You know the best cure for a crappy mood," Sam said. "The moon is full. No harm in getting an early start."

Rosie turned to him, and the familiar gleam of mischief in his eye sent a little tendril of excitement up her spine, melting her glum mood like hot water on ice.

She started to get up, but he pushed her down as he jumped off the bed ahead of her.

"Last one there is a rotten egg!"

"No fair!" She slid out of bed and took off after him.

By the time she reached the backyard, he was halfway to the trees. She sprinted through the grass, feeling the cool blades under her feet. Pausing behind a tree, she whipped her clothes off, then she leaped back out to the grass, shifting to her wolf form. Her large paws landed on the ground—much larger than she remembered. Her gangly limbs had started to fill out. After a quick shake of her auburn fur, she was off, racing through the pines.

Though Sam was stronger, Rosie's lithe body made her faster, and she nipped at him as she bolted past. He gave a low growl as he nipped back. Leaping over broken tree branches and dodging bushes, she made her way through the forest, her legs pumping like a heartbeat.

Rosie listened closely to the sounds of critters running through the dead leaves of the forest floor and birds chirping in the sky. In the distance, water rushed through the ravine, and memories flooded her mind. The last time she had been there, she'd faced her father's killer.

As she approached the spot where he'd died, she slid to a stop. After a few moments, Sam caught up to her, rushing to her side. He followed her gaze, and she could feel the sadness from him as his memories no doubt turned in the same direction.

"I visit that spot every once in a while," he said. *"More than his grave. I can feel him there more than I can in a cemetery, you know?"*

"I know," Rosie said. *"Could you..."*

Sam seemed to sense her need to be alone. *"I'm going to go find a few rabbits to bother."*

Rosie slowly walked through the brush, keeping her nose low to the ground, smelling her way to the spot. Sam's smell got stronger as she neared the area, and she knew he visited the spot more than every once in a while.

She sat on her haunches, closing her eyes, and could feel her father's presence. Leaning her head back, she let out a long, low, mournful howl. When she lowered her eyes to the horizon, a patch of blaze orange in the distance cut through the greenery. A hunter. She sniffed the air. Tobacco... cologne.

As she jumped to her feet, her heart hammered. She watched him turn, and a moment later, she jumped at the *brrapp* of an ATV engine starting. The hum grew faint as the hunter drove away.

FIFTEEN

LUCAS

Glowing streams of water tumbled over rocks and down the steep riverbed. Droplets that sprayed off the falls caught the moonlight and glittered like magic.

Beyond the sound of rushing water, the heartbeat of Lucas's pack thumped against the ground as they ran through the forest. *His* pack. Generations of his ancestors had run through the same land, and their legacy flowed through his veins to the beat of the pounding feet in the distance. Lucas closed his eyes. He'd never known how much he wanted this. How much he *needed* this.

In his short time with the Becketts, he'd found a sense of belonging he'd never experienced before.

Home.

Beckett Falls called to something deep inside him. It would have devoured him whole, but for one piece of him that didn't belong there. That would never belong there. One piece of him would always burn for a different need that couldn't be filled by a place.

He closed his eyes. That piece would remain a painful, burning void for the rest of his life.

A howl broke through the night, and his tail

thumped against the ground as he raised his head to answer his alpha. Turning toward the sound, he leaped forward, running through the trees to rejoin the pack.

It didn't take long to find them. Roger ran ahead to greet him, and he nudged his head against his father's flank. He felt so grateful that his father had pushed him to come here, but of course he couldn't say that out loud.

He jogged forward and tackled Travis from behind. His cousin spun, attempting to pin Lucas to the ground, but Lucas gained the upper hand and had him in seconds.

"Yield." Lucas gave a good-natured growl.

"Showoff." Travis huffed. *"Yeah, yeah. I yield."*

Lucas let him up then bent down, inviting him for another round. Travis took the bait, leaping up and hopping on his paws before he jumped forward to tackle Lucas. They scuffled in the dirt for a while before Lucas pinned him again.

Brody ran circles around them, yipping. No longer a pup but not quite fully grown, he was smaller than the other wolves, but he begged to play. *"Me next, Lucas! Me next!"*

Since his arrival in Beckett Falls, Lucas had spent more time at the river house Marcus had built than at the pack house. Every minute Brody wasn't at school, he and Lucas were together. They played games, read books, and talked. The kid brought out something in Lucas. Maybe it was memories of his youth. Maybe it was that innate protective drive that wolves had for their young. Maybe it was just being part of a pack.

Lucas tackled Brody, gently pinning him to the ground, then let Brody make a counter move to tackle him back.

The older wolves watched, laughing and encouraging them as they wrestled.

Shawn lowered his head and limped off toward the edge of the bluff. The alpha's fall in the factory still caused him pain, and in wolf form, he was unable to put weight on his right front leg. He turned to Lucas and pinned him with a stare before he moved forward again. The message was clear. *Follow.*

Trotting off to join his alpha, Lucas watched as the others shuffled away.

"Are you happy here, Lucas?" Shawn's voice in his head sounded hopeful.

"You know I am."

"Have you given any more thought to taking over?" Shawn nudged him. *"I really want to get back on the road, kid. And you've got this. The pack loves you. You're a leader. You were born for this. You were meant to do this."*

"I have been thinking about it." Lucas looked back toward the pack as they disappeared into the trees. He would protect them with his life. They needed him. And he was ready to answer their call. *"I would be honored to take over."*

Lucas caught up with the rest of the pack after Shawn decided to head back to the house on his own. The alpha's sore shoulder had been bothering him.

As Lucas approached, he snuck up behind Brody, who trailed behind the others. He tackled him from behind, pinning him to the ground.

"You scared me, Lucas!" Brody giggled.

Lucas let him up.

"Come on!" Brody jogged toward the trees. *"Let's play—"*

Brody froze, his wagging tail slumped, and his ears perked. He stared toward the woods and leaned forward as though about to run.

Lucas perked his own ears, listening. Nothing sounded out of the ordinary. He sniffed the air. Nothing. *"What is it, Brody?"*

The boy stood still as though Lucas hadn't even spoken. His attention was on something in the woods. He took a step toward the trees.

"Brody!"

Brody tucked his tail between his legs and crouched low to the ground, swiveling his head in Lucas's direction. *"Sorry, Lucas."*

"What did you hear out there?"

"N-Nothing."

"Are you sure?"

Keeping his body low, Brody slunk past Lucas and jogged ahead to catch up with the rest of the pack.

Odd.

Lucas followed the others back to the pack house then walked Brody down to the other house. They shifted, dressed, and headed inside. Lucas just wanted to make sure Brody got in okay and say good night to Shawn before he headed back to the pack house for bed.

As they stepped through the front door, Lucas's attention was drawn to a pale-faced Shawn sitting on the sofa. His tense posture and worried frown made Lucas pause in the foyer.

Shawn glanced at Brody, and a smile erased the worry lines. "Hey, bud. How was the run?"

"It was good." Brody nodded then stared down at

his feet. The infectious, happy energy from earlier had been replaced by nervous fidgeting. Something wasn't right. He'd been quiet since they left the forest.

"Why don't you go get ready for bed." Shawn nodded toward the stairs.

Brody drifted across the room to the staircase. After he jogged up the stairs and was out of sight, Lucas focused his attention on Shawn. The worry lines were back on the alpha's forehead.

"What is it?" Lucas moved forward and sat next to Shawn on the sofa.

"I heard from the hospital." Shawn sighed. "Marcus is gone."

"Dead?"

Shawn glanced toward the stairs then shook his head. "I wish. No. He disappeared. Apparently, he's been awake for weeks."

"What?" Lucas raised his voice then flinched, glancing toward the stairs. "How could they not tell you about that?"

"He asked them not to." Shawn peered at Lucas. "He's up to something."

THE DARK FOREST LAY BEFORE ROSIE. SCREAMING pierced the silence of the night. Her feet moved forward, and a large house stood in the distance. The memory tugged at her brain. She'd been here before. It was the old Hart House from her dream. The screaming... That was her grandmother.

No. She couldn't go back to that house again. She didn't want to watch, but it was no use. She'd seen it already, and the horrific images were burned into her brain. They played again in her head in vivid detail—fangs, claws, torn flesh, blood. She squeezed her eyes shut and fisted her hands in her hair.

"Please forgive me, Rosie," Stuart called to her from somewhere in the woods. His voice echoed as though coming from a dozen different directions.

Her eyes popped open, and she spun in a circle, trying to pinpoint where the sound was coming from. Out of the corner of her eye, she saw movement.

Her father appeared in front of her, smiling. "Don't forget, Rosie."

Her heart thumped wildly. She always found comfort in her father's arms, but now she needed to get away from him. He asked too much. They all asked too much. As she turned to run, she suddenly stared into her mother's green eyes.

"Don't run away, Rosie. You can do this. Remember."

Rosie woke with a start. She shot up in bed, panting. A cold breeze touched her damp cheek. She wiped the tears away as she stared at her open balcony doors. The curtains billowed in the late-night breeze.

It was the third time in a week she'd had the nightmare.

Each day, she shoved the memories of her dreams to the back of her mind. They were dreams, nothing more.

Gods didn't *actually* visit her. She didn't talk to her dead parents. She didn't talk to her dead great-uncle. She didn't witness her grandmother getting eaten by her ancestors.

Right?

She blew out a long breath through her mouth and lay back onto her pillows. Staring at the ceiling, she hoped it was almost morning. There was no way she would get any more sleep tonight. She grabbed her phone, turned it on, and looked at the time. Ugh. It was only 3:00 a.m.

This had to stop. She had to tell someone, or she would go crazy. But no way would she talk to the guys about it.

Becca would freak out. Definitely couldn't tell her.

It had to be her grandma. She would know what to do. Nodding, Rosie made a plan to visit her grandmother first thing in the morning. She glanced at her phone again and hoped that *Candy Crush* was still a thing. She had some time to kill.

~

"Is the Jeep still in the garage?" Rosie asked casually at breakfast, but she might as well have asked if a meteor was headed for earth.

Sam, Michael, and Daniel stopped eating to stare at her, their mouths agape.

Sam cleared his throat. "Um, Rosie, do you think it's wise to drive so soon after..." After glancing around the table as though looking for help, he pinned Daniel with a pleading stare.

"He's right, Rosie." Daniel put his fork down. "Maybe you should practice driving first or something. Make sure you can still—"

"I can still drive," Rosie grumbled. "I don't think the concept has changed in the past year."

"Where do you need to go?" Sam asked warily. "I can take you anywhere."

Rosie carefully placed her own fork down. She was afraid she might stab it into Sam's hand. "I want to go and visit my grandma."

"Oh." Sam smiled. "I can take you out there. No problem."

"I got it," Michael said. He downed the last of his juice and dropped the glass onto the table with a loud *clink*. He grinned at Rosie. "I have to go into town this morning. I can drop the invalid off at the old witch's house."

"Michael!" Sam and Daniel both shouted at him, and Michael laughed.

Half an hour later, Rosie sat in Betty's passenger seat. Michael had kept the Jeep in good condition. She tried not to think about how she was sitting in Lucas's spot.

"Don't mind Sam and Daniel," Michael said.

"They hover like old ladies, but they mean well. They worry. That's all."

"I know." Rosie looked out the window at the blur of trees as the Jeep raced down the road. Michael drove fast and recklessly. If Sam and Daniel worried so much, they'd have been better off letting her drive.

"So, what's on the agenda with good ol' Clara today?"

Rosie smiled at Michael. His carefree spirit was uplifting, so unlike Stuart and Daniel. He was much more like his father, Jack. What would Michael and Daniel say if she told them about the things she saw in her dreams?

"Nothing. I just really need to talk to her."

"Couple hours be enough time?"

Rosie nodded.

"Good. I might have Daniel with me when I come back. We have to check up on some repairs they're doing to the deck on cabin five. I can handle it myself, but you know Daniel. He wants to see it for himself." Michael rolled his eyes. "I'm picking up some contracts from the warehouse to take back to the house. We should be able to check on the cabin and be back to get you before lunch."

Michael pulled the Jeep into Clara's driveway. He sped up the small path to the front of the house and stopped with a jerk. Rosie had to brace herself against the dashboard. She shot him a look, and he laughed.

She climbed out and shut the door, waving goodbye as he sped away. When she turned toward the house, Clara stood on the porch, watching her closely.

"Oh dear." She shook her head. "Something is troubling you."

SEVENTEEN

ROSIE

Clara tapped a fingernail against her cup, studying the wall for a moment, before she took a sip of her tea. She placed the cup back on the table then nodded as though agreeing with her own thoughts.

"Care to let me in on that internal conversation you're having?" Rosie raised an eyebrow.

She'd told her grandmother everything. About the gods and what they said. About her father and their conversations. About watching Stuart participate in killing her other grandmother.

About seeing her mother.

After Rosie told Clara that she had seen Gwen, her grandmother had turned five shades whiter, and tears streamed down her cheeks.

"You don't *really* believe it was just a dream, do you?" Clara narrowed her eyes at her.

Letting out a huff of air, Rosie averted her gaze. She ran her finger over a knot in the wood on the table. "I guess not."

Strange. To anyone else, it would seem odd for her to say it *wasn't* a dream. To her grandmother, it seemed odd for her to say she thought it *was* just a dream.

"I think we both know the truth." Clara reached across the table and took Rosie's hand. "You've been sent messages from the gods. You can't ignore that."

"I don't know what to do."

"Be alert," Clara said. "Look for signs."

"What kind of signs?"

Her grandmother shrugged. "You'll know them when you see them."

Rosie rolled her eyes. "Thanks. That helps."

WHEN MICHAEL and Daniel picked Rosie up from Clara's, lunch was on everyone's minds. Daniel wanted to go to the diner, but Michael and Rosie both voted for Miller's. They parked by the lake and headed toward the boardwalk.

As they walked, a soft wind blew Rosie's hair into her face, and she pushed it out of the way. Out on the water, a speedboat pulled a large tube with three kids. It bounced over the waves while the kids held tight to the straps. She smiled as she remembered doing the same thing when she was young.

A few people wandered in and out of the shops along the boardwalk, but it wasn't overly busy. The day was beautiful.

Next to her, Daniel shoved his hands into his pockets and frowned.

"What's wrong?" Rosie nudged him.

On her other side, Michael laughed. "He's mad because we didn't go to the diner."

"Shut up, Michael." Daniel glared at his brother.

Rosie frowned. "I'm sorry. We could have gone to the diner."

"Don't feel bad, Rosie," Michael said. "He just wants to gawk at his girlfriend."

"Michael, I said *shut up!*" Daniel growled. He scowled.

"Girlfriend?" Rosie's eyes widened. "Daniel..."

Daniel huffed. "She's not my girlfriend. We're friends. Good friends."

"Who undress each other with their eyes every time they're in the same room."

"Michael, I swear to God—"

"Hey, we're here!" Rosie grabbed both the boys' shirts and pulled them through the doors and into Miller's.

Becca stood next to the bar, talking to her father. She glanced toward the door as they entered, and her face brightened. "Rosie! Boys!"

"Hi, Becca!" Rosie rushed forward and embraced her friend.

"You guys here for lunch?"

Rosie nodded.

Becca grabbed some menus and led them to a corner booth and waited for them to slide in. "Let me guess. Michael will take a Miller, Daniel will have water, and Rosie will have cherry cola."

"Sounds about right," Michael chirped. He leaned back and slung his arm over the booth. "So back to what I was saying about Greta."

"Michael, you're relentless." Daniel's face reddened, and he rubbed his forehead.

"Not to add fuel to the fire," Rosie said, eyeing Daniel, "but I'm pretty curious. What's the story?"

"There's no story." Daniel shot Michael a look. "Greta likes horticulture. We talk about plants and flowers. It's only been a couple of weeks."

"Yeah, but you've been gawking at each other for months."

"Michael, leave him alone."

He frowned and crossed his arms. "Fine. Killjoys."

"Seriously, though, Daniel." Rosie reached across the table and took Daniel's hand. She sent him soothing energy and watched the tension in his features ease. "I'm happy you found someone you like talking to. You've always been so quiet. Just like Stuart."

At the mention of their grandfather, Michael and Daniel both frowned, and the energy at the table darkened.

Rosie closed her eyes and took a deep breath. "I got to say goodbye to him."

When she opened her eyes, both boys were staring at her. Her cheeks grew hot. "I had dreams while I was... sleeping."

"You mean..." Daniel swallowed. "You mean while you were in the coma?"

Rosie nodded. She found it hard to speak past the lump in her throat, but she had to tell them. They deserved to know. "He told me... Well, he said that Amos pushed him down the stairs."

Michael straightened. All traces of the mischief and laughter that had glimmered in his eyes moments ago dissolved to anger and hate. Next to him, Daniel studied his hands and bit his lip.

"I tried to ask him more, but he didn't seem to want to talk about it. He wanted to talk about... Well... He and I had... We had some things..."

"We heard about what he did to Simon's mother," Michael said.

"You did?" Rosie tried, but she couldn't keep the tears away. "He apologized. Said he wasn't the same person. He would change it all if he could. I think talking brought us both peace." A tear dripped down Rosie's cheek. "Even if it was just, you know, a dream."

"A dream." Michael nodded.

The thick emotions brought more tears to Rosie's eyes. They were still mourning their grandfather, and she'd just told them he might have been murdered.

Daniel stayed quiet for a few moments before he spoke. "He didn't say why Amos pushed him?"

Rosie shook her head. "Just that we didn't need to worry about Amos anymore. Sam would take care of him. That we needed to worry more about someone named..." Rosie thought for a second. "What did he say the name was? Frank. He said to worry more about Frank."

"Okay, here we go!" Becca's chipper voice cut through the tension. "You guys know what you want to eat?" After she placed the drinks down, Becca looked at each of their sad faces and frowned. She raised her hands and shook her head. "You know what? I don't think I want to know what you're talking about. I'll come back for your order."

EIGHTEEN

LUCAS

THE NUMBER OF LEGO PIECES THAT LITTERED
the floor in front of Lucas made his head spin. How
on earth were they supposed to construct a Death
Star from this? He looked over the instructions again
as Brody went to work clicking pieces together.

"Wait," Lucas said. "Don't you want to read the
instructions?"

Brody shrugged. "I've put this together like three
times. I know where everything goes."

Lucas looked at the mess on the floor again and
raised an eyebrow. "If you say so. What do you want
me to do?"

"Here." Brody grabbed a handful of Lego men
and held them out.

Lucas opened his hand and accepted them.

"Put the helmets on the storm troopers."

"I guess I can handle that." Lucas examined them.
"I never played with these much when I was little."

Brody swept his brown hair off his forehead.
"What did you play?"

"Hmm." Lucas thought while he started putting
the helmets on the storm troopers. "We played outside a lot. Hide-and-seek was always a favorite. And

hunters-and-prey. And Rosie made us make mud pies sometimes."

Brody's forehead wrinkled. "What's hunters-and-prey?"

"It's like hide-and-seek, but we played it in wolf form. Someone was hunter, and everyone else was prey. The hunter had to sniff out the prey."

"That sounds fun." Brody frowned. "I wish I could have played something like that."

Lucas studied him. "Did your dad ever play any games with you to sharpen your hunting skills?"

"Nah." Brody shook his head. "We only phased for the full moon, mostly. Dad didn't like leaving the house."

Lucas swallowed. "Why?"

Brody frowned, concentrating on the Lego pieces. He shrugged.

Lucas stayed quiet, waiting.

Finally, Brody sighed. "Dad got sick a lot. It made him not want to go anywhere. We stayed home most of the time so I could help him feel better. We played cards and board games. Sometimes we watched movies. Dad didn't like having Ginny around when he was home, so usually it was just me and him."

"Why didn't he want Ginny around?"

Brody looked at Lucas as though he'd asked a dumb question, but he didn't answer.

"Things changed when he started going to visit the Cramers all the time. He would leave, and we couldn't hang out anymore."

"He would just leave?"

"Yeah." Brody's voice turned hard. "Sometimes he didn't even tell me. I would get home from school, and he would be gone. He wouldn't come back for weeks."

"That must have been really hard."

Brody shrugged.

"I'm sorry you went through that, buddy."

Brody concentrated on clicking Lego pieces together and stayed silent.

"Well, I will definitely teach you to play hunters-and-prey."

Brody peeked at Lucas through the curtain of hair that had fallen into his face again. "Really?"

"Yeah." Lucas smiled. "Every wolf needs to know how to hunt. That's the best game to help you learn."

Brody's face brightened. "I've never been hunting. Dad didn't let me go on the full-moon hunts."

"Well, after a few months of playing hunters-and-prey, you'll be hunting with the rest of the pack. Guarantee it."

~

Teaching Brody to hunt was like teaching a fish to swim. The kid was born for it. His natural instincts were uncanny. Everywhere Lucas hid, Brody found him in minutes. They raced for rabbits, mice, and squirrels. Brody outhunted Lucas every time.

"Are you sure no one ever played hunting games with you?" Lucas tackled Brody to the ground and gave his ear a playful nip.

"Come on! My turn to be prey! Bet you can't find me!" Brody took off through the trees.

Lucas chuckled. He gave Brody a few minutes to hide then started to sniff him out. It didn't take him long to pick up on the boy's scent, but the other scent that mingled with it raised the fur on his back.

Another wolf.

It had the smell of a Beckett pack member but

with a distinction Lucas hadn't smelled before. There was only one Beckett pack member he hadn't smelled yet.

With his heart in his throat, he crept forward, his nose taking him in the direction of the smell. Through a tangle of bushes, he spotted Brody in a small clearing. The enormous wolf that stood over him was bigger than any Lucas had ever seen. He bet it was even bigger than Michael.

And Michael was huge.

No time for fear. Lucas's pack needed him to be strong. He lunged forward and leaped in front of Brody then crouched low and laid his ears flat against his head. He bared his teeth, and a low rumble rattled in his throat. His eyes stayed focused on Marcus.

The beast was even bigger up close. Marcus's dirty, matted brown coat was peppered with black and white markings. His eyes narrowed, and his lips curled back. He crouched low to meet Lucas's challenging posture and growled.

"Back off, Marcus."

"You must be Roger's boy," Marcus ground out. *"Aren't you a little far from home?"*

"This is my home," Lucas snapped. *"Brody is my pack. Back off."*

"Your pack?" Marcus laughed. *"You're no alpha, pup."*

"Not yet. Give it a day or two."

"You've got to be kidding me." Marcus laughed again. *"Shawn is something else."*

"Leave, Marcus." Lucas inched forward. He stayed steady and didn't break eye contact. *"Before I make you."*

Marcus crouched lower, showing his teeth again. *"Do you really think you can make me leave, pup?"*

Lucas's heart hammered as he stared at the enormous beast, but he wouldn't let Marcus see his fear. *"Do you want to find out?"*

"You aren't worth my time, pup. Don't worry. I'll be out of your hair in a minute." Marcus huffed a breath out his snout. *"Come on, Brody. Let's go."*

Lucas tensed. Marcus wasn't there to try to take back his place as alpha. He was there for Brody. No. He couldn't have him.

The low rumble started in Lucas's throat again, and he snapped out a warning. *"Brody isn't going anywhere."*

"Get out of my way." Marcus growled. *"Brody. Come here."*

Lucas turned to Brody. The pup cowered on the ground behind Lucas. Poor kid was terrified and confused.

"Stay put, Brody," Lucas ordered. *"Just stay right there."*

"Why don't you go back to the Hart pack? Back to that female werewolf?" Marcus's words cut deep, and Lucas winced. *"Oh right. Shame what happened. William Cramer told me all about her. She was a feisty one. I would have liked to have a turn with her."*

Lucas spun, going straight for Marcus's throat. His limbs trembled with rage and hate.

Marcus dodged then flipped Lucas onto his back. He had Lucas pinned in seconds. Marcus was even heavier than Lucas had imagined, and he fought to breathe under the crushing weight.

"Stop! Dad, stop! Don't hurt him! Please!"

Brody's cries barely filtered through Lucas's brain. As he fought for breath, the world started to spin. Just when he thought he would black out, Marcus let him go.

"That was a warning, pup," Marcus said. *"Stay out of my way."*

Lucas rolled onto his side, panting. Marcus approached Brody and said something to him. He said it only to Brody—Lucas couldn't hear the projected words. He fought to make his limbs work.

With a low growl, Marcus turned and darted toward the woods. He disappeared into the trees.

Lying in the dirt, Lucas waited for the world to stop spinning. When he was sure he could get up without passing out, he fought his way onto his unsteady legs and approached Brody. The pup cowered on the ground, still scared.

"Are you okay?" Lucas nudged him.

Brody hopped onto his feet, but he didn't answer.

Lucas led Brody back to the house. After they shifted, dressed, and went inside, Lucas searched for Shawn, but the alpha wasn't home. Deciding to stay until he came back, he sat Brody down on the couch to talk to him about what had happened.

"Are you okay?" Lucas asked again, just to be sure.

Brody bobbed his head.

"What did he say to you?"

Brody fidgeted with his fingers. "He wanted me to come with him."

Lucas furrowed his brow. "That's all?"

"Yes."

"Did he say where?"

"No."

"Are you sure?"

"I'm sure."

Lucas took a deep breath. Brody wouldn't meet Lucas's eyes.

"Is this the first time he's come to you?"

After a few moments, Brody sighed. "No. The night of the full moon, he called to me in the forest."

Lucas nodded. It made sense. Brody had seemed shaken that night. "Why didn't you say anything?"

Brody shrugged.

"Brody." Lucas tried to get the boy to look at him. When Brody finally did, he tried to keep his voice even as he asked, "Do you want to go with your father?"

Relief flooded through him when Brody shook his head.

"No. I want to stay with the pack," Brody said. "I want to stay with you."

"Did he say if he'll be back?"

"No." Brody's eyes trailed to the window. "But I don't think he will be."

"Why?"

"I told him he didn't need to worry about me anymore. I have you now."

NINETEEN
SAM

THE THREE MEMBERS OF THE UNITED STATES Werewolf Council sat on one couch, each of them studying Rosie intently as she sat next to Sam on the couch across from them. Rosie shifted under their stares. She looked like a child. She'd borrowed some clothes from Becca, but they were too big. Her hair fell around her shoulders, and she slumped in her seat, picking at her nails. An uneasy tingle worked its way up Sam's spine. The moment he'd become alpha, the instinct to protect his pack became physical. When a member was threatened, his body tensed and reacted in a way he couldn't completely control. That it was Rosie—his little sister—only amplified the physical twinge.

Behind the couch where the Council sat, three of their famous bodyguards stood sentry. Sunglasses, suits, herculean builds. They looked like the Secret Service on steroids. Sam knew from stories he'd heard over the years that the Council selected the strongest, most powerful werewolves for the small army they kept on hand to do their bidding. He'd never seen them in person before, and when they'd arrived with the Council, Sam's hackles rose. What made the

Council decide the presence of their bodyguards was necessary?

"It's good to see you up and around, Rose." Jagger ran a hand over his thick beard when he finally spoke after a full five minutes of silent staring. "Though we're surprised to see your quick recovery."

Clearing his throat, Sam leaned forward. The presence of Michael and Daniel standing behind the couch reassured him. "The doctors were impressed by her fast recovery, but everything checked out fine."

"Still," Roland said. "It's unnatural for someone to recover so fast from such an injury. Werewolves don't have the ability to heal quickly, as we're all aware. Neither do humans." Roland sat forward. His silver hair was carefully combed, his suit neatly pressed. His eyes were hard and his voice menacing. "So tell me, Rose. What are you?"

Sam stood, his fists clenching at his sides.

"Let's not be hasty, Roland," Jagger hissed. "No need to point fingers before they've had the chance to speak." Jagger focused his gaze on Sam. "We've heard rumors that your father kept something from us. That your sister, the only female werewolf ever known to exist, is the product of witchcraft."

"We're giving you the chance to come clean with us." Garrett looked at Rosie then back at Sam. His posture was much less rigid than that of the other two Council members. He sat back, one hand slung over the back of the couch, the other running a hand through his long hair. He propped one leg on the coffee table, his bare toes peeking out from his sandals. "To tell us the truth. You haven't lied to us yet. Don't start now."

"As you know," Jagger spoke again, "the hatred

werewolves have for witches goes back hundreds of years."

Roland made a sound and rolled his eyes as he crossed his arms. "Here we go."

Sam unclenched his fists, but he didn't take his eyes off Roland as he sat down again.

Ignoring Roland, Jagger continued, "Witches and werewolves worked together to protect the people in their tribes and villages. Werewolves provided food and safety for the witches, and witches mothered the werewolf young. It was a symbiotic relationship. However, when humans started hunting witches, the witches turned tail and ran, abandoning the werewolves and going into hiding. They doomed werewolves to extinction. Werewolves needed to carry on their legacy. Human women were their only option. The old traditions, as brutal as they may seem, were a desperate attempt to keep our race alive."

"See?" Roland glared at Rosie. "Witches can't be trusted."

"So, what is it, Sam?" Jagger spoke up again. "Do you have a witch in your pack?"

Sam's heart picked up speed. He had no intention of telling the Council that Rosie was a witch, but it seemed they already knew. They'd already made up their minds what they would do. The reason for the presence of the security guards became all too clear. They expected a fight.

Before he could speak, Rosie laid a hand on his arm. He watched in horror as she stood.

"It's true. I'm a witch."

The air left Sam's lungs. He wanted to stop her, but he couldn't. Something held him back... froze him in place. Across from them, the Council members watched Rosie with wide eyes.

"I'm only a witch in the same way that all of us are werewolves. Those are labels given to us by those who don't understand what we are. My father and my mother were both members of the Chosen. My father was a Chosen male—a werewolf. My mother was a Chosen female—a witch. Together, they formed a bond blessed by the gods. A mate bond." Rosie glanced at Sam before she turned back to the Council. "My mother gave birth to me then died. My father raised me with the pack. I was blessed with the gifts of both the Chosen men and the Chosen women."

"How is that possible?" Jagger whispered.

"The gods came to me while I was asleep." Rosie wrinkled her nose. "While I was in a coma. They told me that they needed my help to bring the Chosen men and the Chosen women back together again."

A sinking feeling pulled at Sam's stomach. What was she saying? His sister had dived straight off the deep end, and he hadn't even seen it.

"She's crazy." Roland screwed his face up in disgust. "The Chosen are myths."

"They are not myths," Jagger snapped. "We are the Chosen. Are we myths? The girl is right. Werewolf was just a name given to us by scared people centuries ago. The God gave us these gifts to protect mankind."

"That's all a bunch of nonsense." Roland rolled his eyes. "Just stories our ancestors told."

"It's not nonsense." Jagger furrowed his brow. "And if you truly believe it is, then you have no place on this Council."

"I think we all need to calm down." Garrett held up his hands. "This is bigger than us. We need to take this to the World Werewolf Council."

"It's going to divide us even more than we already

are!" Roland yelled. He stood, and his face reddened. "Those meetings are full of disagreements about our traditions and our history. Do you really want to sit in a World Werewolf Council session all day, listening to everyone argue over..."

Rosie moved to Roland's side and placed a hand on his shoulder. Roland's eyes rounded, then his body relaxed. Behind the couch, the henchmen tensed, but Jagger held up his hand, keeping them still. As the tension left Roland's face, he studied Rosie in confusion.

"What was that?" His voice lost its bitter edge.

"What happened between werewolves and witches was a long, long time ago," Rosie said. "We lived in peace once. Don't you think we could live in peace again?"

"What else did the gods tell you in your dreams?" Jagger whispered.

Rosie rubbed her forehead. "If the werewolves change their ways, the witches will come."

After a long beat of silence, Garrett cleared his throat. "I think we have a lot to discuss with the World Werewolf Council."

"And the girl needs to come with us." Roland straightened, avoiding Rosie's gaze.

"Over my dead body." Michael stomped around to the front of the couch, putting himself in front of Rosie.

"We can arrange that." Roland gestured to one of the security guards.

"Stop." Garrett stood. "We can go to the World Werewolf Council without Rose." He looked back to Rosie. "For now."

Something shifted, and Sam was able to move again. What was that? He'd been frozen. As though watching what happened but unable to participate. As he stood, his face heated. He stared at his sister, needing to yell, but that would have to wait until after the Council left. Letting them know she'd just used witchcraft on her alpha probably wouldn't help her case.

He walked the Council members out to their SUV and held his breath as they piled into the vehicle with their security guards.

After they drove away, Sam stormed into the house and cornered Rosie in the living room. "What did you do?"

"What do you mean?" Rosie smiled bashfully.

"You know exactly what I mean. Can you control people now? Because that's really freaky, Rosie."

"I can't control people." Rosie rolled her eyes. "I just put you on pause. Just for a bit."

"On pause?" Sam put his hands on his hips and paced the length of the living room, taking deep breaths in through his nose and blowing them out slowly through his mouth. Finally, he turned back to Rosie. "Why?"

"So that you wouldn't get yourself into trouble with the Council." Rosie shrugged like it was the most obvious thing in the world.

Sam stared at the ceiling then closed his eyes. "I don't need you to protect me from the Council, Rosie." He looked at her. "It's my job to protect *you*."

"I know." Rosie studied her hands. "But you didn't have all the information. And you were going to lie to them for me. I couldn't let you do that."

"Rosie, what you told them—"

"Was the truth." Rosie pinned him with a hard stare and crossed her arms. "I can feel your skepticism, but it really happened, Sam."

"You were visited by gods while you were in a coma?" Sam cocked his head. "You know how ridiculous that sounds?"

"Oh, I'm well aware, but just trust me, okay? Please?"

Trusting Rosie always came easy to Sam, and it had never led him down the wrong path. He hoped this time wouldn't be the first.

TWENTY

SAM

"ANY OTHER TOWN BUSINESS?" ED, THE VILLAGE president, sounded bored as he addressed the sleepy crowd. Listening to a forty-five-minute discussion about sidewalk easements would put anyone to sleep.

Holding his breath, Sam ran his eyes over the number of gruff men who didn't normally frequent the village board meetings. He knew why they'd come. Certainly not to hear about sidewalk easements. They'd come to gripe about hunting land. The same argument happened every year. Sam's father had dealt with it for as long as he could remember, and Sam had been dealing with it ever since Simon died.

His gaze landed on Lenny Beckinsale, head of the area hunting club. They'd had a conversation not long ago, when Lenny asked Sam to open Hart land for hunting. Sam declined, of course. He should have known that wouldn't be the end of it. Scanning the crowd some more, Sam scowled at Mason Lewis when their eyes met. Mason smirked, jutting his chin out as he held Sam's stare.

"I have business." Mason broke the staring contest to look at Ed. "What is the board going to do about all the wolf attacks around here? Plenty of us hunters are ready to take care of the problem, if certain greedy landowners would give hunting rights for their land."

Shouts of agreement rioted through the room, and Sam closed his eyes.

"The wolf attacks have slowed down," Ed said. "I haven't heard of one in more than two weeks."

Thanks to the shift in leadership and a break in attacks by the rogue wolf, the Cramers had stopped killing area livestock and pets. It had been two days since the Council's visit, and everything had been quiet.

Almost too quiet.

"So we just sit around and wait for the wolves to start attacking again?" someone hollered from the back of the room. "I don't think so."

"How do we even know there are wolves around here?" Sam rolled his eyes to the ceiling and crossed his arms. "There were a few sightings and some horrible attacks but then nothing. Maybe they were just moving through."

"No." Mason shook his head. "They're out there. And the red one is back."

Sam clenched his teeth. Rosie had told him she'd seen a hunter out in the woods. He'd prayed she hadn't been spotted, but that wasn't their luck.

"Friend of mine saw it." Mason sneered. "It was the wolf that killed my dad."

It took a moment for Sam to find his voice. "How do you know a red wolf killed your dad? And where did your friend see a red wolf? I find that highly unlikely. They're endangered."

"He saw it, all right," Mason said. "On your property. Same one I saw the night my dad died on *your* property."

Another chorus of shouts filled the room, and Sam tried to keep a lid on his temper. "How did your *friend* see a wolf on my land? Was he trespassing? Because you know I don't tolerate trespassers."

Mason shrugged. "Guess you'll have to ask him."

His patience wearing out, Sam sat up straight. "If you've been on my land, I'll have you arrested. You didn't learn your lesson last time? You going to come back and kill the rest of my family now?"

"Never said it was me." Mason smiled, showing his nasty teeth. "Said it was a friend."

"This wouldn't happen to be the same friend who's been missing the last year and half, would it? The one the sheriff has been looking for? The one who was there the night my father was killed?"

Mason crossed his arms and stayed silent. He shrugged.

Sam's cheeks grew hot.

Ed sighed. "It's late, and I'm tired. Sam isn't going to allow hunting on his land, and we're just going to have to live with that. You will all have to hunt on designated hunting land when hunting season opens."

The disgruntled moans barely registered in Sam's mind. He again locked eyes with Mason. Sam wanted nothing more than to knock the rotted teeth out of his mouth.

AFTER THE MEETING, Sam headed for Miller's. He'd planned to meet Michael, Daniel, and Rosie there for dinner. He was grateful to his pack for keeping Rosie safe and felt the need to make it up to them. Michael and Daniel would do anything for Rosie, but they went out of their way to do what Sam asked.

The loud music rattled his brain as he stepped inside the restaurant, and an ache worked its way up the back of his head. He spotted his family at a table near the bar, and his mood lifted when he saw Becca sitting with them. When he approached, he touched her shoulder and bent down to kiss her cheek. "I thought you had to work tonight."

"I did." Becca smiled. "But I got off a little early. We trained someone new the other night, and she's already doing tables on her own. Dad doesn't need me. How was the meeting?"

Sam grunted as he sat next to her. "Awful. I don't want to talk about it."

"Oookay." Becca winced. "Well, I talked your sister into a big day of shopping tomorrow followed by a sleepover."

Sam caught Rosie's scowl behind Becca and suppressed a laugh.

"That reminds me." Sam reached into his back pocket for his wallet. He opened it and pulled out a new credit card. "This is yours. Get what you need. Don't be frugal, but don't go out and buy a car or something."

Rosie's frown wasn't really the reaction he'd hoped for. She took the card and stuffed it into her back pocket. "Thank you, Sam."

"Also, I heard you want to get your GED. I got you a laptop. It's at the house. It has a hotspot on it, so you should be able to use internet anywhere." Sam nudged her. "Happy belated birthday."

"Oh! I'll bet the burgers are up." Becca jumped up from the table. "Rosie, will you help me grab them?"

Rosie nodded and gave Sam a tight smile before she stood and followed Becca to the kitchen. Sam rubbed his temple. He'd hoped for more excitement. Turning back to the table, he tried to listen to whatever Michael and Daniel were talking about.

Michael glanced toward the kitchen before he looked at Sam. "Any leads on who broke in at Clara's?"

"Nothing." Sam shook his head. He watched the girls, who stood off to the side, chatting. The burgers must not have been up yet. "Do you remember Stuart telling Amos he knew who was behind the rogue attacks? What if this is connected? Something isn't adding up."

"Amos didn't want him talking about it, that's for sure." Michael scowled. "Do you think Amos pushed him down the stairs to keep him quiet?"

Sam nodded. "I do."

Michael cursed, and Daniel averted his gaze.

"Daniel." Sam touched his cousin's arm. When Daniel turned back to Sam, his eyes were wet with tears. "Do you think you can look through Stuart's journals and see if you can find something?"

Daniel sniffed. "Like what?"

Shaking his head, Sam shrugged. "I don't know. But your grandpa knew something that Amos didn't want him to share with us. Let's hope he wrote it down somewhere."

TWENTY-ONE
LUCAS

THE CLANGING OF BOTTLES AND THE WHIR OF
machinery filled the air. Loud. So loud. Lucas had always known a lot happened in the brewery, but the
bottling area would give him a splitting headache if he
had to spend all day there. He preferred to watch the
fermenting process.

"Lucas!" Travis hopped down from the scaf-
folding and pulled out his earplugs. "You have to
meet the bottling crew. I've been telling them about
you. We have a euchre night once a month. Told them
you're going to mop the floor with them. They don't
believe me." Travis laughed. "I can't wait to see their
faces."

Lucas looked over Travis's shoulder and spotted
the crew eyeing him while they worked. They muttered to one another and pointed, and heat spread up
his neck. He would have to bring it at the card game.
Or maybe he would piss them all off if he beat them.
Dammit, Travis. Way to set him up for failure.

"Shawn said he wants to talk to you." Travis
batted his gloved hand against Lucas's chest.
"Sounded important."

"Where is he?"

Travis jutted his chin toward the second level. "Up in his office."

Lucas nodded and waved goodbye as he jogged toward the stairs to the second floor. He climbed the steps to the top and peeked into the windowed office, where Shawn sat at a desk covered in a sea of paperwork. The alpha rested his forehead in his hand, his fingers massaging his scalp as though he had a headache.

With a quick knock on the doorframe, Lucas stepped inside. "Shawn?" He moved forward and eased into the chair across from his uncle. "Travis said you needed to see me. Please don't tell me it's to sort through that mess of paperwork, because that looks like a stroke waiting to happen."

Shawn laughed. "No. Thank God for your father. He's taking all this stuff over. Christopher and I have muddled our way through it for years, but your dad has finesse. He'll have us back in shape in no time."

"I noticed you didn't mention Travis. He's no help with the paperwork?" Lucas grinned.

Shawn laughed. "He might not be able to fill out a form to get a library card, but the guy manages the employees in this warehouse like no one else can. The people here love him."

"I can see that." Lucas picked up a paperclip and started spinning it around on his finger. "So, what did you want to see me about?"

Shawn averted his gaze. "I have something I need to tell you, Lucas. And it might affect your decision to take over as alpha."

Lucas furrowed his brow and dropped the paperclip back onto the desk.

Shawn studied his fingers, avoiding Lucas's eyes.

"I thought about not telling you, but it's not something I can keep from you. I talked to Sam Hart."

Worry for the Harts caused his stomach to churn. "Is everyone all right?"

Shawn nodded. "Everyone is fine. The Harts have a new alpha. Sam challenged Amos and killed him."

Relieved, Lucas let out a breath. "I know it sounds harsh, but that's actually really great news. I'm proud of Sam. He finally took his place. The Harts will be okay now." Lucas sat back. "Man, that's a weight off my shoulders. I can't imagine how Sam must feel. I just..." Lucas eyed Shawn. The alpha still wouldn't meet Lucas's eyes. "Is there something else?"

"Rose Hart woke up from her coma."

Shawn's words speared Lucas through the heart and stole the oxygen from every cell in his body. The walls closed in on him, and somewhere deep inside, the fire of his mate bond burned brightly, using every bit of oxygen his starved lungs craved. The room swam. Whether he was crying or about to faint, he wasn't sure. When he had enough breath to find his voice, he stuttered, "Is s-she... Is she okay?"

"She's doing amazingly well." Shawn furrowed his brow then eyed Lucas, his gaze calculating. "She's already back at Hart House."

His head became too heavy, and he dropped it into his hands. Awake. Rosie was awake.

"Lucas... I won't try to keep you here. I don't think I can. But please, I'm begging you to think about the pack."

Lucas raised his head and met Shawn's gaze. A tear slipped down his cheek. "I have to..." He swallowed. "I have to get to her."

Shawn squeezed his eyes shut as though Lucas

had hit him. "Go to her. But please come back, Lucas. Bring her with you. We'll welcome her. Just come back and take your place here. Promise me."

Could he make that promise? "Shawn, I..." Lucas blew out a breath. "I'll try my best."

Lucas's hands shook as he grabbed clothes from his dresser drawer and stuffed them into his duffel. He couldn't move fast enough. The drive would be too long. He needed to be in Hanks Hollow now.

Rosie was alive. Awake. God, what the hell?

He paused, put his hands on his hips, inhaled a deep breath through his nose, and blew it out slowly through his mouth.

"Lucas!" Roger's voice carried from the main level.

Closing his eyes, Lucas cursed as his father's feet pounded down the basement steps. He didn't have time for this. He went back to grabbing clothes from drawers. Some T-shirts, some flannels. Jeans.

"Lucas."

He didn't look at his father as he stuffed the clothes into the duffel and zipped it closed. "I'm going, Dad." His voice shook. "Don't try to talk me out of it."

He shouldered past Roger, storming across the main area to the bathroom. He grabbed his deodorant, toothbrush, and toothpaste and stuffed them into the side pocket of his bag. The heat of his father's presence behind him made his neck itch. He *really* didn't have time for this.

"What about the pack?" Roger's angry words made Lucas's chest tighten. "What if Marcus comes back?"

Lucas paused. He closed his eyes when he felt the sting of tears. "I have to go to her, Dad."

"And do what? Stay with her in Hanks Hollow for the rest of your life?" Roger raised his voice. "Abandon your pack?"

Lucas glanced at Roger, and the desperation in his father's eyes almost broke him, but he set his jaw, stormed across the floor to the stairs, and took them two at a time. He raced across the floor to the front door, barely aware of Travis and Christopher standing in the living room.

"Lucas?" Travis called out to him, but Lucas ignored the plea.

Outside, Lucas ran across the driveway to the car Roger had bought in Hanks Hollow. His father had given him a set of keys for the vehicle, and he dug them out of his pocket. He opened the back door and tossed his duffel inside. When he was about to climb into the driver's seat, he heard a small voice in the distance.

Crap.

He glanced at his phone. It was 3:45. Brody was home from school. Normally, Lucas would have been down at the house, playing with him by now.

"Lucas!" Brody called to him. "Lucas!"

Brody ran up the hill toward the driveway. He still had his backpack on. He must have come straight over after school when Lucas wasn't at the house. A megawatt smile lit Brody's face as he waved. His figure blurred, and Lucas wiped furiously at the tears clouding his vision. What would he tell the kid?

"Hey!" Brody eyed the car. "Are you going to the brewery? Can I come?"

"I'm not going to the brewery." Lucas leaned against the car and sighed. "I have to leave, Brody. I have to go back to Hanks Hollow."

The smile slid off Brody's face, and the light left his eyes. "You're coming back, though. Right?"

"I..." Lucas bit his lip and turned away when he felt the burn of tears again. "I don't know."

"What do you mean, you 'don't know'?" Brody's voice wavered. "Why do you have to go?"

Lucas swallowed. "Do you remember my friend Rosie? She needs me. I need to go to her."

"*We* need you!" Brody screamed.

"I'm sorry," Lucas said. "We'll see what happens, okay?"

Brody's breath hitched, and a tear slid down his cheek.

Lucas turned and climbed into the driver's seat, shut the door behind him, and started the car. When he pulled into the driveway and accelerated toward the road, he held his breath. He tried not to look, but he couldn't help it. In the rearview mirror, he watched Brody standing alone in the driveway. Tears streamed down the kid's cheeks.

He choked on a sob and pulled the car onto the road, leaving the Beckett pack behind.

TWENTY-THREE
ROSIE

"Becca, do I really need all these clothes?" Rosie struggled to make all the hangers fit on the little hook in the dressing room, but it wasn't big enough to hold everything. She dropped three dresses. Grumbling, she picked them up. She would have been perfectly happy with some new T-shirts and a few pairs of jeans, but Becca had insisted Rosie needed to branch out.

In the dressing room next to her, Becca was trying on her own pile of clothes.

They had already been to five other shops. A collection of bags sat at Rosie's feet, stuffed full of sweaters, jeans, shoes, and undergarments. The lingerie store had been embarrassing, to say the least. Who knew being measured for a bra was actually a thing?

"Ugh, for crying out loud, Rosie!" Becca huffed at her over the wall. "Stop complaining, and try them on!"

Rosie looked up at the ceiling and closed her eyes, counting to ten. "When am I going to wear a dress?"

"*Fine*, you don't have to buy a dress."

"Thank you."

Rosie tossed the dresses aside and chose a top. She put it on then pulled at it, trying to adjust it to fit on her body. It was no use. *Nothing* fit right. She still hadn't gotten over the shock of seeing herself in the mirror. She had the hourglass figure she'd coveted at sixteen, but she just wanted her old body back. The new body came with a new life that she struggled to fit into.

Giving up on the tight-fitting shirt, she grabbed some yoga pants that Becca had *insisted* she try. As she pulled them on, she regretted giving her friend a hard time about it. Becca was right. The pants were the most comfortable thing she'd ever put on.

She collected the three pairs just like it that Becca had shoved into her arms earlier and a few T-shirts then joined Becca at the cash register. Rosie's cheeks heated as the items were rung up and the total climbed. Money had never really been an issue, but something felt strange about spending it now. She knew it was her family's money, but it didn't feel like *her* money. She wasn't a kid living under her father's roof anymore.

"All right." Becca's voice broke through Rosie's thoughts. "We have clothes, we have shoes, we have underwear... what else do we need? Oh! A swimsuit!"

"Becca, it's September. I don't think I'll need a swimsuit for several months."

"Rosie, come on! It's like eighty degrees today. We could go out on the boat. I can get a tan. You can get burned. It will be like old times."

"Pass."

Becca growled. "Fine."

After paying for their purchases, Rosie juggled with the bags as she maneuvered her way through the door and outside to the sidewalk. She didn't manage well, and several of the bags fell to the ground as the door closed behind them.

"Crap," Rosie murmured.

"Ugh, you're still a klutz." Becca laughed at her.

"Shut up, and help me." Rosie giggled, giving her friend a small shove.

As they scooped the spilled contents back into the bags, a passerby stepped on one of Rosie's new sweaters, leaving a dirty footprint.

"Hey, jerk! Watch where you're walking!" Becca yelled.

Rosie looked up as he turned toward them. She dropped her bags as she rose from the ground, her jaw dropping.

Mason Lewis stood on the sidewalk in front of them. Surprise flickered in his eyes before an angry grimace spread across his face.

"Rose Hart," he sneered. "Have a nice nap?" He ran his eyes up and down her figure and raised an eyebrow. "Guess the beauty sleep did some good."

Rosie crossed her arms over her chest, dropping her head and taking a step backward. She remembered that predatory look on his face. She had ignored it back then, eager for him to like her. Now it gave her the creeps.

He smiled, flashing rotted teeth. Rosie winced then noticed his ratty clothes and greasy hair. He looked awful.

"Get lost, Mason." Becca picked up the bags from the ground and shoved them into Rosie's hands.

Rosie forced her numb fingers to work, gripping the bags tightly to her chest as Becca pushed Rosie behind her.

"Don't you have a liquor store to rob so you can

get another meth fix? Come on, Rosie." Becca turned Rosie in the opposite direction and steered her down the sidewalk.

"You ruined my life, you know," Mason called out behind them.

Rosie froze, turning slowly toward him. His emotions rolled off him in waves. Anger. *Hate.*

"You're a lying slut, and you ruined my life!" Mason's mouth foamed, and spit shot from his lips as he spoke. "I hope you die, you bitch!"

Becca spun Rosie away from him, urging her forward, and she stumbled before she found her footing and started walking quickly down the sidewalk, her heart racing. They darted into a café, and Becca pushed her into a chair.

"Are you okay?"

Rosie could barely hear Becca over the rushing in her ears. Her chest heaved as she tried to catch her breath.

Becca placed a hand on Rosie's shoulder. "I'm going to get you some water. I'll be right back."

Rosie nodded as she stared at her shaking hands and concentrated on catching her breath. Becca returned with a glass of water, and Rosie took it from her and gulped greedily at the cool liquid.

"What the hell was that?" Her voice came out in a rasp. "What happened to him?"

"That," Becca said, sitting down across from her, "was a walking, talking antidrug commercial. Mason has been messed up for years. He's a meth head. He was even dealing for a while."

"You're kidding," Rosie whispered. Old emotions stirred in her gut as she tried not to think about that night. His hands on her, pulling up her skirt.

"Yeah," Becca said. "He's been arrested a few

times." Rosie glanced through the window toward where they had seen him moments ago, her mind working overtime. Did he really blame her for the way his life had turned out?

"Don't give it another thought, Rosie," Becca said. "He's a loser."

Rosie closed her eyes, and images flashed before her of that night in the woods. Mason had been there with his family. Hunting. He had a gun.

She nodded absently, still thinking about the hate she sensed from him. It chilled her to the bone. She shivered and closed her eyes, praying she never saw Mason Lewis again.

THE BRIGHT SUN DID LITTLE TO WARM THE CRISP morning air as Becca and Rosie made their way up Main Street toward the diner the following morning. Rosie tucked her hands into the sleeves of her sweater as she crossed her arms over her chest. She was in the mood for pancakes, and her stomach growled in anticipation when she saw the large red-and-white awning in the distance. Though the diner wasn't far from Becca's apartment, the walk back would be miserable. Rosie planned to stuff her face, like she used to when she and Becca went for breakfast after a sleepover. After their day of shopping yesterday, Rosie had spent the night at Becca's new apartment for a movie marathon. Just like old times when they had sleepovers at Becca's dad's house, complete with popcorn fights, makeovers, and junk-food binges.

Crowds of tourists buzzed along the sidewalks, already out shopping. Fall leaf garland decorated the light posts, and pumpkins and mums littered the storefronts in pretty displays of fall colors. The decor coupled with the crisp air gave a hum of excited anticipation for autumn. The trees had changed to shades of orange and red. The colors would reach their peak in a couple of weeks.

A prickle tingled along Rosie's neck. She stood still, momentarily paralyzed. The eerie feeling of being watched unnerved her, and she shifted her gaze back and forth, searching for the source of her unease. Dozens of people milled around. Tourists swarmed the streets, wearing gaudy sunglasses and hats. Nothing seemed out of the ordinary, and she tried to brush the feeling aside.

"Ugh, damn tourists." Becca threw her arms into the air and frowned as they neared the restaurant. The crowd of people waiting to be seated at the diner stretched out the door. Rosie sighed in disappointment as her stomach growled. She couldn't wait an hour to eat.

"I guess we can grab a breakfast sandwich from the gas station," Rosie said.

Becca wrinkled her nose in disgust. "A gas-station breakfast sandwich sounds horrible. I have some cereal back at the apartment."

Rosie nodded in agreement as they turned to head back toward Becca's place. The prickle returned, and Rosie looked around nervously, rubbing the back of her neck.

"You working today?" Rosie tried to strike up a conversation to distract herself from the uneasy feeling.

"Nope," Becca said with a smile. "I'm going hiking with some friends. Do you want to come?"

"Thank you," Rosie said, "but I need to get started working on my GED. I'm going to look for some online study guides and prep courses. It's nice out. I think I'll work out on the boardwalk. I need to get out of Hart House for a while."

"You're welcome to use my apartment if it gets too hot." Becca nudged her. "I have an extra key. It's all yours."

"Are you sure?"

"I'm positive." Becca put her arm around Rosie's shoulders. "Sam is coming by tonight for dinner and a movie. Stay at my place today and study. By dinnertime, you'll be ready for a break, and you can join us."

"That actually sounds..." The uneasy feeling of being watched hit her again, and she looked around.

"Are you okay, Rosie?" Becca gave her a funny look.

"I'm fine." Her stomach fluttered, a nervous feeling settling there. She searched the street one last time for any sign of something out of the ordinary, but all she saw were the throngs of people happily wandering in and out of shops.

ROSIE PULLED a deep breath in through her nose as the wind wisped through her hair. The fishy lakewater smell mingled with pine and popcorn. Charlie always turned the popcorn maker on late at night when the barflies got the munchies. The late-night quiet on the boardwalk had replaced the daytime bustle of the popular tourist spot. Only the sounds of boats bumping against the pier and water lapping against the concrete steps filled the air. Streetlights cast white halos on the wood planks of the walkway, giving an eerie feel to the evening.

The day had been productive. She'd found out she could take the GED test one module at a time. If she took the test modules in person, she didn't need to go through an entire prep course. Instead, she could use online study guides. The drive to the community college would take about twenty minutes each way, so avoiding the prep course was a bonus. She'd also found some information about a massage program at the same college. It would be a commute, but she could cross that bridge when she got to it.

After her day of studying, she'd joined Becca and Sam for dinner. She'd never felt more like a third wheel in her life. After dinner, she could tell they needed some alone time in the apartment. They had been watching a movie, and she sensed the sexual tension. She made up a story about meeting Michael and Daniel downstairs at Miller's and stepped out to give them some privacy.

As she paused to watch how the moonlight reflected on the water, an uneasy feeling made the hair on her arms rise—the same feeling she had that morning, walking down Main Street. Looking around warily, she didn't see anyone. She turned and started dashing back toward Miller's.

A trash can tipped over in an alley as she passed, and she paused, her heart hammering.

"Who's there?"

Only silence answered as she stared into the alley, watching the trash can roll on its side. She turned back to the boardwalk and looked toward the lights of Miller's a few yards away. The hum of music and the buzz of conversation floated through the open door. She paused, considering whether running would be ridiculous, when a hand suddenly wrapped around her chest, pinning her arms to her sides. Rosie screamed, but another hand clamped over her mouth, muffling the sound. She wiggled and thrust, trying desperately to free herself, but she couldn't get out of the strong hold.

Her attacker began to drag her backward into the alley, and she screamed into his hand over and over, trying to bite his palm. She kicked and bucked, but he held firm.

A sudden jerking motion to the left sent her sprawling, and she landed with a hard thud on the ground. Her attacker landed next to her, and her breath caught in her throat when she got her first look at his face.

Mason.

Mason disappeared from view as he was pulled to his feet from behind. After the sound of a fist connecting with skin, Mason appeared on the ground next to her again. Rosie spun onto her back, trying to get a look at who was there, but the face was hidden in the shadows.

Next to her, Mason jumped to his feet and leaped at his attacker. The two of them scuffled in the dark. After a series of grunts and curses, the sound of feet running away mingled with the sound of heavy breathing.

Rosie backed up and managed to get her unsteady legs under her as the heavily breathing shadow moved forward. The figure stepped into the light, and Rosie gasped and stumbled back to the ground, clutching her heart.

The fire within her burst to life.

"Lucas?" A tear slipped down her cheek, and her breath hitched.

Lucas knelt in front of Rosie, his face contorted in a mix of emotion. Tears welled in his eyes, and he reached a hand toward her face. He hesitated for a moment, meeting her gaze, asking permission, before his fingers brushed against her cheek.

As she closed her eyes, tears cascaded down her face, and a sob escaped. Her fingers grasped his hand, and she opened her eyes. "Are you real?"

"Rosie, I—"

"Rosie!"

Pounding footsteps and the sound of Sam calling to Rosie snapped her attention away from Lucas. Behind her, Sam ran toward them.

Sam froze in his tracks. "Lucas?"

"Sam." Lucas straightened. "I'm sorry for coming here without permission. I had to see her."

Sam shook his head and looked at Rosie. "What happened? I heard you scream. Are you okay?"

It took a moment for Rosie to find her voice. "Mason grabbed me from behind. Lucas..." She stared at him, still in disbelief he was there. "Lucas stopped him."

The emotion that came from Sam as he studied

Lucas hit Rosie like a tidal wave. The innate territorial alpha drive fought with the relief at seeing his friend again. The war within him reflected in his tortured gaze as he struggled with his next move.

"We need to call the police, then Rosie needs to go back to Hart House where it's safe." Sam clenched his jaw. "I don't want to leave Becca alone."

"I can take her home, Sam," Lucas said softly.

Sam huffed out a breath. "We can talk tomorrow. I'll tell Michael and Daniel you're coming."

Rosie's stomach twisted in knots as Lucas steered his car up the long driveway that led to Hart House. Lucas had told her the car belonged to his father. That was the extent of their conversation. The rest of the drive had been silent.

Lucas pulled the car into the garage. They sat in silence for a few moments, the engine making little clicking sounds as it settled.

After Rosie had given her statement, the sheriff sent the entire Hanks Hollow police force out looking for Mason. The anger and hatred she'd felt from Mason when she'd seen him on the street while out shopping had been frightening, but she'd never dreamed he would actually attack her. That sort of thing only happened in horror movies.

"How... How did you show up at just the right time? I'm glad you did, but how..." Rosie shook her head.

Lucas winced. "I was watching you today."

"What?" As she remembered the creepy-crawly feeling she'd had all day, anger inched its way up her spine. "Why?"

"I was trying to get the courage to talk to you." He rubbed his forehead. "When I heard you were awake, I just couldn't believe it. And when I saw you... It was just... I didn't have the courage to face you."

"What do you mean?" Rosie frowned. "Does this have anything to do with why you never came to see me in the hospital?"

Lucas jerked his head toward her, and a tear dripped from the corner of his eye. "I'm so sorry, Rosie. I couldn't stand to see you in a hospital bed. Not when..." Lucas made a choking sound and wiped his eyes.

"Not when what?"

A muscle ticked on his cheek as his jaw clenched, and he shook his head.

"Lucas?"

"Not when it was my fault you were there." Pure agony passed over his features before he turned to look out the window. "My fault you lost your father. All of it was my fault. How can I ask you to forgive me for that?"

The pain in his voice tore at her. How long had he been carrying this guilt? "Lucas, how could you think this was your fault?"

"I was the one who led you away from the pack. If I hadn't done that, you would have been safe from the hunters." Sobs erupted. "God, Rosie. I'm so sorry. I'm so, so sorry."

With her heart bursting, Rosie crawled over the middle console and into his lap. She wrapped her arms around his neck, hugging him close as he sobbed into her hair. She wanted to take his pain away. Not temporarily with magic—she wanted to take it away for good.

He kissed her forehead, and she looked into his

eyes. Blue as ever. She leaned forward and kissed him. The electricity was immediate and just as intense as she remembered. Her fingers brushed over his cheeks, and she deepened the kiss. God, she'd missed him so much.

He ran his hands gently through her hair and over her back. The blissful euphoria of his touch made her head spin. Inside, the flames of her mate bond roared, warming her in a way she hadn't felt before.

"I love you so much, Rosie." His whispered telepathic words brought fresh tears to her eyes. *"I always have."*

She ran her fingers over his face, looking into his eyes again. "From the moment I woke up, all I wanted was you. I was so alone. So lost. I didn't feel like I had a home anymore. It's you, Lucas. You're my home. As long as I have you, the rest will get figured out."

TWENTY-SIX
LUCAS

SOFT CURLS TICKLED LUCAS'S NOSE. MORNING sunlight warmed the fluffy down comforter that covered Rosie's bed. Her arms had been wrapped around him while she slept, and Lucas thought he must be in heaven.

He bent forward to gently kiss her heart-shaped pink lips and freckled cheeks, careful not to wake her. Rosie moaned and snuggled closer to him, tightening her hold on his torso. They had spent hours kissing and holding each other before they finally fell asleep.

Yesterday had been a whirlwind. As Lucas had sped to Hanks Hollow in his father's car, he had time to let his fear take over and paralyze him. When he had spotted Rosie on Main Street, she took his breath away. Always beautiful. His Rosie. But he just couldn't get himself to go to her. He spent all day watching her like a stalker. When Mason attacked her, Lucas froze in fear for a moment before fury drove him forward, and he barreled into Mason, ready to rip out his throat. How had he not seen the attack coming? He'd been too distracted with watching Rosie. Guilt washed over him. He'd let her get hurt again.

The flames of his mate bond burned steady and warm. Running his hands through her hair, he considered where Mason might be hiding. If the police didn't get him, Lucas would.

Another low moan, and Rosie's soft eyelashes beat a few times before her cherry-chocolate eyes looked up at him. "How long have you been awake?" her soft morning voice purred.

"Not long." Lucas ran a hand over her arm. "You ready for some breakfast?"

She bobbed her head. "I'm starving."

"I'm assuming Martha still has breakfast on the table at seven."

"Every morning."

"Well..." Craning his neck, Lucas stole a glance at his new phone on the nightstand—the one Shawn had gotten for him the day after he arrived in Beckett Falls—and checked the time. "It's quarter after. If we want any eggs, we'd better hurry."

Throwing back the covers, Rosie hopped out of bed.

Lucas grinned. Nothing got the girl moving like the promise of food.

Both still fully clothed from the night before, they headed downstairs. Lucas trailed behind Rosie and laughed at the tangled mess of her uncombed curls.

"What's so funny?" She narrowed her eyes at him.

"Your hair is a mess."

"I'll take a shower after breakfast." Rosie shrugged. "Must have food first."

When they entered the dining room, Michael and Daniel stopped eating to greet them. Daniel stood and threw his arms around Lucas. "Good to see you."

Michael stayed put. "Dude. Leaving without a goodbye? Dick move."

"I'm sorry, Michael." Lucas frowned. "We couldn't risk Amos finding out."

"I get it." Michael nodded and took a bite of his eggs. "If Sam forgives you, then I guess I do too."

Choosing not to speak, Lucas smiled and nodded. Truthfully, the jury was still out on whether or not Sam had forgiven him for leaving the pack.

Rosie took a seat and started piling food onto her plate, and Lucas followed her lead. He felt like he was imposing, and it didn't sit right with him. Hart House had been his home for as long as he could remember.

"Lucas!" Martha's shriek cut through the air as she came out of the kitchen with more eggs. She rushed to his side and wrapped her free hand around his head, hugging him to her large chest. "It's so good to see you, kiddo!"

"Hi, Martha." Heat crept up Lucas's cheeks. Her gushing attention was both endearing and humiliating. "It's good to see you too."

"You let me know if you need anything." She ruffled his hair as she set the plate on the table and shuffled back to the kitchen.

At Michael's chuckle, Lucas glared.

"So... How do you like Beckett Falls?" Daniel speared a piece of sausage with his fork. "I know you've always wanted to go."

"It's amazing, actually." Lucas paused, careful not to let the conversation venture into pack business. "There are waterfalls everywhere, and the architecture is so interesting. And the brewery..." He caught Rosie frowning.

"Are you going back?" Michael narrowed his eyes.

Silently cursing him, Lucas clenched his teeth.

He looked into Rosie's tortured eyes. "I haven't worked that out yet."

"Sam called this morning." Daniel cleared his throat. He looked at Lucas then Rosie. "He asked if the two of you would meet him for lunch at Miller's. Noon."

Great. He'd get an earful from both Sam *and* Charlie. When he'd left Hanks Hollow, he didn't exactly give Charlie a two-week notice. Lucas lowered his gaze to his plate and nodded. "We'll be there."

"I think I'm full." Rosie stood from the table and turned toward the hall.

Lucas swore and jumped up from his chair to run after her. He caught up to her in the foyer. Grabbing her hand, he pulled her toward him before she could bolt up the stairs. When she turned to him, tears glittered in her eyes.

"Can we talk?" Lucas pleaded. "Outside?"

As she bit her lip, tears spilled down her cheeks, and she gave a short nod.

Lucas led her outside to the porch. Taking a seat on the top step, he pulled her down to sit next to him. After a deep breath, he found the words he needed. "I'm with you, Rosie. Always."

Wiping at the snot dripping from her nose, Rosie sniffled. "But you said—"

"I want to go back to Beckett Falls. I really do." As he took a deep breath, his heart ached with hope. "But not without you."

Shock and confusion crossed over Rosie's face. She looked out toward the trees for a moment. "Lucas, I don't know..."

"I know it's a lot for you right now. I'm willing to wait. You need time. I get that."

"It's not just that." Rosie sniffed again. "I don't know if the Council will allow it."

"That's the thing, though." Excited, Lucas sat up straight. "I'm going to be alpha. Soon. Shawn wants me to take over as soon as possible, so—"

"Lucas... There's more to it than that. The Council was here. Just the other day. They know I'm a witch."

Fear clamped his heart and squeezed. "What?"

"I'm going to tell you something, and I want you to keep an open mind."

The worry in her gaze set him on edge, but he nodded.

"When I was in a coma, I had... dreams... or something. Visions, maybe? I was visited by the gods. They told me I'm here to bring the Chosen back together." She bared her teeth in a nervous smile, eyeing Lucas carefully.

If it had come from anyone else, Lucas would have written them off as crazy. But from Rosie, it made sense. It was out there... really weird. But Lucas had no doubt it had happened. "Okay."

Her eyebrows shot to her hairline. "Okay?"

"Did you tell the Council about this? Because I believe you, Rosie, but I have to say anyone else is probably going to put you in a straitjacket."

"They're taking it to the World Werewolf Council." Rosie frowned. "The jury's still out on the straitjacket."

"Okay. So we wait here for now. But I want to come up with a plan. Just in case they decide..."

"That I'm a crazy, rabid witch-wolf that needs to be put down?"

A shiver coursed through his body. "Don't say that."

"Lucas, there isn't anything we can do if they decide that. The Council's little army is more than we can beat."

"We'll see." He wasn't willing to give up so easily.

"There's one more thing."

"There's more?" Lucas rolled his eyes. "I forgot how adventurous life can be when I'm with you."

"I also saw Stuart... and my dad... and my mom." Rosie smiled and squeezed Lucas's hand. "My parents had a mate bond like ours."

TWENTY-SEVEN
LUCAS

"Your hands are sweating." Rosie dropped Lucas's hand and wiped hers on her shirt. "What is wrong with you? Why are you so nervous?"

Not bothering to answer, Lucas arched an eyebrow. They were approaching Miller's, and an ice chunk the size of a glacier floated in his stomach.

"It's just Sam." Rosie sighed. "He loves you."

"I came onto his land without his permission, I'm dating his sister, I abandoned his pack..." Lucas ticked the transgressions off on his fingers. "If the situations were reversed, I'd be pissed."

"So maybe he is." Rosie shrugged. "He'll get over it. It doesn't change how he feels about you."

Lucas grunted in response as he opened the door for Rosie. Inside, the restaurant was empty. Strange, even for a weekday. Usually, Miller's drew a large lunch crowd. Glancing at the door, Lucas saw the sign had been flipped to Closed.

Maybe Charlie had decided to close early. They would have to catch up with Sam somewhere else. Taking a step back, Lucas was ready to leave before he heard Sam call to them from inside.

"Are we seriously having a private lunch?" Rosie's eyes widened.

Sam approached from the back of the restaurant. "I have an in with the assistant manager."

"I hope you gave her a good tip."

"Yeah, I did." Sam waggled his eyebrows.

Rosie swatted his arm. "Pig."

Sam leveled his gaze at Lucas. "Thank you for coming, guys." He turned and headed toward the back of the restaurant.

Rosie took Lucas's hand and pulled him along as she followed Sam to a booth. Sam sat on one side, and Rosie slid in on the other. Lucas sat next to Rosie. He glanced at Sam but quickly averted his gaze.

After a few moments of awkward silence, Rosie cleared her throat. "Sam..."

"Sorry I'm late." Becca burst into the room, carrying three bottled beverages. As she got closer to the table, Lucas recognized the label—his favorite nonalcoholic beer. "Don't worry. I won't stay while you talk pack business or whatever, but I wanted to bring you these and let you know I've got some burgers cooking for you in back. They'll be ready shortly."

Becca set the beer on the table and bent down to kiss Sam on the cheek. Her whispered "Behave" caused Sam's cheeks to redden, then she disappeared back into the kitchen.

"This is new to all of us," Sam said. He cleared his throat. "Me being alpha... Lucas coming from another pack... the two of you... doing whatever you're doing." He shook his head. "I think we need to understand each other." He sighed. "I love you like a brother. You know that. But you need to understand you're putting me in a tough spot. The Council is watching us closely. I need to know whether you're here to stay or you're going back to Beckett Falls. You know I'll take you back into my pack. But I can't really allow someone from another pack to stay in my territory." His gaze flitted to Rosie. "And I can't let you take Rosie with you."

"Excuse me?" Rosie sat up straight. "How is that for you to decide?"

"You know the answer to that, Rosie." Sam furrowed his brow. "I'm your alpha. I know it's going to take some getting used to, but I need you to follow the rules I put in place. It's my job to protect you. It's too dangerous for you to leave right now. The Council is watching. Any wrong move could set them off. You can't make them angry."

His heart hammering, Lucas closed his eyes. The thought of turning his back on the Becketts made him sick to his stomach, but there was nothing he wouldn't do for Rosie.

"What about the time I spent with the Cramers?" Rosie's chin jutted out defiantly. "I was a visitor on their property. I was there to get to know another future alpha."

"Yeah." Sam dipped his brow in confusion. "What are you getting at?"

"Lucas is a future alpha." As the words left Rosie's mouth, Sam's eyebrows shot to his hairline. "Couldn't you allow him to stay here to court me as a future alpha?"

When Sam's gaze flitted his way, Lucas nodded.

Sam blew a long, slow breath out through his mouth. "If that's your request, Lucas, then I will honor it."

"That's my request." Lucas's mouth twitched in a smile. "Thank you, Sam."

"Lucas Beckett!" The sound of his name being

shouted in anger from across the restaurant drove his heart to his throat. Charlie Miller stomped across the dining room toward them. "You have some nerve, kid."

Lucas shot to his feet. "Charlie, I'm so sorry. I had a family emergency. We had to leave in a hurry."

"Yeah." Charlie crossed his arms. "I heard all that from Sam."

Glancing toward Sam, Lucas mouthed a quick thank-you. Sam shrugged.

Charlie frowned. "Everything okay now? Your family all good?"

"They're doing better. Thank you." Lucas cleared his throat. "I'm really sorry, Charlie."

"Well... you can make it up to me." Charlie pursed his lips. "One of my guys has a broken arm, so I'm down a bartender." He rolled his eyes. "Idiot fell off his water skis. If you can fill in for him while you're in town, you'd be doing me a big favor."

"Of course." Lucas's shoulders sagged with relief. A couple of nights working the bar sounded great, actually. "I can do that."

"Great. Your burgers are up. I'm going to go get them." A small smile twitched at Charlie's mouth, and he winked at Rosie before he turned and disappeared into the kitchen.

Lucas collapsed into the booth and let his heartbeat return to normal.

"And you were worried." An I-told-you-so smile graced Rosie's lips.

Charlie came back out a moment later with three plates of burgers and set them on the table. "Hey, Rosie, I heard what happened last night, sweetie. I'm sorry. Whole town is talking about it already. Guess we know who broke into your grandma's place the other night. Sure hope the boys are keeping an eye on you till that little creep is found and put behind bars."

Just as his heart rate had returned to normal, it sped again. What break-in?

"Thank you, Charlie." Rosie put ketchup on her burger as she responded casually, but her hands shook ever so slightly. "Hopefully they'll find him soon and get him the help he needs."

"Well, you let me know if there's anything I can do." Charlie shook his finger at her. "I'm going to get you some mace just like I got for Becca. You girls need to stay off that boardwalk at night."

Lucas watched Charlie march back to the kitchen then turned to Rosie.

"When were you going to tell me he broke into your grandmother's house?" Trying to control the volume of his voice, Lucas spoke slowly. "What happened?"

"It was nothing." Rosie shrugged. "He left dead roses in my hospital room and on my bed at my grandmother's house."

Sam and Lucas spoke at once. Over Lucas's curse, Sam asked angrily, "What the hell are you talking about, Rosie? You never said anything about anyone leaving dead roses in the hospital."

Rosie's face paled. "It didn't seem important at the time, then I didn't think about it until long after the break-in."

"And you didn't think this was important information for the sheriff?" Sam rolled his eyes. "Seriously, Rosie. What's wrong with you?"

"Hey." Lucas wasn't pleased with Rosie either, but his hackles raised at Sam's tone. The wolf inside him growled. "Chill out a little bit, Sam."

Eyes rounding, Sam threw his napkin down on

the table. "Really? Do you know how serious this is, Lucas? There was blood mixed in with the roses. Someone was sending a clear threat."

Every muscle in Lucas's body tensed.

Rosie massaged her forehead. "I know I screwed up, okay?" She sighed. "I'll call the sheriff and tell him about the roses in the hospital room. I don't see the point, though. They already know who did it."

"I'm not so sure." Sam scowled.

"What do you mean?" Rosie asked.

Sam looked toward the kitchen then scanned the dining room before he leaned forward. "I sniffed around at Clara's place the day after the break-in. I thought I smelled one of the pack, but it smelled like Amos."

Paling even more, Rosie swallowed. Tears clouded her eyes. "You said Amos is dead."

"He is." Sam furrowed his brow. "Something doesn't add up." An angry shadow passed over his face. "If I would have known the same person was at the hospital, I could have sniffed around there to see if I could find a scent."

Rosie's small shoulders sagged. "I'm really sorry, Sam."

Feeling the need to reassure her, Lucas took Rosie's hand and squeezed.

Sam's eyes flitted down to their entangled hands, and he sighed. "I know, Rosie. I'm sorry I lost my temper."

"We'll figure this out," Lucas promised. "No one is going to hurt you."

TWENTY-EIGHT
ROSIE

IN THE DAYS THAT FOLLOWED, THE TOWN GOSSIP centered around Mason stalking Rosie. Most people agreed he'd done it to get back at the Hart family. The rivalry between the Harts and Paul and Mason Lewis had become famous. Rosie spent her life trying to stay out of the spotlight, so being the center of attention put her anxiety level off the charts.

Rosie squeezed Lucas's hand and bit her lip as they walked down Main Street. All around her, people glanced her way and nudged one another, pointing. She'd heard several of the whispers yesterday when she sat on the boardwalk outside Miller's while Lucas worked. She'd thought it would be a good idea to sit with her laptop and study while he worked but regretted it as soon as she felt the stares of the people around her.

"Did you hear?"

"He's been stalking her since she woke up from the coma..."

"I bet he did it to get back at Sam for not letting him hunt on their land..."

"She's always been weird. I doubt it even happened the way she said it did..."

She tried to ignore them and focused on the shops. They hadn't changed much in her time away. The Sconnie Scoop still served the best ice cream—she'd already stopped there a couple of times. The popcorn shop smelled just as heavenly. Tourist shops still sold Northwoods T-shirts and souvenirs. The only marked difference was the diner. For years, it had been Dave's Diner. Now, the sign above the red and white awning had changed to read Greta's. Not Greta's Diner... just Greta's. Becca had promised Rosie the best pancakes ever if she gave the restaurant a try, so Rosie and Lucas made the late-morning trip for breakfast before Lucas's afternoon shift at Miller's.

She also *needed* to check out Daniel's crush. It sounded like he had it pretty bad for Greta. From the way Daniel talked about the restaurant owner, they sounded so right for each other.

As she and Lucas stepped out of the cool fall wind and into the small, crowded diner, a whoosh of warm air filled with the smell of maple syrup hit Rosie's face. Her stomach rumbling, she scanned the restaurant for a place to sit.

"Hey, guys!" a woman called out to them from behind the counter as she poured a cup of coffee for one of the customers. Her long, lean body bent forward as she spoke. Dark hair stuck out in short, choppy wisps around her face. Red lips popped against flawless porcelain skin. "I think there's a table in the corner."

The woman turned back toward the kitchen and placed the coffeepot on the coffee maker. Even from across the room, Rosie could feel her energy. Familiar, electric. Like Rosie's grandmother...

A hand on her back startled her, and she jumped.

"Sorry." Lucas creased his forehead, looking from Rosie to the woman and back again. "Are you okay?"

"Yeah." Rosie moved through the maze of tables, chairs, and people toward the table the woman had gestured to, and she slid into a chair. Lucas sat across from her and picked up a menu.

The woman sashayed toward them, a bright smile on her face and a small pad of paper and a pencil in her hand. "Hi, kids. I'm Greta. You here for some pancakes?"

Not able to find her voice, Rosie nodded.

Lucas creased his brow again as he studied her. "Yeah, we'll both have pancakes. And some coffee. Thank you."

Greta winked before she spun on her heel, doing a little twirl and calling, "Whoopsie!" as the busboy almost collided with her. She returned moments later with a pot of coffee and filled their cups, humming, before she fluttered away.

"What's up?" Lucas spoke quietly. "Something's wrong."

"She's a witch." The words tumbled out of Rosie's mouth, and she flicked her gaze toward Greta. The woman stared back at her, a small smile playing at her lips. No doubt Greta could read Rosie just as easily as Rosie could read her.

Lucas turned to look toward the kitchen. "Are you sure?"

Rosie blew out a soft huff. "Positive."

"Wow." He arched an eyebrow. "That seems like a weird coincidence."

"What do you mean?"

"I mean... I don't think there are very many witches, from what you've told me. Seems weird that one would show up in this little town where there are two others."

Curiosity gnawed at Rosie. What was this woman's story?

"You have your laptop." Lucas patted Rosie's hand. "You planning to study in the park?"

Nodding, Rosie felt a knot of worry. She planned to drive to the community college to take the first module of her GED test tomorrow. She'd taken a practice test, and it seemed like material she'd learned in high school. Still, test anxiety gnawed at her.

"That was fast." Lucas leaned back as Greta scampered to the table, holding two plates with heaping piles of pancakes.

"Fresh off the griddle." Greta put the plates on the table and smiled. "Peter keeps 'em coming until lunch."

"Thank you, Greta." Finally finding her voice, Rosie smiled at the woman. "They smell really good."

Their eyes met for a moment, and something passed between them. A shared knowledge.

"Enjoy." Greta smiled at Lucas again before she turned to walk back to the kitchen.

When Rosie focused her attention on her plate, her stomach growled again, and her mouth watered. She grabbed the syrup from the table and doused the pancakes then grabbed her fork and took her first bite. Syrupy deliciousness melted in her mouth, and she quickly shoved another piece into her mouth.

"Slow down. They aren't going anywhere." Lucas laughed at her as he poured syrup over his pancakes.

"I'm hungry. Back off." Rosie kicked him under the table.

"Ow. Okay, okay. I know better than to get between you and food."

Lucas took a giant bite. His lips ticked up in a smile between his bloated cheeks, and she laughed.

Lucas's phone vibrated on the tabletop, and he swallowed before he picked it up. "Hey, Charlie. What's up?" Rosie watched his face fall. "Yeah, okay. I'll be right there." He stuffed his phone into his pocket as he stood from the table. "I'm really sorry. Charlie had a big shipment come in, and no one's there to help him with it. The restaurant is opening soon, and there are boxes everywhere. I wasn't supposed to go in until later, but he needs me."

"You're kidding, right?" Anxiety crawled through her at the thought of eating alone in a crowded restaurant.

"I'm really sorry." Lucas bent down to kiss her cheek. "I'll see you later?"

Rosie forced a smile, and Lucas turned to make his way through the crowd of people and out the door.

"That's insulting."

Rosie jumped at the sound of Greta's voice. She hadn't even heard her approach the table.

"He barely took two bites. Better not let Pete see that." Greta started to take the plate away, but she paused and studied Rosie's face. "Everything okay, doll?"

"Fine," Rosie said with a tight smile.

"You know..." Greta sat down in the chair Lucas had just abandoned. "That boy is head over heels for you."

Rosie's cheeks warmed. "I know. The feeling is mutual."

"I know." Greta placed a hand on Rosie's.

Rosie sighed deeply as euphoria surged through her body, and her anxiety left her. She recognized the feeling immediately and gasped.

"What brought you to Hanks Hollow?" Rosie whispered.

Greta's expression shifted, and she seemed to be in a different place. "I can't explain it. I had to. Almost like a calling."

Sucking in a breath, Rosie thought about the words of the Goddess. *If the wolves change their ways, the witches will come.*

"I know what you are," Greta whispered. She winked and stood from the table, taking Lucas's full plate of pancakes with her.

Happy hour was in full swing. The locals occupied their usual barstools, nursing their usual cheap pilsners and rolling their eyes at the tourists. The fall tourism season brought in hordes of vacationers. They perused the beer menu for several minutes before asking for recommendations on the best craft-beer experience.

Lucas plopped a fresh bottle of cheap, big-name beer in front of one of the regulars. "There you go."

Ernie grunted in response as he finished the bottle he had been working on and reached for the new one. A permanent fixture there every afternoon, Ernie always came in right after he finished work at the distribution center outside town and sat on the barstool closest to the back wall of the bar. He spent an hour and a half nursing four beers before he hefted himself up and headed home to his wife and kids.

"Have you seen Rosie today?" Becca plopped her tray on the bar, leaning over it to get Lucas's attention. Her voice came out in a wobbly rush. The early-dinner rush had her juggling at least five or six tables.

"Yeah, I had breakfast with her this morning. Why?" Lucas watched her out of the corner of his eye as he delivered a beer sample to a waffling tourist. He turned his attention to the man briefly. "Try that one. I think you'll like it."

He grabbed a rag from under the bar and wiped his hands as he approached Becca. Loose strands fell from her ponytail into her face, and her smudged black eye makeup framed her eyes, which glittered with tears. "Are you okay, Becca?"

She huffed a breath grabbing her tray and turning back toward her waiting tables. She called to him over her shoulder, "Fine. Tell her I'm looking for her."

"Oookay." Lucas creased his brow.

"You're right, young man." The tourist held up the empty sample cup. "I like that one. I'll take one of these."

"You got it." Lucas reached under the bar for a bottle of the expensive ale and jumped when someone tugged on his hair.

"Hey, slacker." Rosie leaned over the bar, stretching her short body as far as she could reach, her lips puckered for a kiss. Her red curls spilled around her face and pooled on the bar top, getting wet as they dipped into some spilled beer.

Lucas smiled and leaned forward, kissing her before he pushed her hair behind her shoulder and out of the beer. He swiped his rag across the spill then went over to the waiting vacationer and handed him the beer. "Becca is looking for you. She looks upset about something."

Rosie's smile dropped, and she crinkled her brow. She glanced behind her toward the dining area.

"She's got a lot of tables. Just let her know you're here," Lucas instructed. He knew Rosie would immediately want to take her best friend aside and find out what was bothering her, but that would only put Becca behind.

Rosie went toward the dining room and came back a few minutes later. She found an empty stool and plopped down. Her freckled face creased in a frown. "She's been crying."

"I'm sure she's fine," Lucas said. "Maybe she has her—"

"Do *not* finish that sentence." Rosie scowled. "Not every female problem revolves around her menstrual cycle."

Lucas laughed as he leaned over the bar, took Rosie's delicate hand, and started playing with her fingers. "Did you get lots of studying done today?"

"Yes, I did." Rosie's lips curled into a grin as she leaned forward, her face inches from his. Her breath smelled of sweet peppermint. "But I was constantly distracted, thinking about a tall, handsome bartender."

A smile stretched across Lucas's face, and he brushed his lips over hers. He tasted her cherry lip gloss as he deepened the kiss. The familiar spark ignited like a firecracker. The noises around them fell away, and he deepened the kiss further. He wanted her. God, he wanted her.

"Hey, Lucas! Think you can pry yourself away from your girlfriend long enough to get me a beer?" Ernie's snarky growl hit his eardrum with a smack, and the noises of the bar came back in a cold crescendo of idle chatter, loud televisions, and raucous laughter.

Lucas groaned and dropped his head to the bar top, and Rosie massaged her hands through his hair soothingly. He straightened and made his way over to Ernie, grabbing a beer along the way.

"Be careful, kid," Ernie said. He smirked and winked at Lucas. "They draw you in with their feminine wiles, but they have the bite of a wild dog."

A smile lit Lucas's face as he glanced back toward Rosie. "Don't I know it."

"Speaking of wild dogs..." the man next to Ernie drunkenly chimed in. Lucas wasn't sure of his name. He was a local who only came in on occasion. "Anyone hear anything about Mason Lewis? He still hiding out somewhere, or did they find 'im?"

Narrowing his eyes, Lucas reined in his temper. "What does that have to do with wild dogs?"

"Because he's so obsessed with that red wolf." The man teetered on the edge of his barstool, looking like he would fall off, but he righted himself again. "Him and that other hunter. The one always wearin' them sunglasses."

Sure his heart was beating louder than the music, Lucas glanced toward Rosie. She played with the new phone Sam had given her, oblivious to the conversation. He tried to act casual and interested in the gossip. "I didn't hear about that. They going to hunt it down?"

"Pssshhh." The man waved a hand through the air and almost fell off the stool again. "Nothin' gonna stop Mason from getting that wolf. He is absolutely one hundred percent positive it killed his dad. Hates it more than he hates that little red-headed girl and all the rest of the Hart family."

Quickly glancing toward Rosie again, he sighed in relief. She still played with her phone and hadn't heard any of it.

"You mean that little red-headed girl?" Ernie asked. He pointed toward Rosie.

The man turned, and his eyes widened when he saw Rosie sitting at the other end of the bar.

"Ralph, you're such a dumbass," Ernie said. "Go home."

"Oh." The man did a hiccup-burp combination and slid off the stool. As he passed Rosie, he put a hand on her back. "Sorry!"

Lucas stepped forward, ready to throw him out, but the man moved on, stumbling out the door. Rosie watched him go, confusion etched all over her face. She turned her gaze toward Lucas, and he gave his best attempt at a smile as he shrugged.

"Rosie!" Becca rushed to Rosie's side, and the two of them began talking softly.

Turning back toward Ernie, Lucas almost asked him if he wanted another, but the man slid off his stool. "Forget Ralph." Ernie shrugged. "He talks a lot, but he don't know shit."

As Ernie sauntered toward the door, Lucas's phone buzzed in his back pocket. He pulled it out and cursed under his breath when he saw his father's name on the caller ID. He'd checked in with Shawn each morning over the last few days. The alpha had assured him all was quiet.

"Dad?" Lucas held the phone to one ear and held a hand over the other to block out the noise in the bar.

"Lucas." Roger's voice came through clear and urgent. "You need to come home."

"What is it? What's wrong?"

"Marcus came back."

Lucas almost dropped the phone. "What?"

"Christopher and Travis managed to chase him away, but, Lucas, you have to get back here. Your pack needs you."

THIRTY

ROSIE

THE COOL NIGHT AIR BIT AT ROSIE'S CHEEKS AS Becca pulled her outside Miller's and rushed her to the door that led to Becca's second-story apartment. She quickly unlocked it, grabbed Rosie's hand, and pulled her up the stairs.

"I have to talk to you, Rosie."

"I gathered that." Rosie stumbled over the stairs as she tried to keep up with her friend. "What's wrong?"

As Becca pulled Rosie into her apartment, something in her energy hit Rosie. She couldn't place it. Underneath Becca's anxiety and fear was something new.

"I think I'm pregnant." The words came out in a rush, and fresh tears sprang to Becca's eyes.

Rosie gasped. Pregnant? Her eyes trailing down to Becca's belly, Rosie gently reached out and touched her fingers to the area. A faint energy wisped over her hand. Not Becca's normal energy—something new.

"We have to talk to my grandma," Rosie said. "She can tell us."

"Tonight," Becca said. "Please. I have to know

now. I already told my dad I'm sick. He's covering my tables."

"Okay." Rosie ran her hands through Becca's soft blond hair and sent a calming energy through her fingers. She watched the tension leave Becca's shoulders. "It's going to be okay."

Tears slid down Becca's face. "Will it?"

"Hey." Rosie gently pushed Becca onto the couch and took her hand. "Sammy loves you. If you're carrying his child, he'll be over the moon."

"It's complicated." Becca rolled her eyes as she wiped her tears away.

Complicated—yes. Rosie tried to shove that aside. For Becca's benefit, she giggled. "Sam isn't going to lock you up and let the pack eat you."

"It's not funny, Rosie!" Becca sobbed. "I was in that cell, remember?"

A shudder ran through Becca's body, and Rosie winced in sympathy. Her own memories of the cell came back in a rush, and her stomach tightened. "I'm sorry. We'll figure this out, okay? Get changed. We'll go see Grandma."

~

CLARA'S DOOR opened as Rosie and Becca climbed the steps to her front porch.

"Rosie?" Clara's face pinched with concern. "What is it? What's wrong?" Clara's gaze flitted to Becca, and her mouth dropped open. A knowing glint touched her eyes.

Clara stood aside, inviting Becca and Rosie into the house. The smells of incense, lavender, and an assortment of spices hit Rosie's nose as she pulled Becca to the scratchy couch, and the two of them sat down.

Clara knelt in front of Becca and gestured to her stomach. "May I?"

Becca's face scrunched tightly, and she let out a little sob as she nodded. Clara put her hand on Becca's lower abdomen.

"It's a werewolf." Clara nodded to herself.

"How do you know that?" Rosie had barely felt something off until Becca told her she was pregnant. How on earth could her grandma sense it was a werewolf?

"Aside from the fact that she and your brother have been glued to each other? I've felt that energy before, when your mother was pregnant with you. You'll get to know the energy, then you'll recognize it when you feel it again. Just like the energy of any living thing. It's unique."

Becca sobbed. "What am I going to do?"

Rosie took Becca's shaking hand and sent her soothing energy. "You're going to talk to Sammy, and the two of you will figure it out together. You're not alone, Becca."

Contemptuous energy wafted in the air, and Rosie shot her grandmother a look. She knew how Clara felt about the chauvinistic world of werewolves, and a small tickle of worry nagged at her. Clara wouldn't hesitate to speak her mind, but Becca didn't need that. Not now.

"Grandma," Rosie warned.

Clara huffed and grunted as she climbed off the floor. "Men are stupid."

A smile tugged at Rosie's lips. No one would argue with that.

Clara made her way to her kitchen and rummaged around in the cabinets until she found what she was looking for then came back to the living room with a bottle of oil.

"Here," Clara said. She handed the oil to Becca. "This is ginger. It will help with the queasiness. If it gets bad, come and see me or Rosie. We can help."

Rosie squeezed Becca's hand. "Do you want to go out to Hart House with me tonight to talk to him?"

"God, no." Becca wiped her hand across her nose and sniffed. "I need some time to think."

Rosie nodded and squeezed Becca's hand again. Hopefully Becca wouldn't wait too long. Sam would have a lot of thinking to do himself. She knew her brother. He would try his hardest to do what was right for Becca, but his actions and decisions would be influenced by more than a sense of obligation. His primal instinct to protect the pack could drive away logic and reason. Rosie wondered if love would win over instinct. She prayed they wouldn't need to find out.

THIRTY-ONE
ROSIE

Rosie pried her sticky eyelids open to peek at the morning sun coming through the bedroom windows. With a long, low groan, she checked the clock on her phone. She had just enough time for a shower before breakfast. Mentally, she ticked off all the things she should do to prepare for a big test. Study? Check. Get a good night's sleep? Check. Breakfast? Getting there...

Beside her, Lucas stared up at the ceiling. Tense lines crinkled around his eyes. He'd been quiet the night before when she returned to Miller's with Becca to ride back to Hart House with him. She couldn't read Lucas's energy the way she could with everyone else, but it didn't take an empath to feel his tension. Something bothered him.

His warm skin felt soft under her fingers as she ran them over his arm. Letting her energy run through her body and out through her fingers, she watched the tension leave his face as he relaxed under her touch.

Blue eyes met hers as she let her fingers trail over his chest. "Good morning."

"You didn't have to do that."

Rosie frowned. "I don't like it when you look tense. It makes me feel tense."

"Sorry." Lucas turned and leaned on his arm. "I definitely don't want that, especially not today. You ready for your big test?"

"Ready as I'll ever be, I guess." Rosie shrugged. "I'll feel better after a shower, though." Watching Lucas closely, she nudged him. "Are you okay?"

"I'm good."

Rosie rolled out of bed and grabbed her towel on the way to the bathroom. She pulled her sweats off and stepped into the shower, flinching as the water hit her face. The relaxing smell of the lavender soap her grandmother had made put her at ease. After washing her hair, she stepped out onto the tiled floor, feeling much more ready to face the day.

After wrapping herself in a towel, she ran a comb through her tangled, wet curls before she stepped out of the bathroom to get dressed.

As she went into the bedroom, Lucas pulled a T-shirt over his head then buttoned his jeans. He leaned down and kissed her. "I'll see you downstairs after you get dressed?"

Rosie nodded, and he left, closing the bedroom door behind him.

Deciding on a sweater and a pair of jeans, she quickly dressed then went back to the bathroom to dry her hair. Her red curls frizzed under the heat of the blow dryer, and she tamed them with some conditioning spray.

After she was finished getting ready, she bounced down the stairs, rounded the corner, and moved down the hall to the dining room. Everyone was already at the table.

"Good morning!" Rosie plopped into the chair closest to Lucas, grabbed a piece of bacon, and stuffed it into her mouth.

"You're in a good mood." Daniel's grin reached his eyes. "What's got you so happy?"

"She's taking the first part of her GED today," Lucas supplied.

"And that puts you in a good mood?" Michael raised an eyebrow.

Rosie shrugged. "I guess it's just nice to have a little piece of something normal." She rolled her eyes. "And to get out of Hanks Hollow for once."

At the head of the table, Sam froze. "Where are you going for the test?"

"North Lake Community College."

"You didn't tell me that, Rosie." Sam's face reddened. "Is anyone going with you?"

The tension in the room notched up, and it ate at Rosie's nerves. The last thing she needed was to exhaust herself on negative energy. She huffed. "I'm driving myself. The Jeep is still in the garage, and I still have my license."

"Rosie..." Sam shook his head.

"Sam, it's fine!" Rosie grumbled. "I'm driving there, taking the test, then driving right back. I won't stop anywhere else."

"Maybe I should go with you." Lucas touched Rosie's knee. "I can wait in the car. It's not a big deal."

"No." Rosie scrunched her face. "I don't need a babysitter. Besides, you have a shift at Miller's today."

"Fine." Lucas raised his hands and chuckled. "Just call me when you get there, okay?"

"Shoot me a text too," Sam grunted.

She rolled her eyes. "Fine."

"Mason is still out there somewhere," Sam said. "We'll all feel better when he's locked up."

Rosie frowned. "I know. I'll be careful."

~

"Remember to call me when you get there." Standing on the front porch of Hart House, Lucas wrapped his arms around Rosie and squeezed then kissed the top of her head. "You'll do great. I know it."

Face smooshed against his chest, Rosie felt safe and warm. Like nothing in the world could touch her. If he wanted her to, she would go with him to Beckett Falls. She would go with him anywhere.

Hart House had always been her home, but things change. Lucas was her home now. Wherever he went, she went too.

With a final kiss goodbye, Rosie turned and headed down the porch steps.

When she entered the large garage, the red Jeep Wrangler sat ready for her. Michael had told her he "tuned her up and topped her off" that morning, so she was good to go. As she settled into the driver's seat, nostalgia brought a sting to her sinuses. Her first and only vehicle. She'd missed it. She and Lucas had spent a lot of time together in the Jeep.

When she turned the key, the engine roared to life. Deep breath. Could she still drive? She *felt* fine, but the whole being-in-a-coma-for-a-year thing made her hesitate. Guess she would find out. Easing her foot onto the gas, she pulled the jeep out of the garage, then she coasted down the driveway to the road. After making a left, she picked up speed, feeling the rough pavement beneath the large tires. It would just take a little getting used to. Just like riding a...

A scream erupted from her throat as a blur of black ran out in front of her. Time froze as the black wolf stopped in the middle of the road and stared directly at her. She stomped her foot on the brake and jerked the wheel to the left, screaming as the Jeep careened down the embankment, into the trees.

HER HEAD POUNDING IN TIME WITH HER HEART, Rosie looked up at the cracked windshield and tried to steady her breathing. Shakily, she reached to her forehead and felt the sticky wetness from a cut.

Her door was cracked open. She tumbled out of the Jeep and found her footing, staggering away from the vehicle. A nearby tree provided the stability she needed when everything started spinning. She leaned against it and glanced back at the wreckage. The front end was wrinkled like an accordion against a tree.

Michael would be pissed.

Her phone. She needed her phone. Rosie reached into her back pocket and pulled it out. She was about to make a call, but her hand froze when a low growl rumbled behind her. A memory hit her. The black wolf in the road. Amos? She turned slowly.

Yellow eyes popped against pitch-black fur. He crouched, ready to attack. Dropping the phone, Rosie ran. She shifted, and on all fours, she ran faster.

Behind her, the beat of Amos's feet quickened and went to the right. She went to the left and tried to run faster.

It didn't make sense. Amos was supposed to be dead. Sam had assured her he was.

Ahead, a large crop of pines gave way to a clearing. She headed straight toward it and shot through the grass. Amos kept pace with her then went to the left. She went right.

Just as she reached the rocky base of a bluff, she felt a pinch on her front right paw before she heard a snap. She was jerked backward and pulled to the ground. Something squeezed her paw. She shook it, but it wouldn't release. The silver glistened in the sun, and it hit her. She'd been snared by a foot trap. Panic overwhelmed her, and she shook her paw, trying to get loose.

Amos paused behind her. He had her cornered. Had he corralled her?

"*Amos?*" she projected, but he stayed silent.

He held her gaze for several more moments until the hum of an ATV engine in the distance grew louder. As it neared, the black wolf took off, disappearing into the trees.

Rosie didn't have time to shift before the ATV came into view. As the clatter of the engine neared, she tucked in her tail and lowered her body to the ground. She finally got a view of the person driving, and she desperately made another attempt to free herself from the trap.

Mason Lewis jumped off the ATV. "I got you!" he yelled. "I finally got you!" Mason reached for his shotgun. "I've been waiting for this day a long time."

The sound of another ATV revved to life somewhere nearby, as though it had just been started. It picked up speed then spun around the trees. It skidded to a halt next to Mason. The hunter climbed off the vehicle and approached, aiming his gun at Rosie.

He was the hunter she'd seen that day in the woods behind Hart House. The one who shot her father. Sunglasses. Blaze-orange beanie. Up close, she could see black hair that jutted from under the cap and unkept stubble that lined his chin. The overwhelming smell of cheap cologne and tobacco assaulted her senses.

Frozen in place, Rosie watched the man smile. Something was familiar about that smile.

"Come on, Frank," Mason whined. "You have to let me be the one to shoot her."

Rosie's heart skipped a beat when she heard the name. Stuart's warning rang in her head.

Frank.

THIRTY-THREE

LUCAS

After saying goodbye to Rosie on the porch, Lucas went back into the house to get ready for his shift at Miller's. He'd had a quick shower after breakfast, so he just needed to grab a flannel to throw on over his T-shirt.

He was halfway up the stairs when Michael called out to him from the foyer. Lucas paused and turned toward him, resting his hand on the banister.

"You going to Miller's?" Michael scratched the back of his head and squinted through a yawn, slurring the words.

Lucas narrowed his eyes. "Yeah, I have a shift starting in half an hour. Why?"

"Can I catch a ride with you?"

"Where's your truck?"

Michael smiled sheepishly. "On Lake Street... in front of Miller's."

"Michael..." Lucas grinned. "Were you too drunk to drive home last night?"

"I came home with Sam." Michael shrugged. "It's a little blurry, but I do remember some shots."

Lucas shook his head and turned to jog up the rest

of the stairs. "You're a terrible influence. Meet me in my car in five minutes."

"Thanks, Lucas!" The giddy shout was followed by a laugh.

Upstairs, Lucas opened the door to Rosie's room and rummaged through his duffel on the floor. His old room still sat empty down the hall because he slept in Rosie's room every night. He hadn't really gotten around to unpacking his things in the few days he'd been there.

Grabbing a flannel and pulling it on, he stole a glance at the potted plants on the windowsill. They were flourishing, the leaves healthy and green. So much livelier than they had ever looked while Rosie was away. He touched one of the leaves.

God, he hoped she would come with him. Time had run out for him. He had to get to Beckett Falls. The pack needed him. Christopher and Travis had managed to chase Marcus away when he showed up, but what about next time? He needed to be there.

But he couldn't leave Rosie...

Squeezing his eyes shut, he ran a hand through his hair.

He would talk to her tonight. After her test. Ask her to come with him. Sam would be furious. They would have to answer to the Council. He didn't care. If she was willing, they would face the consequences together.

"Lucas, come on!"

The shout from downstairs reminded him Michael was waiting, and he walked to the door. Jogging down the stairs, Lucas glared at Michael. "I'm coming. I'm coming."

"Aren't you going to be late for work?"

"Yeah, yeah." Lucas checked the time on his phone and cursed. "We need to go."

Outside, a mild, sunny day greeted them. They hurried down the porch steps, across the paved driveway, and through the garage to Roger's car. Michael barely had his door shut before Lucas stepped on the gas and blew down the driveway. After whipping the car to the left toward Hanks Hollow, he accelerated quickly, hoping to make the ten-minute drive in seven or less.

When they were barely a mile down the road, Michael's shouts nearly made him drive off the road. "That's Betty! Lucas! Stop! That's Betty!"

Putting all his strength behind his foot, he slammed it into the brake pedal. The car screeched across the pavement as it slid to a halt. Lucas stared through the windshield, watching for something in the road. Chest heaving, heart hammering, eyes wide, he waited.

Nothing came.

Anger bubbled to the surface, and just as he turned to lay into Michael, the sun glinted off red metal and caught his eye. Looking closer, he saw it.

"Jesus."

At his whispered curse, they both leaped from the car and hurtled toward the wrecked Jeep.

Please, please, please let her be all right. The thought of her flying through the windshield made him sick to his stomach.

Lucas leaped into the ditch and ran to the open driver's-side door. Cracks spiderwebbed across the windshield, and he winced. The Jeep lay empty, and he sniffed. Blood but not much. Hopefully she wasn't badly hurt.

After turning toward the forest, he took a step forward and sniffed again. Rosie's scent hit him. Her *wolf* scent. Why did she shift? He searched the ground and spotted her torn clothes a few yards away.

Sniffing again, he sought her unique smell. It mingled with the fresh scent of another wolf. Another Hart. "Someone is with her."

"Impossible." Michael took a deep breath in through his nose. "It smells like Amos. I can smell that oily bastard anywhere. But he's dead. I burned his body. I don't get it."

Michael's tracking skills outmatched everyone else's in the pack. If he smelled Amos...

"Take the car, and go get Sam and Daniel." Lucas shook himself out of his flannel and tore off his T-shirt. "I'm going to look for them."

Michael clenched his jaw. "You'll need help."

"Which is why we need the whole pack." Lucas pulled off his jeans and took one last look at Michael. "Go!"

After turning on his heel, Michael took off up the ditch to the road.

Lucas moved in the other direction, leaping through the air and shifting into wolf form. When all four paws hit the ground, he paused only long enough to sniff out the right direction before he pushed his legs as fast as they would go.

After a few minutes of following the scent, the sound of an ATV speeding across the terrain hit his ears. The little vehicle was headed in the same direction he was, and his stomach dropped. Michael couldn't have gotten to Sam and Daniel so quickly. Only one other type of person rode an ATV in the middle of the wilderness.

A hunter.

Trying to push his legs harder, he pressed on.

Ahead of him, the ATV slowed to a stop. The sound of voices hit him, but he couldn't make out the words.

When the ATV and two hunters came into view, Lucas slid to a stop and crouched behind some bushes. Scanning the area, he spotted Rosie, and his heart leaped to his throat. Pinned against a rock wall, she had two guns trained on her. She pulled desperately at her paw, and Lucas let a low whine escape from his throat. She was stuck in a trap.

"Come on, Frank. You have to let me shoot her."

Lucas's blood boiled in his veins at the sound of Mason's voice, and hatred consumed him as Mason took aim at Rosie's head. Lucas ran out from behind the bushes, leaped onto Mason's back, and tackled him to the ground.

THIRTY-FOUR

SAM

THE TICKING OF THE GIANT GRANDFATHER CLOCK in the corner of the office beat against Sam's brain. The level of its annoyance competed with the hum of the computer. Sam stared at the screen, but the numbers on the spreadsheet couldn't hold his attention. Too much was going on for him to focus on work. He rubbed his forehead and contemplated taking a couple of aspirin.

"Sam?"

The shaky voice startled him, and he swung his gaze to the doorway. Becca shifted from one foot to the other, twisting her fingers together nervously. She looked like she would run away at any moment. He hadn't even heard her drive up. He definitely needed a break.

"Becca?" Sam stood and moved to her. "I wasn't expecting you. Is everything all right?"

A tear made its way down her cheek, and Sam's stomach clenched. He took her hand and led her to the large leather sofa. They both sat, and Sam squeezed her hand.

"What is it, Bec? What's wrong?"

"Sammy..." Her breath hitched in a sob as she met his gaze. "I'm pregnant."

Sam dropped Becca's hand as a wave of dizziness hit him. He stood, pacing to the fireplace. Bracing his hands on the mantel, he took a few deep breaths. *Don't freak out. Stay calm.*

An image filled his head—Becca in the cell downstairs, crying, terrified. He squeezed his eyes shut. Not the same. They didn't do that anymore. They could work around it. Garrett said they were inviting women into the packs to live in the Pacific Northwest.

"Sam?"

"Okay." He turned back toward Becca. "Okay. This is... This is a surprise, but it's good." He smiled reassuringly as he took a seat next to her. "This is great, Becca. A baby."

Her brow creased with confusion. "You're not freaked out?"

"Are you kidding? I'm thrilled! Becca, I love you." He plastered another smile on his face.

"You're pretending, Sam. Don't do that."

Damn. She knew him too well. "I *am* happy. Really." Sam took her hands in his. "But if we keep this baby, it comes at a cost for you."

Becca's hands tensed inside Sam's. "What do you mean?"

"You know what I am." She searched his face, and it made the words harder. "You know I'm bound to the laws of my kind. If we have this child, you'll need to join us. Here."

"You mean... like move in together?" Becca didn't look appalled by the idea, and Sam was relieved.

"It's more than that." Sam took a deep breath. "Humans who are taken in by a pack are bound to the pack forever. You can never leave."

"You mean... I would be locked up? I would never see my dad again?"

Sam smiled. "I would never lock you up. But you would need to live here. You could still visit your dad, but I don't think you would be able to work at the restaurant anymore."

Becca shrugged and raised an eyebrow. "That doesn't sound so bad."

So far, so good. He dropped his smile before he told her the last bit. "There's one more thing. When I say you can never leave, I mean it. Werewolves don't have a lot of laws, but the secrecy of our existence is first and foremost. That means no human with knowledge of the werewolf world is allowed to live outside a pack."

"You mean—"

"The pack is obligated to kill any human who tries to leave."

Becca pushed Sam's hands away and stood. "*What?* Are you kidding me? Sam, that's messed up! So if things don't work out between us, you have to kill me?"

"No, not exactly." Sam stood and reached for her, but she shook off his hand. "If things didn't work out between us, we wouldn't date anymore, but you would still have to stay here."

She crossed her arms and rolled her eyes before turning her back on him. "Oh my God. This is insane. Insane!"

Placing his hands gently on her shoulders, he could feel her tension. "It *is* insane. I get that. But is it really that much more insane than the fact that you're dating a werewolf?"

She turned to him and glared. "Cute." She shook him off again and paced back and forth a few times. "I have to think about this, Sam."

"I understand." Sam bit his lip. "I love you, Becca. If you decide this isn't for you, I get it. I do. But you'll need to make your decision soon. If you decide not to do this, you'll have to terminate the pregnancy." He flinched as the words left his mouth. Allowing her to have an abortion went against his instincts. He needed to grow the pack. A primal part of him wanted to claim the child inside her as his. Fighting past it, he knew he had to let her choose.

Becca's eyes welled with tears, and she nodded silently. "I need to go."

She turned, about to run out the door, but she collided with Daniel as he ran into the office.

"Sorry, Becca." Daniel barely looked at her as he glided past her and rushed to Sam, waving a journal in the air. "I found it. Sam, I found it."

"Found what?"

"The answer. To everything." Daniel shook his head. "Did you know that Amos had a brother? A *twin* brother?"

"What?" Sam grabbed the journal from Daniel's hands and glanced at Stuart's barely legible penmanship.

"Grandpa said they were identical. Looked the same in both human form and wolf form. And, Sam, they smelled the same too."

"So I could have been smelling him at Clara's."

"And he could have been roaming around here for years, and we wouldn't have known it," Daniel said. "He's the rogue."

"Son of a bitch..."

"Also, Rosie said that while she was in a coma, she dreamed that Stuart warned her about someone named Frank. Sam, Amos's brother's name is Frank."

Sam paced. This was all so bizarre. "Why did Frank leave the pack?"

Daniel's eyes darkened. "After Rosie was born, he challenged Simon. Simon won and banished him. Sam, he challenged your father because Simon refused to kill Rosie."

"Oh my God," Becca said, remnants of tears still sprinkled on her face. "When I thought I saw Amos in Rosie's hospital room before she woke up, it must have been Frank. He had longer hair. He was messier. He looked like Amos but rougher."

"Oh God." Sam sprinted toward the foyer just as the front door flew open, and Michael charged in, barely avoiding a collision.

"Sam!" He pulled on Sam's arm as he shouted desperately. "We need to move!"

THIRTY-FIVE
ROSIE

Rosie's heart thundered as she stared into the barrels of the two guns pointed at her head. She tried again to pull her paw out of the tight hold of the trap, but it wouldn't budge. Her breath came in sharp pants as fear overwhelmed her. She squeezed her eyes shut, waiting for one of them to pull the trigger.

A terrified shout made her jump, and her eyes popped open in surprise.

Mason fell to the ground, and his gun tumbled away from him. On top of Mason, Lucas bared his teeth and snarled.

Mason screamed and held his arms out in front of him. "Help! Oh God! Help!"

Lucas latched onto Mason's arm, and the crunch of bone split the air. Another scream exploded from Mason's throat, and a new kind of terror filled Rosie's gut. Lucas would kill Mason.

"*Stop, Lucas!*" Praying she got through to him, she projected her voice into his head. In his rage-filled state, she wasn't sure he could hear her. The fury in his face as he curled his lips over sharp teeth and stared Mason down made Rosie's stomach ache.

"Please stop. Don't kill him. He's a human. A person. You aren't a murderer."

He paused, his face softening slightly. Another low whine vibrated in her throat. A plea. He looked toward her, and after a moment of hesitation, he lowered his head.

Glancing at Mason, he gave one last growl, then he moved forward and stood over Rosie, placing himself between her and Frank.

Wide-eyed, Mason scurried to his feet and backed up toward the trees. He held his arm to his chest and looked at Frank. "Let's go!"

Frank lowered his gun and smiled. After tossing the gun to the dirt, he slowly raised his hand to his head and pulled the orange beanie off. Next, he slid the sunglasses down his nose and tossed them to the ground.

Rosie's heart skipped a beat. *Amos?* But... not Amos. The man grinning at her had long, greasy hair, stubble, and a dirty face. Pristine, impeccably dressed Amos wouldn't be caught dead looking like that.

In a blur of movement, not-Amos shifted to wolf form. His smell turned from obnoxious cologne to the unmistakable Amos wolf smell. Confusion rocked Rosie's brain, but before she could think any further, he turned on Mason and growled.

"What... What the..." Mason backed toward the trees. His face ashen, tears coursing down his cheeks, he asked, "How did you..."

The black wolf lunged, and Mason never finished his question.

A spray of blood shot across the dirt, and Rosie squeezed her eyes shut. She turned her head away, but she could still hear the guttural cries, the tearing of flesh, and the cracking of bones. A weight brought comfort as Lucas lowered his body onto hers and shielded her from the gruesome view of the slaughter happening a few feet away.

When silence replaced the screams, violent growling, and gnashing of teeth, Rosie tentatively raised her head. Lucas didn't move, keeping himself between her and the monster.

"*Why did you do that?*" Rosie's projected voice shook. "*He was leaving.*"

"*I'm done with him.*" The voice didn't sound like Amos's. "*He's served his purpose.*"

"*What purpose was that?*" Lucas growled.

"*I needed a face for you to fear. I couldn't show you mine.*"

"*Who are you?*" Sitting up a little straighter, Rosie watched the black wolf warily from behind Lucas.

"*Family.*"

"*You look like Amos,*" Rosie said.

"*Amos was supposed to bring me back into the pack after we took care of you and Simon. My bastard brother turned his back on me. Went back on the plan. Turned me away.*"

A whine vibrated in Rosie's throat, and her heart picked up speed. "*You killed my father. Why?*"

"*The plan was to kill you. Your father got in the way.*"

Rosie took a moment to let that sink in. She tried not to let herself spiral into thinking her father's death was her fault, but he'd taken the bullet meant for her.

Lucas nudged her then addressed Frank. "*What about Paul Lewis?*"

"*I killed Paul and let everyone think he killed Simon.*" Frank snarled.

"*Why?*" Rosie cried. "*Why did you do all this?*"

"*I spent years as a rogue. Do you know how awful*

it feels to be without a pack? I wandered from place to place, trying to find somewhere to fit in. They put me in mental hospitals and pumped me full of drugs. Half the time, I didn't know where I was. My life has been hell. Your father cast me out because of you. A witch. An abomination. You should never have been born."

"Rosie is the best thing that could have happened to this pack." Lucas took a step toward Frank. "To all werewolves."

"A lot of us strongly disagree, pup. We were going to get rid of your girlfriend. It didn't exactly go as planned, but killing Simon was a nice bonus. I went to my brother that night, thinking I would have a pack again, but he turned me away." A low growl rumbled from his throat. *"I've spent the past couple of years trying to get back at Amos the only way I knew how. By turning the other packs against him."*

"You're the rogue." Lucas bared his teeth. "You've caused a lot of damage. Hurt a lot of people."

"Waste of time. Damn fool got killed by his own pack." Frank took a step forward. *"At least I'll get the pleasure of finally finishing off Simon's little abomination."*

In a flash, the black wolf before them shifted, and Amos's twin crouched in front of them in human form. A quick smirk crossed his face as he reached to his right for the rifle he'd thrown down earlier.

Before Rosie could think, Lucas launched himself at Frank.

A shot rang out loudly, echoing off the rocks behind her. Rosie squeezed her eyes shut and flinched, crouching low to the ground. When she peeled her eyes open, a whimper of panic tore through her. Still crouched with the gun leveled in her direction, Frank smiled at her.

Lucas lay at his feet, blood pooling around him.

The world came to a standstill, and Rosie lost her breath. The flames of her mate bond roared, burning furiously. For the first time, the witch in her overpowered her werewolf, and her shift to human form came with a feral scream. Birds flew from the trees, and animals scurried everywhere, unnerved by her tortured energy.

She released the trap from her hand and stepped forward, but the cock of the gun stopped her. Frank pointed it at her head, his finger on the trigger.

Seething rage flowed through her veins, pulsing with each beat of her broken heart. Drawing on all of the energy within her, she called out to every living thing within her reach. Worms, spiders, birds, ants, mice, beetles—they all heeded her call.

Weeds from the forest floor twisted around Frank's legs, wrapping tightly around his calves and slicing at his skin. Spiders and ants swept up his legs, hundreds of them covering him from head to toe.

Dropping the gun, he screamed. "Witch! What are you doing?"

Not enough.

She called to the mice, and they crawled up his legs, gnawing on him. His screams tore through the air. Faintly, she was aware that someone was calling her name, but she ignored it. The insects made their way to his face and invaded his mouth and nose, suffocating him.

As he dropped to his knees, choking, his body jerked. Birds swarmed around his head, pecking at his eyes, his forehead, and his cheeks, tearing bits of flesh away. His body collapsed to the ground and jerked again and again before it went still.

The silence that followed pressed against her

ears. Tears streamed down her cheeks as she tore her gaze away from the dead man to look at Lucas. A hole tore through her gut, and her breath stuttered.

"Rosie?"

She turned her head to the right. Behind her, Sam, Michael, and Daniel stood by the rock face. They must have come in wolf form. She looked down at herself, and her own nudity caused a slight flare of insecurity. It quickly left her as she turned back to Lucas.

Still a wolf.

That meant there was a chance.

She ran to him, knelt, and placed her hands on his back. More tears dripped down her cheeks as she closed her eyes and concentrated on bringing the healing energy from within. She visualized it. A glowing ember that radiated down her arms, through her hands, and out her fingertips.

At first, there was nothing. No movement. A crushing weight settled in her chest. Then the soft fur beneath her fingers shifted, and she opened her eyes. Lucas's ears twitched, and he raised his head. He gave a soft whine and nudged her with his snout.

She shifted into wolf form and nestled into him, rubbing her head under his chin and against his chest. They huddled together in the dirt, and she soaked him in. Her limbs shook with the shock of what happened and how close she'd come to losing him.

Sam would never have believed it in a million years if he hadn't just watched it play out in front of him. Rosie's magic had always fascinated him, but what she'd just done almost terrified him.

He'd called to Rosie over and over, but she focused only on Frank. Her eyes glowed, and her hands stretched out as though controlling the movements of the bugs and rodents that overtook Frank and suffocated him.

His sister had taken a life.

Granted, the life she'd taken had threatened hers and those she loved. She was justified in her actions. It was just not the Rosie he knew. The Rosie who would never hurt another living thing. She'd snapped.

They'd heard the gunshot and come running—they were only a few hundred yards away. By the time they got there, she was too far gone. Sam couldn't get through to her. He'd shouted her name over and over, but it was as though she didn't hear them. And Lucas... Sam thought he was dead. Apparently, Rosie did too.

"Michael, Daniel, come with me." Keeping his tail low, Sam kept his eyes on Rosie and Lucas as he ma-

neuvered around them to Frank. With the bugs cleared away, no evidence pointed to what had caused his death. His lifeless eyes stared up at the sky —so much like Amos's eyes. Sam shivered.

What to do with the bodies? Mason could be left for the authorities to find. Or Sam could call the sheriff and tell him he'd found Mason's body on his land. Like father, like son. Trespassing on Hart land only to be mauled by the thing they hunted.

Frank... that was more complicated. Did anyone anywhere miss him? He would be identified as one of the Hart family, for sure. That would raise questions Sam didn't know how to answer.

"Burn Frank's body, and scatter the bones. No one will be looking for him."

Michael and Daniel would make sure it was done.

Sam turned back toward Rosie and Lucas. They were huddled together, oblivious to everyone else. A few short barks, and Sam had their attention. They scrambled to their feet and approached, their heads lowered.

"Sorry, Sam," Lucas projected quietly.

"Let's head back." Sam nudged them and started walking in the direction of Hart House.

On the long walk, Sam shared what Daniel had discovered in Stuart's journal, and Rosie filled Sam in on the awful details of their run-in with Mason and Frank. Hearing that Frank had murdered their father, Sam suddenly wished he could have helped Rosie kill him. His gruesome, violent death at Rosie's hands felt less frightening and more satisfying.

When they reached the house, Lucas shifted and went inside to get some clothes for Rosie. Sam took human form and retrieved the clothes he'd left on the patio. After he got dressed, he sat in one of the patio chairs and watched Rosie pace the lawn like a caged tiger. Her red fur glowed under the afternoon sun.

The patio door slid open, and Becca stepped out. "I'm going to pretend I didn't just see Lucas's bare ass when he ran up the stairs. Thank God I only saw him from behind."

A low growl rumbled from Rosie, and Becca's eyes widened. The color drained from her face, and her jaw dropped as she focused on the big red wolf in the yard. Her mouth opened and closed a few times before she finally spoke. "Is that..."

"It's Rosie." Sam stood and went to Becca's side. Placing a comforting hand on her shoulder, he spoke softly. "It's okay. She won't hurt you."

As if to emphasize his point, Rosie lowered herself to the ground, lying on her belly. She rested her head on her paws and stared up at Becca.

"Do you think it's okay if I... go to her?" Becca whispered, as though she were afraid of offending Rosie.

Sam chuckled. "Knock yourself out."

Slowly, Becca shuffled across the patio and took the steps down to the lawn one at a time, her hands out in front of her as though she were approaching a rabid dog. Rosie stayed perfectly still until Becca neared. When Becca reached forward, Rosie's tail thumped against the ground, and she closed her eyes as Becca stroked her head gently.

"Oh my God." Becca laughed, and a tear slipped down her cheek. Rosie raised her head and licked the tear away, and Becca laughed again. "This is incredible."

Warmth spread through Sam's chest. Of course Becca would react like this. The woman was a walking ray of sunshine and positivity. Hope flared.

He was asking so much of her. Giving her life to the pack was a heavy burden. But God, he hoped she would say yes.

When she looked up at him from her spot next to Rosie, the twinkle in her eye told him he might not need to worry.

Lucas rummaged in Rosie's closet and grabbed a T-shirt, a hooded sweatshirt, and a pair of jeans. His cheeks heated when he pulled her dresser drawer open to find a pair of underwear for her.

He reached into his duffel for his own T-shirt and jeans. The clothes he'd worn that morning still sat in a heap next to Rosie's wrecked Jeep. Hopefully Michael and Daniel would grab them when they cleaned everything up. Those were his favorite jeans.

After pulling on the pair he took out of the bag, he buttoned them and put on his T-shirt. He sat down on the bed and took a calming breath. The day had him reeling. Picking up his phone, he silently thanked Michael for bringing it back to the house with him when he came for Sam.

He squeezed his eyes shut when he saw five missed calls and a message. Cursing under his breath, he dialed his voicemail, then he listened to his father's urgent plea.

"You need to come, Lucas. I know you're torn, but this is your family. Please. We need you."

Staring at his duffel and the contents that spilled

out around it, he bent down and started stuffing his things back inside.

Now or never...

Lucas jogged down the stairs with Rosie's clothes in hand and rounded the corner then quickly made his way down the hall, through the dining room, and out the patio door. Outside, Sam and Becca sat in the grass next to Rosie. Becca was stroking Rosie's fur.

Lucas winced. "Since when did werewolves become household pets?"

"You're just jealous." Sam leaned back on his elbows. "No one will pet your flea-ridden fur."

"Do you guys really get fleas?" Becca wrinkled her nose in disgust.

"Gross. No." Lucas rolled his eyes. "Rosie, I'm putting your clothes behind the tree over there."

After Lucas walked to the closest tree and set her clothes behind it, Rosie stood and jogged over to the tree then disappeared behind it.

Lucas crossed his arms as he watched Sam and Becca paw at each other. Sam took Becca's hand and kissed it.

She smiled at him and nodded toward the house. "I think we should go talk."

They stood.

Pausing in front of Lucas, Sam patted his shoulder. "I'll come back to talk to you guys shortly."

Lucas turned to watch them walk into the house. When Rosie emerged from behind the tree, he nodded toward the grass where she'd been sitting with Sam and Becca. "What was that all about?"

Rosie's brown eyes rounded. She glanced toward the house then stepped closer to Lucas. "She's pregnant."

His jaw dropped. "What?"

"She was getting comfortable with me. Seeing what it felt like... you know... to be around us like that."

"What is Sam going to do?"

"He invited her into the pack. He told her what the decision means for her future."

"Heavy." Lucas bit his lip. "Are you okay?"

"I'm okay now." Rosie met his eyes. Tears pooled in hers. "When I thought you were dead, I..."

"I know."

Lucas pulled her to him, and she pressed her face into his chest. Her back hitched with soft sobs. When she pulled away, Lucas used his thumb to wipe the tears from her cheeks.

"I need to talk to you." Gesturing toward the patio chairs, Lucas nudged her elbow. "Let's sit."

Rosie sniffled as she moved to a chair and sat down. Lucas sat across from her. He ran a hand through his hair and scratched his head before he took Rosie's hands and looked into her eyes.

After clearing his throat, Lucas started. "This is awful timing. I know I promised you that I would give you time to think about..."

"Going with you to Beckett Falls."

"Yeah." Lucas frowned. "The thing is I need to ask you to make a decision a little bit sooner. Like... now."

"Now?" Rosie's eyes widened.

"My pack is in danger."

"What kind of danger?"

"Marcus keeps coming back. I don't think he's trying to take his place as alpha again, but I can't be sure. Even if he isn't, what he wants I can't let him have."

"What does he want?" Concern flitted across

Rosie's face. Red splotches still marred her cheeks from crying.

"It's a long story. But Shawn is hurt. He can't fight. Christopher and Travis are doing their best to work together to keep him away, but they need me to step up."

The fear that passed over Rosie's face tore at him. "What are you going to do?"

"I'm going to be there to protect the pack if he comes back." Lucas took Rosie's hand again. "It's my duty, Rosie. It's time for me to take my place as alpha."

Tears sprang to her eyes, but she set her jaw. Determination crossed over her features. "Then I'm with you." She squeezed Lucas's hand. "All the way."

THIRTY-EIGHT

ROSIE

After grabbing the duffel at the base of her closet, Rosie set it on top of her bed. She took a deep breath then turned to her dresser, pulled out undergarments, and tossed them into the bag. Next, she went to the closet, where she hesitated for only a moment before pulling a handful of T-shirts from their hangers. She rested them on her shoulder and bent over to pick up a few pairs of jeans. She carried it all to her bed and stuffed them into the duffel.

Lucas had told her to pack light and promised if she couldn't come back for the rest of her things, he would buy her new stuff. The thought of never coming back to Hart House or Hanks Hollow made her feel cold and empty. It was her home.

No.

Lucas was her home. If Beckett Falls was his home, then it would be hers too. After zipping the duffel closed, she slung it over her shoulder and crept to the door. Lucas had told her to meet him at the car. Sam and Becca were still tucked away in Sam's room, talking. Michael and Daniel were still cleaning up the mess from earlier.

Tiptoeing down the stairs, Rosie glanced over her

shoulder at Sam's closed door. She didn't see the figure standing at the base of the stairs until she almost ran them over.

"Martha!" Rosie winced at her screech and looked over her shoulder, making sure Sam didn't come out of his room. "You scared me."

"Were you going to leave without saying good-bye?" Martha's teary gaze stabbed through Rosie's heart. "I don't know what you're up to, but be careful, dear. I hope to all the heavens I get to see you again someday."

Rosie's vision blurred, and her body jerked forward as Martha pulled her into a tight hug. Martha's squishy hugs would always be her favorite.

Without another word, Martha patted Rosie's shoulder and waddled away. Rosie watched her go, and a small part of her wondered if she was doing the right thing. The thought left as soon as it came. Nothing in the world would keep her from Lucas.

She opened the door as quietly as she could then crept out and slowly closed it behind her. She jogged down the porch steps and across the driveway to the garage, where Lucas waited.

"You ready?" He took her duffel from her and put it in the back seat of the car.

Rosie peered back at Hart House. The large structure seemed to frown as it looked down on her. This wasn't how she wanted to leave. Turning back to Lucas, she forced a smile. "I'm ready."

Drool puddled at the corner of Rosie's mouth when she snapped her eyes open. Her head pressed against the passenger window of Lucas's car. Blurry scenery whizzed past. The sun was just below the horizon, painting the sky pink. She sat up and ran a hand through her hair. Drowsily glancing at Lucas, she yawned. "How long was I asleep?"

"About an hour." Lucas grinned. "Good timing, actually. We're almost there."

Rosie wiped the drool from her mouth. "Have you heard from your dad?"

Lucas nodded. "I sent him a text and told him we're coming. He said meet them in town for dinner."

"We? They know I'm coming?"

"They know." Lucas laughed. "I wish I could tell you they'll lay out the red carpet, but truthfully, it's kind of like a frat house there. No food, and all they do is sit around and drink and play games. I'm sure that's why they opted to meet for dinner in town. Didn't want to scare you away."

"Oh." Great. Her new home. Rosie tried to smile. "That sounds... interesting."

"Sorry. That sounded worse than it is. They're a great bunch. You'll love them. It's just... they don't have a Martha, and it shows. We'll stay in the other house, okay? Ginny keeps that place immaculate, and she's a great cook. Almost as good as Martha but not quite."

"I still can't believe you have *two* pack houses."

"Only Brody, Ginny, and Shawn live there now. There's plenty of room for us."

During the first part of the trip, Lucas had filled Rosie in on the basics of the pack. He told her about Brody and about Marcus coming back for him. It sounded like the poor kid had been through a lot.

Lucas pointed out the windshield. "Here we are."

A sign on the side of the road read Welcome to Beckett Falls. A town straight out of a fairytale lay before her. In the distance, a towering waterfall with a bridge stretched across it looked like something from a Tolkien fantasy. Beautiful buildings, cobblestone streets, a river running through town...

"Lucas, this is amazing. It's beautiful."

His smile radiated pride and relief. "I'm so glad you like it."

He pulled in front of a pizza place, and they climbed out of the car. Numbness from the long drive prickled her feet, and she stomped them against the ground to get some circulation going. She joined Lucas on the sidewalk, and they entered the shop. Rosie had barely stepped inside before she found herself wrapped in Roger's warm embrace.

"I'm so glad you're here." He pulled back and looked her over. "Gosh, you've grown. You look as beautiful as ever."

"Roger." Rosie studied his face. No worry lines or tight expression. He just looked happy. "It's so good to see you."

With a hand on her back, Lucas gestured to the only other people in the room. He first pointed at a red-haired man in his twenties and introduced him as Travis. Then he indicated an older man and introduced him as Travis's father, Christopher. They nodded in an almost identical manner, welcoming smiles spreading across their faces.

A boy approached, a small frown on his face as he studied Rosie. His immense anger surprised her, and she averted her gaze. The look he shot her told her the anger was directed at her. Underneath the anger was sorrow. He'd been hurt. Badly.

"This is Brody." Lucas reached out to ruffle the boy's hair, but the boy batted his hand away. "And this is my uncle Shawn. The pack alpha." Lucas gestured to a very tall man. She realized Lucas looked more like Shawn than Roger. They had the same tall, lean frame, bright-blue eyes, and shaggy brown hair.

Shawn offered his hand to Rosie. She shook it gently.

"I'm glad you've come to Beckett Falls, Rosie. We're happy to have you here."

"Can we eat now?" Travis slid a chair out and sat down. "I'm starving."

Shawn scowled at Travis. "You can eat now. And you can keep Rosie company while I speak with Lucas alone in the back room."

A sly smile slid across Travis's lips, and he stood and approached Rosie smoothly. He put his arm around her shoulders. "I'll keep her company."

"Don't scare her," Shawn scolded him.

"Travis," Lucas said. "Rosie likes to play euchre."

"Hey!" Travis pulled a chair out for her. "Now we're talking."

Feeling a little more at ease, Rosie sat down. She stole a glance at Lucas, and he winked at her.

"I should warn you, though," Lucas said. "She taught me how to play."

THIRTY-NINE
LUCAS

Lucas followed Shawn to a room in the rear of the restaurant. It looked like a spot reserved for private parties.

"I'm really glad you came back, Lucas." Shawn picked a table and sat, stretching his long legs out in front of him. "I'm sorry you didn't get more time in Hanks Hollow."

Lucas sat across from Shawn and rested his elbow on the table. He rubbed his chin. "Not your fault. Not like you had any control over this."

"Maybe Marcus won't even show up again." Shawn shrugged. "If he does, we need to be ready." Shawn's brow creased. "Our pack can't survive under his leadership. He can't become alpha again. And even if alpha isn't what he's after, he can't take Brody—"

"He won't." Lucas clenched his jaw. "I won't let that happen."

A smile of relief pulled at Shawn's lips. "Are you ready to become alpha?"

Ignoring the nerves making his stomach cramp, Lucas replied, "I'm ready. How does this work?"

"In the old days, there was a whole big ceremonial

thing." Shawn rolled his eyes. "Pomp and circumstance and all that. All that really matters is the pack and the Council accept you as alpha."

"Do they?"

"What do you mean?"

"We've had these conversations in private. Do Travis and Christopher know you intend to make me alpha?"

"We haven't talked about it, but they know."

"How do they know?" Lucas knit his brow.

"The same way I knew I was going to ask you. Lucas, you were born to do this. I can't really explain it. When you walk into a room, everyone just knows you're destined to lead the pack. It's in you."

Lucas could see that in Simon and in Sam. Could others really see it in him?

"I scheduled an emergency call with the Council tonight," Shawn said. "When we get back to the house, we'll call them and let them know I'm handing the reins over to you. Then we'll go for a run and make it official."

Huffing out a deep sigh, Lucas thought of Rosie. "Only one other thing to talk about."

"You're going to have to tell the Council you're bringing her into the pack." Shawn furrowed his brow. "Don't keep the fact that she's here from them. They won't like it."

"I need to keep her safe."

"Lying to the Council won't do that."

Lucas nodded. "Okay."

~

AFTER THEIR MEETING, Shawn and Lucas moved back out to the main restaurant area to rejoin the rest of the pack. The laughter that filled the air and the genuine delight on Rosie's face as she immersed herself in cards and conversation filled Lucas with an overwhelming sense of relief. She looked happy. Relaxed.

Empty pizza pans, beer bottles, and soda cans littered the tables. Travis was blathering on about something. No doubt he'd filled Rosie in on at least a dozen stories. Her musical laugh danced through the air again when Christopher yelled, "Bump!" and Travis cursed a blue streak. Getting beaten at euchre again.

Lucas ran his hands through Rosie's soft hair before he bent down to kiss the top of her head. She turned to him and took his hand.

"Everything go okay?"

"Fine." Lucas smiled. *"Shawn is making me alpha tonight."*

Rosie bit her lip, concern flitting across her face.

"It will be okay."

He squeezed her hand reassuringly as Shawn berated the rest of the pack for eating all the pizza. They ordered another, and after it was polished off, they made their way out to their vehicles.

On the dark drive out to Beckett House, Rosie spoke softly. "I like them. I see you when I look at them, and they have your same intelligent humor."

"If you got intelligent humor out of the conversation, then Travis must not have been talking as much as I thought he was."

Rosie laughed. "He puts on a show. He's smarter than he lets on."

"If you say so." Lucas shrugged, but he knew what she meant. Travis liked the attention and laughs he got when playing the part of the village idiot. Of course Rosie would pick up on that right away.

"What's going to happen tonight?" Rosie asked. "How is Shawn going to make you alpha?"

The moon hid behind the clouds, and Lucas peered at the road, where the headlights cut through blackness. "First, we have to talk to the Council."

After a beat of silence, Rosie asked what he knew she would. "Are you going to tell them I'm here?"

Lucas cleared his throat. "I think it will be best."

Rosie nodded. "I trust you."

FORTY
SAM

THE FAINT LIGHT OF DUSK HIGHLIGHTED THE TIPS
of the pines and formed an eerie silhouette of the forest. Bats bobbed and weaved around the trees, their
occasional screeches piercing the silence. Sam sat on
the patio, staring out over the backyard. Lucas and
Rosie were gone. No warning, no goodbye, no expla-
nation. Just gone. Sam clenched his fists when he felt
the sting of tears.

How could they do this?

When he'd gone looking for them earlier, he'd
thought maybe they'd decided to go to town for lunch
or something. When two hours turned into four, he'd
checked Rosie's room. Lucas's duffel was missing.
Rosie's dresser drawers were open, and most of her
clothes were gone.

For the second time, Lucas had left without a
word. This time, he took Sam's little sister with him.
Lucas was supposed to be his best friend. And Sam
had never dreamed Rosie would do something to hurt
him. Not in a million years.

"Sam?"

Becca's voice soothed some of the ache, and he
reached for her hand as she crossed the patio toward

him. She crawled into his lap and wrapped an arm around his neck.

"Martha said supper will be ready in a few minutes." She kissed his cheek. "Are you okay?"

Sam nodded, but he couldn't look her in the eye.

"I'm sure they had a reason for leaving," Becca said gently.

"Why would they do this to me?"

Becca rolled her eyes. "Don't be so self-centered, Sam. They didn't do this *to* you. They did this *for* them. It had nothing to do with you."

That stung more than it should have. "I'm her alpha. I told her not to leave."

"Why?"

"Because it's not safe."

"You think Lucas won't keep her safe?"

"I didn't say that."

"So why isn't it safe for her to be with him?"

"Well..." Sam rubbed his forehead.

"Are you sure you didn't want to order them to stay here to keep them close to you?"

"I..."

"Sam, you guys grew up together. The three of you have always been close. You're all older now, though. It's time for the baby birds to leave the nest."

Sam fought the urge to curse. "What if he hurts her?"

The way Becca cocked her head made Sam feel like a jerk for asking the question.

"Do you really think Lucas would ever do anything to hurt Rosie?" Becca asked.

"He's a guy, isn't he? Aren't girls always saying guys are dumb?"

Sam waited, and Becca bobbed her head back and forth in a "kind of" gesture.

"Remember what Lucas was like when Rosie was in a coma?" Becca nudged his shoulder. "He loves her, Sam. I'm not saying everything will always be perfect. Love is complicated and messy. But that's their business. She's an adult."

"Barely."

"Yeah, but she's still an adult. You have to let her make her own decisions. And you have to accept that they are ready to move on with their lives, and moving on might not include staying with you and your pack."

Sam flinched like Becca had hit him. That was the real nitty gritty of it. He wasn't ready to let go, and it hurt that they were so ready move on without him.

Not to mention that the weight of the Council and what they would do with Rosie still hung heavily on his shoulders.

The front doorbell rang.

Becca raised an eyebrow and pressed a hand to his chest. "Try not to take it personally. Let them explain it to you when they're ready."

She climbed off his lap, and he stood. As he took her hand and let her lead him into the house, he avoided her gaze. After they stepped inside, Becca turned and kissed his cheek.

"I'm going to help Martha."

Sam watched her go as she turned toward the kitchen. Their morning conversation had gone well. She was willing to stay at Hart House on and off for a while to see how things went. Every bone in his body vibrated with the hope that she would decide to carry their child and stay with him. The people he loved most seemed to be leaving him left and right. Sam didn't think he could handle it if she was the next to go.

He headed down the hall toward the foyer. When Sam opened the front door, the sheriff stood out on the veranda.

"Hey, Craig. Come on in." Sam stood aside to let the sheriff in.

"Thank you, Sam." Craig stepped into the house. "I won't stay. I can smell you've got supper going. I just wanted to let you know that we have the area taped off where you found Mason's body. I think you're right. Looks like a wild-animal attack. Unfortunately, the coroner said it was probably a wolf, so the hunters will be in an uproar again."

Sam groaned and leaned his head against the door.

"I'll be releasing a statement tomorrow. We'll try to keep them off your land."

"Thank you, Craig," Sam said. "You want to stay for supper?"

"Hell, I'll never say no to Martha's cooking." Craig stuck his hands into his pockets and grinned. "Lead the way."

FORTY-ONE
LUCAS

None of the Council members looked particularly happy to be joining a late-night emergency meeting, and Lucas swallowed the cantaloupe-sized lump in his throat. They used Shawn's office—the only room on the upper floor of the pack house. Shawn sat in his chair, facing the webcam, but he told Lucas to stay off camera until he gave the go-ahead to join him.

"As you know, I took over when Marcus could no longer carry on as alpha," Shawn said. "I named Lucas Beckett as my successor when he and Roger rejoined the pack."

"We're aware." Roland's impatient tone brought the lump back to Lucas's throat. "What's the point?"

"You may have heard that Marcus is missing from the hospital. His mind was deteriorating even before he got sick. I'm afraid of what he'll be like now. If Marcus comes here, looking to challenge his way back to pack alpha, I want the best line of defense between him and our pack. That isn't me. I've never been a fighter, and I injured my shoulder recently. I can't defeat Marcus in a fight. Lucas is ready to take my place, and I'm ready to relinquish control of the pack to him."

The Council members each perked up, no longer looking bored with the meeting.

"Are you sure about this, Shawn?" Garrett asked. "You're young. You could be alpha for many more years before handing over control."

"I'm sure," Shawn answered quickly. "I want to go back to travelling for the beer business. Lucas has agreed to take care of things here so that I can do that."

"Very well," Jagger cut in. "Give us a moment to speak in private."

Shawn's connection to the web conference was muted, and silence filled the office for a few minutes. Lucas didn't realize he was tapping his foot like Thumper until Shawn raised his eyebrow. When the screen blipped, indicating that Shawn was no longer muted, Jagger addressed him.

"Is Lucas there?"

"He's here," Shawn said.

After wiping his sweaty palms on his jeans, Lucas stood and moved to the seat next to Shawn so that the Council could see him.

"Lucas," Jagger said. "The Council accepts your appointment to alpha of the Beckett pack. Do you understand your obligations with this role?"

"Yes, sir." Thank God, his voice didn't sound as weak as he felt. "I have a matter of business for the Council."

"Not wasting any time, are you, boy?" Roland laughed. "Go ahead, then."

"I would like to bring in a new member." He tried to clear the cantaloupe out of his throat again. "Rose

Hart left Hart House with me. She wishes to join the pack, and I would like to accept her."

"Rose Hart had no business leaving Hart House." Roland's face reddened. "She was to wait for word from us on our meeting with the World Council."

It felt like his heart was trying to pound its way out of his chest. God, he prayed he hadn't just gotten her into more trouble than she was already in.

"Wait a minute, Roland," Jagger said. "We didn't tell her she had to stay put. She hasn't gone into hiding. We know where she is."

"Just curious," Garrett said. "Is there something between you?"

Lucas swallowed again. "Yes."

"This complicates things." Jagger rubbed his bearded chin. "We haven't decided her fate, and we certainly aren't prepared to allow her to bring offspring into the world."

"You don't need to worry about that." The conversation was getting unbearably private. "At least not yet. We haven't... um... Nothing has *happened* between us."

"I see." Jagger cleared his throat. "Unless there are any objections from the other Council members, I see no reason you can't bring her into your pack for now. However, we'll be following up with you in the very near future. Be sure nothing... *happens*... until then."

Heat flooded Lucas's face. "Of course."

~

STEPPING onto Beckett land as alpha, Lucas felt a new rush of adrenaline. The blood of a dozen alphas before him ran through his veins. They all walked these grounds. A primal desire to protect his pack vibrated in his bones.

He stepped to the rocky edge of a cliff and raised his head to the sky. Thick clouds spread, revealing a bright moon. A long, low howl crept from his throat, bouncing off rocks and trees and ringing through the valley. Behind him, his pack echoed his call.

FORTY-TWO
ROSIE

WATCHING LUCAS TAKE HIS PLACE AS ALPHA filled Rosie with a level of love and pride she couldn't believe existed.

Running with the Beckett pack felt right. As though she belonged. She felt whole. It didn't make sense. She'd just met these people, yet it seemed as if she'd known them her whole life. Maybe because they were so like Lucas or because her bond with Lucas drew her to them in a way she couldn't quite understand.

The river that cut through the Becketts' land ran down from the bluffs, creating a series of breathtaking waterfalls. The pack led her along trails that snaked through the forest, back to the riverbed, and up the rock face to overlooks where she could see for miles.

They skipped over rocks to cross the river where it narrowed and ran back through the trees. The familiar sounds and smells of pine, birch, and wildlife reminded her of home.

When they made their way back toward the pack house, Lucas fell back from the head of the line to join Rosie. He pressed his body against hers, nudging her neck with his nose. She leaned into him, enjoying the closeness.

In the distance, on the bank of the river, near the path, a dark shadow in a clearing caught her attention. As they got closer, the outline of a large house came into view. She paused, taking it in.

The abundance of windows made the home somehow feel like part of the forest. As though the living room sat on the forest floor instead of inside a house. The deck that ran along the second level jutted out so that it sat just over the river—the rushing water only a few dozen feet from the bedrooms.

Paradise.

"We'll change at the pack house then come down here to get settled in." Lucas nudged her then jogged ahead.

Rosie took one more moment to look the house over. Brody glanced in her direction before he jogged over to the pile of clothes by the stone path leading to the front door. Trying to ignore his anger, she looked away, giving him privacy to shift and change.

She followed Lucas up the trail. The pack house was visible at the top of the hill. As she started to make her way up, Shawn and Christopher jogged to her side, and Christopher nudged her.

"Travis, Shawn, and I made a little welcome present for you."

Lucas licked at her face—a kiss. *"I'll come back after I get changed."* He jogged off toward the pack house.

Not sure what to think, Rosie followed Shawn and Christopher a few yards up the hill. A small shed sat among the trees. Freshly cut wood and clean, shiny nails—they'd just built it. Christopher jogged toward it then paused, looking at Rosie as though he expected her to go inside.

Shawn stood next to her. *"I couldn't help build because of my shoulder, but I gave direction,"* he said proudly. *"I'm good at that."*

"If good direction means telling us what not to do after we do it, then yes, great direction." Travis jogged down the hill, holding Rosie's duffel bag in his strong jaws. He dropped the bag in front of the shed. *"Your dressing room, ma'am."*

Rosie laughed and barked, spinning in a circle. *"No way!"* She ran toward it and peeked inside. The doorway was curtained off, and inside, a small space gave her enough room to shift and change clothes. A skylight looked like it would provide plenty of light for her during the day, and lights lined the inside of the roof, enough for her to see at night. *"This is so cool!"*

"It has solar panels on top, so the lights should always be working at night when you need them," Christopher said.

Thank goodness she was in wolf form. No need for them to see waterworks. *"Thank you. This means a lot."*

She sensed their unease. No one wanted a chick-flick moment. They all jogged off toward the pack house wordlessly. As she watched them go, it finally sank in.

She had a new pack.

FORTY-THREE
LUCAS

Lucas stifled a laugh as he watched Rosie make her way around the interior of the house, gaping at the architecture and the view through the windows. She went to the kitchen and looked around before moving beyond the formal dining room, the den, and then the rec room. Her voice carried through the house. "This is amazing! Lucas, I love it."

Her excitement made him so happy. He'd been afraid she would have a hard time adjusting, but she fit right in. Like she really belonged.

When Rosie came back to the living room, Lucas gestured toward the stairs.

"Shawn said we can have the master bedroom upstairs."

Rosie stopped and watched him, her cheeks turning scarlet.

"You want to go see it?"

She nodded, and they went up together. The moment they stepped into the bedroom, Rosie ran to the floor-to-ceiling windows that faced the river then opened the sliding glass door and stepped out to the balcony. The gentle splashing sounds of the river filled the room. She stepped back inside and moved into the bathroom to investigate all the gadgets inside.

When Rosie emerged, Lucas pointed at the view through the skylights. Over the treetops, a navy-blue night sky was speckled with glittering stars.

Lucas climbed onto the giant bed that sat under the skylights and lay back against the mountain of pillows. "There's room for two."

Rosie's cheeks pinkened again, but she smiled as she climbed into bed with him and burrowed into his side. She rested her head on his chest, and Lucas leaned back to gaze up at the stars. His fingers trailed through her soft curls. He wanted her with every inch of his being.

But she wasn't ready.

She hadn't said it, but Lucas knew. In her mind, Rosie was still sixteen. She had a lot to get used to. He would wait however long she needed.

Rosie sighed. "You need to go talk to Brody."

Lucas wrinkled his forehead, trying to wrap his head around the shift in focus. "What? Why?"

"He's angry with you."

Lucas tensed, and Rosie reached for his hand.

"You left him, Lucas. He found someone he trusts, and he was left behind. He's hurt and angry."

"Shit." Of course. Brody had been abandoned repeatedly throughout his life by Marcus. According to Shawn, he'd left him for days or weeks at a time to spend time with the Cramers, and when he was around, he wasn't much of a father. And now he felt abandoned by Lucas. Crap.

"It will be okay." Rosie squeezed his hand. "Just talk to him."

~

Lucas took a deep breath and stared at the door for a moment before he knocked. No answer. Only silence. He turned the knob and poked his head inside. Brody sat on his bed, reading a book.

"Brody?"

The boy frowned and continued to read. Lucas took the hint. He was being ignored.

Shawn planned to move back to the pack house as soon as Lucas and Rosie moved in with Brody and Ginny. It had seemed like a good idea at the time. Now, as Lucas watched Brody avoid eye contact, he wasn't so sure.

A heavy weight settled on his shoulders. Since when did being alpha involve parenting? He was eighteen, for Christ's sake. He wasn't in any position to guide a kid through life. Thank God, he wouldn't be alone raising Brody. He knew he could always count on Rosie's support. He had Roger and Christopher. They were both fathers. Ginny had been looking after Brodie for years. All he could do was make sure the pack knew he had their backs. He would be there for them.

"You're angry." Lucas sighed and sat on the edge of the bed. "I get it. I'm sorry, okay?"

Brody turned a page in his book.

"Someday, when you love someone like I love Rosie, you might understand."

"I'll never let a stupid girl come before my pack," Brody murmured.

"What?"

Brody finally looked at Lucas. Tears pooled in eyes that held so much anger, it made Lucas wince. "She's a stupid girl. They aren't good for anything except—"

"Stop!" Lucas snapped.

Brody huffed and went back to reading his book.

How had he not seen this? Lucas scrubbed a hand over his face. How much damage had Marcus done? Shawn had said Marcus liked the old traditions but never pushed them. He'd been spending time with the Cramers, though. How much had Marcus tried to push that horrible doctrine on Brody?

If Lucas couldn't undo this... If he couldn't get Brody to see how wrong the old ways were, Lucas didn't think he could handle that. He'd grown to love the kid. He couldn't lose him to Marcus and the Cramers. Not now.

"I don't know what Marcus has told you, but you have to know it isn't right. It isn't true." Lucas watched Brody as he spoke. "Somewhere deep inside, you have to know that it's nonsense."

Brody sniffed, but he didn't say anything.

"Do you know what the old ways involve?" Lucas tried not to let himself get angry. "Our ancestors locked people up. They used them then ate them, Brody. Tore them apart. Women. They hunted them down like animals."

Something flickered across Brody's face, but he continued to stare at his book, pretending not to listen.

"What about Ginny?"

Brody flinched.

"Are you telling me you would be okay with them doing that to her?"

A tear leaked out of the corner of Brody's eye. "No."

"The men your father follows... the Cramers. They still lock people up and kill them. They try to justify it by saying the women they lock up are evil or bad or less than human. You don't really believe that, do you?"

Brody looked at Lucas as another tear rolled down his cheek. His forehead wrinkled, and he suddenly appeared so much younger.

"You go to school with the kids in town," Lucas said. "There are girls there. Can you imagine them being forced to do things they don't want to do? Awful things? Then killed?"

His face scrunching, Brody sobbed then shook his head.

"Your father isn't a good man, Brody. If he wants you to believe all that is okay, he isn't good."

Another sob erupted, then Brody spoke softly. "But he's my dad. He's all I have."

"He's *not* all you have." The heartbreak in Brody's voice tore at Lucas. "You have a whole pack, kid. You have Ginny. You have me."

"You left!" Brody barked the words angrily. "You left me."

The vice grip on Lucas's heart squeezed mercilessly. He kept his breath even. "I came back. I won't leave you again. I promise."

"How do I know that?"

"I'm here to protect you. To look out for you. I won't let anything bad happen to you. This pack is my home now."

Brody sniffed.

"Rosie is part of the pack." Lucas nudged Brody's knee. "She's my home too. I want you to give her a chance."

Wiping his eyes, Brody nodded. "Does she cook?"

Lucas laughed. "No, and don't ask her that, or she'll knock you on your ass."

FORTY-FOUR
SAM

"Okay, I'll admit it." Becca's voice broke the silence in the car. "I'm glad you insisted on driving me home."

"It gets dark out here at night, and there are deer all over the place." Sam peered through the windshield, keeping an eye out for wildlife. By the time dinner was done and they'd played a few rounds of cards with Daniel and Michael, it had gotten late. No way would Sam let Becca drive home alone, but she'd insisted she needed to sleep at her place. She had an early shift and didn't have any extra clothes with her.

"Is it just me, or does it actually look like the branches of the trees are reaching for us?"

Sam laughed. "Did I forget to mention the trees come alive at night and start walking around and grabbing people who wander through the woods alone?"

"Sam, that's not funny!" Becca slapped Sam's leg. "Seriously, I've learned that werewolves and witches are both real, so walking trees don't seem out of the realm of possibility."

"You don't need to worry," Sam said. "The trees don't walk. At least, not that I know of. You'll have to ask Rosie. She's the one who talks to them."

"I'll ask her next time I see her."

Sam clenched his jaw.

"Sorry." Becca touched his knee. "What is the Beckett pack like? You said a lot of the other packs still follow old ways that aren't so nice. That's not what the Beckett pack is like, is it?"

"No, they're not bad. Not that I can tell, anyway. I never met their old alpha, but I remember my dad calling Shawn, the new alpha, a hippie once." Sam chuckled at the memory. "I think they're pretty laid back."

"What about the other packs? The ones that aren't 'laid back'? What are they like?"

An uneasy feeling slid through Sam's stomach. "You already know the worst of it. What they did in the past."

"Yeah, but what are they like now? I mean, I just can't picture it. They can't all be like Amos. People aren't like that. Not real people, anyway."

The silence in the car became thick. The way William Cramer had spoken to Martha and Rosie a couple of years back raced through Sam's mind. He couldn't bear to let Becca hear those repulsive words thrown her way. What kind of life was he bringing her into? He could keep that garbage out of his own pack, but what about the rest of the werewolf world? Could he hide Becca from it forever? What about his child?

"Sam, you're kind of freaking me out. Are there really others out there like Amos?"

Lying wouldn't be fair. "There are. But change is happening."

When Sam took his eyes off the road to glance at Becca, his chest tightened at the fear that crossed her face.

"I swear to spend my life trying my hardest to keep that world away from you and our child."

~

THE NEXT DAY, Sam woke late. He'd opted to spend the night with Becca so that she could go back to Hart House with him after her shift was done.

Sunlight reflected off the lake and formed a glittering pattern on the wall above his head. He groaned and rolled out of bed, tripping over mounds of clothes that littered the floor. He stumbled out to the kitchen and groaned again when he didn't see any coffee. When he checked the time, he jerked his head back in surprise. It was nearly noon. How on earth had he slept so late? Becca was already a couple of hours into her shift.

He dressed quickly and made his way downstairs to the boardwalk. Sun and cold air hit his face simultaneously, making him squint and shove his hands into the pockets of his hoodie. He moved to the front entrance of Miller's and stepped inside.

He expected a noon lunch crowd, but he didn't expect the angry shouts and grumbles he heard when he entered the restaurant. He paused in the doorway. Lenny Beckinsale stood in front of a crowd of about ten men. He gestured wildly as he spoke, and Sam closed his eyes and sighed when he caught the tail end of the rant.

"Wolves killing the people of our town. We need to do something about it! It's time to make Sam Hart open up his land for hunting!"

"*If* it was a wolf, it killed a hunter, Lenny! Not some innocent person walking down the street, minding their own business."

Sam's eyes widened when he heard Becca's fury. She stood toe to toe with Lenny, waving her drink tray in the air as she spoke.

"Stop riling people up and making them scared. There's no danger. Mason was out where he shouldn't have been, and you know it! He's been on the wrong side of crazy for a long time, and he wasn't being safe. You can't make Sam open his land for hunting. It's *his* land."

"This has got nothin' to do with you, little lady." Lenny gestured toward the kitchen. "Why don't you go fix me something to eat, sweetheart."

Sam knew something bad was about to happen when Becca's eyes widened and her face reddened. In one fluid motion, she swung her drink tray across the air and smacked it across the side of Lenny's head.

"Get your own damn drink!"

A mixture of laughter, shouts, and gasps rang through the crowd. Becca turned on her heel and stormed across the room, dropping the tray on the bar top.

When her eyes met Sam's, the anger left her face, and she bit her lip and tucked in her chin.

"That girl is crazy!"

"Shut your mouth, Lenny!" Sam took a step toward him, making a fist. "Or I'll come over there and shut it for you."

Lenny held his hands up then turned toward the door and stomped out, mumbling under his breath.

The crowd slowly dispersed, and Sam approached Becca. She kept her chin down as her cheeks reddened again. Sam tipped her chin up with his finger.

"Thank you," he whispered.

"Well..." Tears pooled in Becca's eyes, and she

sniffed. "I couldn't let them talk about the father of my child like that. And if I'm going to be living at Hart House, the last thing I want is a bunch of stupid old hunters stomping around—"

Sam grabbed her around the middle, picked her up, and swung her around. He let out a loud whoop before he placed Becca back on the ground.

"Really?" He couldn't keep the excitement from his voice.

Becca grinned. "You're going to be a dad."

It didn't typically bother Rosie that she couldn't feel Lucas's emotions the way she could with others. The bond they shared filled her with something better than what she felt when she read the energy that came from the people around her. Today, though, she wished she could touch the energy flowing from his body. The way his eyes lit with excitement as he explained every minute, teeny-weeny detail about how to make beer was adorable.

Pretending to be interested in what he said wore her out, but the brewery itself was a cool place. All the people were friendly and seemed to enjoy working there. She'd tasted beer once or twice. Didn't care for it. Still, the culture surrounding the craft appealed to her.

As they got to the packaging area, Rosie stifled a giggle when she spotted Travis flirting with one of the crew members.

Lucas laughed and rolled his eyes. "That's his girlfriend. Christopher said it's not like him to be so into someone, but he can't seem to get enough of her." Lucas leaned down to give her a kiss on the cheek. "I have to run upstairs to say goodbye to Shawn, then we can go get some lunch. I'll be right back."

Rosie nodded and moved toward Travis. As she drew closer, she homed in on the energy of the flirting duo. The attraction Travis felt for the woman was off the charts. When Rosie felt the woman's energy, she froze.

The woman stopped flirting with Travis to look her way. Their eyes met, and they read each other.

Approaching slowly, Rosie cleared her throat. "Hi, Travis. Who's your friend?"

Travis turned and smiled. "Hey, Rosie. This is Sophie. Sophie, this is Rosie."

"It's nice to meet you," Sophie said. "Are you a new employee?"

"No, Rosie is a friend of Lucas's." Travis raised an eyebrow. "A good friend."

Rosie suppressed a groan and turned to Sophie. "Have you lived here long?"

"Not long, no." Sophie glanced behind her toward the rest of the crew. Some of the other members eyed them curiously. "I just moved here a few months ago."

Testing a theory, Rosie asked her next question, almost certain she knew the answer. "What brought you to Beckett Falls?"

Sophie furrowed her brow. "I just really felt like this was where I needed to be." She paused. "Me... and my sisters."

Travis grinned. "She has two sisters almost as beautiful as she is. Can you believe that? Three goddesses working in my brewery."

Three witches. Her heart thumping wildly, Rosie tried to hide her excitement. "Travis, be careful. Sexual harassment suits are a thing."

Sophie giggled. "We all love Travis."

"I'm new in town," Rosie said. "I'd love to get to know some more people. Lucas and I were going to go to lunch, but I'm sure he could eat with Travis. Maybe I could have lunch with you and your sisters." Eating with strangers rocketed her way out of her comfort zone, but she needed to get their story. They would be more likely to talk to her without the boys around.

"Aww, you want some girl time. That's sweet." Travis laughed, nudging Rosie. "Go ahead. I can take Lover Boy off your hands for you."

"We usually have lunch across the street at the café." Sophie's energy tensed. "You're welcome to join us."

~

SOPHIE and her sisters could have passed for triplets. All of them had sleek, straight blond hair, blue eyes, and pointed features. They would make a fortune in the modeling industry. Rosie sat across from them and felt as though her eyes were playing tricks on her. They all wore the brewery uniform, making their similar appearance even more striking.

Sophie introduced the others as Tia and Leslie. The three of them came from the Chicago area.

"Have you ever met any others like you?" Rosie spoke softly, trying to avoid any eavesdropping from the neighboring tables.

"Just our mother," Sophie said. She lowered her eyes to her coffee cup. "She died a few years ago."

"I'm sorry." A dozen questions raced through Rosie's head, and she tried to keep herself from blurting them all at once. "What did your mother teach you about your gifts?"

"She taught us that we're descended from the Chosen. Our gifts were handed down over several generations," Tia said. "The gifts to heal and to share energy with the life around us were a blessing from the Goddess."

"What about the other Chosen?" Rosie hesitated. She was treading on dangerous ground. If they didn't know about werewolves, she couldn't risk giving the secret away. "Did she say anything about them?"

"The werewolves." Sophie nodded. "Our mother said they protected the Chosen women—the witches —until the witch hunts started. Then they turned their backs on them. They started violently abusing women to get what they want. To procreate."

"What if that's changing?" Rosie said. "What if they're putting that violent past behind them?"

Sophie's face softened. "Travis is a werewolf, isn't he? I can feel something different about him. As soon as I saw him, I knew he was the reason I'm here. I want to be with him all the time. I've never felt any-thing like this before."

"Amazing," Rosie whispered. "If the werewolves change their ways, the witches will come."

"This is big, Lucas." Rosie paced the length of the deck that ran along the back of the Beckett pack house while Lucas stood in place, his arms crossed. "This is bigger than big. What do I do with this? In my dreams, the gods told me the witches would come, and here they are. They're coming. They're showing up in Hanks Hollow. They're showing up here in Beckett Falls. I'm willing to bet they're going everywhere there are werewolves who won't lock them up and eat them."

"Did the gods say what to do when the witches get here?"

"No." Rosie dropped her arms to her sides. "They just said I was here to bring the witches and the werewolves back together."

Lucas blew out a long, slow breath through his mouth. "Wow."

"I need something more than that!" Rosie cried. "I need answers."

"I'm sorry." Lucas put his arms around Rosie, pulling her in for a hug. "I don't have any. We'll figure this out, though, okay?"

"Didn't you say you were going to grill out and

light a fire tonight?" Rosie nodded to the rusted fire pit, which was in the center of the deck and surrounded by patio chairs. A thick layer of dirt and leaves covered everything.

"Yeah." Lucas looked around. "I guess I have a little cleaning up to do first."

"I'd say so." Rosie went to the patio door, intent on finding a broom. "I'll help."

As soon as she reached for the door, her phone vibrated in her pocket. She paused then fished it out and looked at the screen. A number she didn't recognize was displayed, and she wrinkled her brow. She answered with a tentative "Hello?"

"Rosie?"

Her breath left her lungs in a rush, and she glanced at Lucas. His concerned gaze held her captive for a moment before she averted her eyes and stared at the patio floor. "Calvin?"

Lucas scowled. "Why is he calling you?"

Rosie waved a hand to keep him quiet, and Lucas crossed his arms.

Something rustled on the other end of the line. "I don't have much time. I just needed to tell you... to warn you. Something is happening here."

"What do you mean?" Rosie looked up again to meet Lucas's eyes.

Calvin continued in a whisper, "Marcus Beckett joined our pack."

Her jaw dropping, Rosie sucked in a breath. A few feet away, Lucas's eyes widened. He must have been listening in.

"Rosie, they're talking crazy. They want to get rid of the surrogate agency so that werewolves will be forced to go back to hunting women. They're trying to build a following and recruiting members from other packs. Rumors have been going around about you being a witch. They say that you perform evil witchcraft at Hart House. Some of the werewolves are getting stirred up."

Rosie let out a breath. If they built enough of a following, things could get dangerous. "Have you told anyone else about this?"

"No." Calvin sighed. "I don't know anyone else outside the pack. Just you." Calvin made a startled noise. "I think someone is coming. I have to go."

"Wait, Calvin—"

The line went dead. Rosie held the phone away from her ear, looking at it. She quickly navigated through the screens to try to save the number to her contact list. "Stupid phone. Can never figure this thing out."

"This is crazy." Lucas started pacing, just as Rosie had been doing earlier. "Are they planning to start a war? They have to know most werewolves won't stand for this. I need to go to the Council."

"I know." Rosie bit her lip. "But I don't think you should talk to them alone."

"What do you mean?"

"I think we should go see Sam."

FORTY-SEVEN

SAM

SAM WATCHED BECCA SCOOP A BIG PILE OF EGGS onto her plate and lick her fingers before she picked up her fork and dove in. Closing her eyes, she hummed in contentment.

"Oh my God." A full mouth muffled her words. "How do all you guys not weigh a thousand pounds with all this incredible food. Martha is a genius."

"You work in a restaurant, Becca." Daniel smiled and took a drink of his coffee. "You have access to some pretty incredible food all the time."

"Not like this," she said. "My dad's restaurant is good but not this good." She pointed her fork at Daniel. "Don't you dare tell him I told you that."

Daniel raised his hands in surrender. "Secret is safe with me."

After Becca swung her fork toward Michael, he raised his hands as well. "Wouldn't dream of crossing you."

Becca had spent the night again. Her comfort level in the house continued to grow. In typical Becca fashion, she got along great with everyone. She adored Martha, and the two of them spent hours chatting together in the kitchen.

Things would work out. They had to.

"Have you heard from Rosie?" Becca asked casually then popped a piece of bacon into her mouth.

Sam's jaw clenched, but he tried not to let his anger show. "No. Nothing from Rosie or Lucas, but the Council confirmed that Lucas took his place as alpha, and he's accepted Rosie into the pack. It's just as we thought."

"I can't believe they would just run off like that," Michael grumbled. "No goodbye. No nothing."

Daniel's gaze flitted from Michael to Sam then back again. "Rosie was ordered not to leave. They couldn't exactly announce their departure."

"What was I supposed to do?" Sam gave up on keeping a lid on his anger. "Rosie is part of my pack. The Council wanted her to stay put while they decided what to do."

"I don't think the Council specified that she couldn't join another pack." Daniel always had to be the voice of reason.

Sam scrubbed a hand over his face. "I'll be in my office."

He pushed his chair out and made his way down the hall. As he approached his office, his sensitive ears picked up on the sound of a vehicle turning into the driveway, and he scowled. The entire pack—what was left of it—was sitting at the breakfast table. Who managed to make it past the gate? When he glanced out the window, a spike of territorial anger went through him.

Lucas's car slowly made its way up the driveway. Through the windshield, he could see both Lucas and Rosie inside. The opposing feelings tore at him. Anger, love, hope... the familiar urge to welcome his sister and his best friend home and the primal desire to defend his territory from members of a different pack.

Behind him, Michael and Daniel came forward, sensing the approach of the vehicle as he had.

"Who is it?" Michael asked.

"It's Lucas and Rosie," Sam grumbled.

"What?" Becca screamed, running from the dining room. "Yes! That's awesome!"

After shoving Sam aside, Becca flung the door open. He stood in the doorway, watching in stunned silence as Becca ran down the porch steps to the approaching vehicle, her arms out wide in greeting.

"Rosie!" she yelled. "You're here!"

Rosie jumped out of the passenger side and leaped into Becca's waiting arms, hugging her like they hadn't seen each other in years.

Lucas climbed out of the driver's side and met Sam's gaze. "I'm sorry for the unannounced visit. We need to talk. It's important."

SAM PINCHED the bridge of his nose.

"So witches are showing up all over the place, and the Cramers are building an army? That about sums it up?"

Breakfast had been cleared from the dining table, and everyone sat to listen to what Rosie and Lucas had to say.

"That's about it. The Cramer pack has to be stopped. We need to tell the Council. But we need to put up a united front." Rosie blew a breath out of her nose. "We need to tell them that we're ready to move forward. To put the past behind us. No more hunting women. No more seducing strange women then stealing their newborns. Honestly, while we're at it, I'm not such a huge fan of the surrogate agency either. I mean, of course it's better than hunting women, but duping women into carrying werewolves. They have no idea—"

"One thing at a time, Rosie." Sam raised a hand to stop her.

"She's right, Sam," Becca said. "You can't ask a woman to use her body to help you bring life into the world then not tell her what kind of life it is she's carrying."

"Can we focus on one fight at a time?" Michael rolled his eyes. "The surrogate agency was set up to stop the hunting and killing of women. If you take the agency away, werewolves will turn to killing again. They won't have any other way to bring new members to their packs."

"Unless the witches come out of hiding," Rosie said.

"And you think that's going to happen." Sam furrowed his brow. It sounded crazy. Absolutely insane.

But he trusted his sister.

"It's already happening," she said. "I told you."

The determination in her eyes told him all he needed to know.

Now more than ever, Sam knew how important it was to rise above the barbaric past of the werewolves. He looked at Becca. She was carrying their child. Their future. What future would he give the generations to come?

"Okay." Sam looked at Rosie then Lucas. "What do we need to do?"

FORTY-EIGHT
ROSIE

"This is certainly a surprise." On the computer screen, Jagger raised an eyebrow. "I can safely say we have never had two pack alphas call us for an emergency meeting from the same location at the same time."

"Add in the female werewolf, and everything's gone to hell in a handbasket," Roland groused.

Rosie fought the urge to roll her eyes. The three of them sat at Sam's desk, facing the computer screen, where the three Council members were each tuned into the web call.

"We've received some disturbing news," Lucas began. "About the Cramer pack."

"We heard that Marcus joined them," Garrett said. "If that's what this is about."

Sam shook his head. "It's more than that. We've gotten word that they're gathering followers. The goal is to get rid of the surrogate agency so that werewolves will return to old traditions."

"Are you sure of this?" Garrett's eyes widened.

"Yes." Rosie cleared her throat. "And there's more."

"She should not be allowed to speak at this meeting. She shouldn't even *be* at this meeting. Is nothing sacred anymore?"

Roland's furious growl startled her, and Lucas placed a hand on hers.

"She needs to be allowed to talk," Lucas said. "Please."

"Let her speak." Jagger waved a hand.

"I told you what the Goddess said to me."

"Yes," Jagger said. "We've been in several conferences with the World Werewolf Council over how to proceed. Naturally, there is skepticism and disagreement about your claims."

"Witches *are* coming," Rosie said. "They're coming to packs who are putting the old ways behind them. I've seen it. If werewolves fall back into the old ways, they'll go back into hiding."

Rosie glanced at Lucas and squeezed his hand. "There is an ancient bond between werewolves and witches. You've heard the stories of the Chosen—how they lived together in the beginning. Now that they're coming together again, that bond is coming back."

"What do you mean?" Jagger furrowed his brow.

"My mother and father were drawn together by a mate bond. It's something bigger than love. It's something I have with Lucas."

Roland made a gruff sound. "This is ridiculous."

"Quiet, Roland!" Jagger yelled. He rubbed his beard. "I remember my father telling me that the Chosen were bonded by something stronger than anything on this earth. Could it really be true?"

"We need to talk about how we're going to deal with the Cramers," Garrett cut in. "The surrogate agency was set up by the World Council. If their plan is to destroy it, that's treason."

"Can you show us some of these witches?" Jagger

sounded intrigued. "Proof that they are actually coming out of hiding?"

Rosie nodded, praying she could talk Greta and the sisters into showing themselves. "I can."

Jagger pursed his lips. "Let us talk to the World Council. We'll be in touch."

The Council members disappeared from the screen, and a heavy blanket of silence filled the room. Sam crossed his arms and stared at the desk. Rosie exchanged glances with Lucas.

"Sam." Rosie reached a hand toward him.

"Don't."

She jerked her hand back like she'd been burned. "I'm sorry, Sammy. I'm sorry I left without saying anything. I couldn't—"

"It's my fault," Lucas cut in. "I begged her to come with me. It was urgent. My pack was in trouble."

"Since when do we lie and sneak around behind each other's backs?" Sam scowled.

"If I thought you would have let me leave, I would have told you we were going." Rosie sighed. "I know you're trying to protect me. I love you for that. But Hart House isn't the same place it was before. You'll always be my family, butthis isn't my home. Not anymore."

Sam jerked his head toward her. Anger flashed in his eyes, and he opened his mouth to speak, but he paused. As he watched her, his shoulders sagged, and he blew out a long breath. "You seem happy."

"I am." Rosie's sinuses stung, and she tried not to cry. "I'm going to miss you so much, but I know where I belong."

"You belong with Lucas." Sam nodded then

glanced at him. "The two of you always did like to gang up on me."

"Not true." Rosie laughed and wiped a tear from her eye. "I think I was always the one getting bullied in this trio."

"So what now?" Sam gestured toward the laptop.

"Now..." Rosie sighed again. "We go find some witches."

FORTY-NINE

ROSIE

THE DINER WAS EMPTY WHEN ROSIE STEPPED
through the door. The streets were dark, all the shops
on Main Street closed.

"We're closed!" Greta shouted from the kitchen.
As she walked to the front of the diner, her voice carried with her. "We'll be open first thing in the mor—"
Greta stopped in her tracks when she spotted Rosie.
A small smile played at her red lips as she tossed the
rag she'd been holding onto the countertop. "I wondered when I would see you again."

"Can I talk to you?"

Greta gestured toward one of the booths. Rosie
sat, and Greta followed, sitting across from her.

"Do you want some coffee?"

Rosie shook her head. "Thanks. No."

Greta watched Rosie closely. "Are you the only
other witch here?"

"My grandma lives just outside town."

"The healer." Greta nodded. "Customers talk
about an old lady who sells the best healing ointments
and balms."

"That's Grandma." Rosie smiled. "Her name is

Clara. You should talk to her sometime. I'm sure she'd love to get to know you."

"Is she like you?"

"You mean a witch?" Rosie furrowed her brow. "Yes, I—"

"No. Like *you*. You're not just a witch. You're something else. I don't know what, and it's been bothering me like you wouldn't believe."

"I heard that you and Daniel get along really well. He talks about you."

Greta's eyes widened, and her mouth formed an O. "That's it! Your energy feels a little like his. But not entirely. What is he? What are you?"

"How much do you know about the Chosen?"

"The witch and the werewolf stories?" Greta rolled her eyes. "My grandma used to tell those to me at bedtime. Fairy tales."

Rosie smiled. "Are they?"

"I see." Greta laughed. "So you're crazy."

Rosie frowned. "I haven't even gotten to the part where I've spoken with the gods in my dreams."

"Crazy, it is, then." Greta started to get up. "I think it's time for me to close."

"Please just listen." Rosie's hand shot out, grabbing Greta's wrist. "Is it really so far-fetched to believe the stories? You know what you can do. You know it's not normal."

"Yeah, but... werewolves?" Greta cocked her head. "Really?"

It was going to be harder than Rosie had thought. She sighed. "I can show you."

"It's a beautiful house." Greta looked around as Rosie led her through Hart House the following morning. "I still can't believe I let you talk me into coming out here."

"I told you everything last night," Rosie said. "You didn't run screaming or call to have me committed, so I think part of you believes me."

"If your family eats me, I'll sue."

"We won't eat you." Rosie laughed. "I promise."

As they passed by the kitchen, Greta paused and jerked her head toward the basement. "There's evil here."

"Old evil." Rosie nodded. "A past our family isn't proud of. Follow me."

Rosie stepped onto the patio, and Greta followed closely behind. On the lawn, Daniel stood waiting. The adoration and apprehension he felt when he saw Greta touched Rosie, and she frowned. Poor Daniel.

Greta smiled and strolled across the patio. "Do I finally get to see your gardens?"

Concern pinched Daniel's features as he looked at Rosie. She nodded to him, and he sighed. In a flash, he shifted, his large wolf form appearing in front of Greta.

Greta screamed and backpedaled toward the patio. She grabbed Rosie's arm, and Rosie placed a hand over hers.

"It's okay, Greta. It's just Daniel." Rosie pushed calming energy to her. "He won't hurt you."

Greta's gaze drifted back and forth between Rosie and Daniel. "Part of me wanted so badly to believe you, but I didn't think it was possible. The stories my grandma told... I loved them. It all sounded so magical. I wanted that. I wanted it so badly."

"We can have it again." Rosie squeezed her hand. "If you help us."

FIFTY

SAM

Daniel and Greta walked through the
gardens together. Sam watched from the window as
she brought life to the flowers, just as Rosie always
did. Daniel seemed to hang on her every word, her
every move. Sam had never seen this side of him before. It seemed like the woman was his missing piece.

Sam shook his head. He'd been talking to Rosie
too much.

Michael approached and pulled the curtain back
to get a better look out the window.

"Think she has a sister?"

Sam laughed. "If she does, I doubt she'd let her
within ten miles of you, Michael. She's been in town
long enough to know your reputation."

"Smart-ass." Michael scowled. He nodded toward
Daniel and Greta. "Lucky jerk."

A hand snaked across Sam's stomach as Becca
hugged him from behind.

"I think it's sweet," she said. "Daniel is so quiet.
He never talks to anyone. From what I've seen,
Daniel and Greta could talk for hours."

Sam turned and gave her a kiss. As he brushed the
hair away from her face, he couldn't help but notice

the happy glow in her eyes. His gaze trailed behind her, and he spotted Lucas and Rosie coming down the hall. They carried their bags with them.

"You're leaving?"

Rosie nodded. "We need to talk to the sisters. We'll be back. Hopefully with them."

Becca turned and crossed the dining room to give Rosie a hug. "Text me, okay?"

"I will," Rosie promised. "You take it easy. Make Sam wait on you hand and foot."

"Excuse me?" Sam held his arms out. "What the hell?"

"Hey!" Rosie pointed a finger at him then aimed it at Becca's stomach. "You did this. You keep her happy and healthy."

"You know I will." He shoved his hands into his pockets as Becca moved back to his side.

"Yes, I do." Rosie gave him a warm smile.

∼

It was almost midnight when Sam's cell rang on his nightstand. He quickly picked it up and answered before the second ring. He glanced at Becca, making sure she hadn't been woken by the sound.

He padded out to the hallway. Who was calling so late? He put the phone to his ear and barked out an irritated greeting.

"Sam," Jagger answered gruffly.

Shit. Why did he always answer the Council's phone calls like a grumpy old man?

"Jagger," Sam said. "Is everything all right?"

"I'm sorry. I didn't think about the time there."

"It's okay." Sam cleared his throat and made his way down the stairs to the office.

"We've spoken with the World Werewolf Council. We want to meet the witches Rose promised she can present. Then we'll discuss a strategy to deal with the Cramers."

"She's working on gathering them now."

"Good. Saturday. Hart House. And, Sam..." Jagger sounded amused. "We'll have the leader of the World Werewolf Council with us."

Jagger disconnected the call, and Sam sat in stunned silence. The leader of the World Werewolf Council was the leader of *all* werewolves. He would be at Hart House. As far as Sam knew, few outside the World Werewolf Council had ever seen Lloyd Abrams. In the past few decades, his leadership had brought the werewolf world out of a hideous past. He started the surrogate agency and fought hard to extinguish the old traditions completely. Of course, there would always be those who resisted. Those who blocked progress by glorifying tradition and glossing over the ugliness. Those outliers kept the sweeping change from happening. But Lloyd had made huge strides.

Sam scrubbed his hands over his face. It was too late to call Lucas and Rosie, but he couldn't hold the news until tomorrow. He tapped Rosie's name in his contacts and placed the call.

Lucas answered with a sleepy voice, and Sam closed his eyes. He didn't want to think about Lucas in Rosie's bed. A shiver ran through his body. Stay focused.

"You guys are never going to believe what I just heard."

FIFTY-ONE
ROSIE

Once again, Rosie was sitting across from the three nearly identical sisters. This time, they sat around the dining table at the Beckett pack house. A platter of snacks lay before them. Cookies, cheese and crackers, sausage—all courtesy of Ginny. Lucas hadn't been kidding. The woman's skills in the kitchen were something else. Travis sat next to Sophie, gripping her hand tightly. The two of them were huddled so close it was as though they were melded together. Tia and Leslie sat on the other side of Sophie. They exchanged glances when Rosie finished speaking.

Rosie had laid it all out for them—her half-wolf, half-witch heritage, the recent changes in the werewolf world, the dreams she'd had when she was in a coma, the visits from the Council, the danger the werewolves posed to humans if the Cramers succeeded in spreading their movement, and the part the three of them could play in changing the future.

"What if the werewolves decide to attack us?" Sophie asked. "There will be so many of them there."

"We won't let them hurt you." Travis kissed Sophie's hand and winked. The uncharacteristic sincerity caught Rosie off guard. He really loved her. "That's a promise."

"Do you really think witches and werewolves have a future together?" Tia watched Rosie carefully. "Like the old stories where the Chosen lived together?"

Rosie reached for a sugar cookie. She recognized the hope in Tia's eyes. "I think so."

The sisters glanced at one another, having a silent conversation.

Sophie turned to Rosie. "We'll do it."

Relief mingled with apprehension, but Rosie smiled. If this worked, the future of all the Chosen would be changed for the better.

If it didn't...

She hoped she wasn't giving everyone false hope.

Rosie spotted movement through the patio door, just for a moment. She looked again, and Brody peeked at her through the glass. He caught her gaze and quickly ducked out of sight.

"We have ties," Tia said quietly.

"What?" Rosie snapped her attention back to the sisters. "What do you mean, 'ties'?"

"Our mother was part of a fairly large network of covens in the Chicago area," Tia said. "If the werewolves are willing to stop what they've been doing, we can spread word. It certainly won't reach all witches everywhere. Not all of them operate in covens. But it will be a start."

A little bit of weight rose from Rosie's shoulders. Things could be coming together.

"Sam said the Council will be there tomorrow. We'll need to leave early." Movement out outside caught Rosie's attention again. "If you'll excuse me. I'm just going to get a second of fresh air."

Rosie grabbed two more cookies from the platter and made her way to the patio door. Lucas caught her eye and started to get up, but she held out her hand.

"I just need a minute."

A pensive expression crossed his face, but he nodded.

Stepping onto the patio, Rosie closed the door behind her. Cool air bit at her arms, and she breathed in the scent of fall leaves. Brody's apprehension tickled her senses.

"I know you're out here," she said. "I brought you some cookies."

"What kind?" His small voice came from somewhere behind the grill.

"A sugar and a peanut butter."

"Did you make them?"

"Ginny did."

A head of shaggy brown hair peeked at her from behind the grill. She went to him and handed him the cookies.

"Thanks."

"You could have come in," Rosie said. "You didn't need to hide."

"Lucas said it wasn't a place for kids."

"Oh." The floor of the deck was dirty, but she'd sat in worse. She carefully lowered herself in front of Brody, crossing her legs and resting her arms in front of her. "What did you think about what was said?"

With a mouthful of peanut butter cookie, Brody shrugged.

"It could mean a much better future for all of us." Rosie tried to catch his eye.

He avoided her, instead watching a chipmunk that approached a few feet away. Its nostrils flared as it sniffed the air. Brody tossed a piece of cookie toward it, and it skittered away.

He frowned. "If it works," he said finally. "But I don't think it will."

Rosie's stomach tightened. Lucas had told her about his conversation with Brody. "What makes you think it won't?"

He tossed a few more pieces of cookie onto the deck, trying to lure the chipmunk closer. The little creature nibbled at the pieces of crumb but wouldn't come near.

"Because of people like my dad. Like the Cramers."

"There are a lot of people like them." Rosie nodded. "But there are a lot of people like Lucas and the rest of the Beckett pack too. And the Hart pack. I think we outnumber the people like your dad and the Cramers. And I think that gives you a chance at a much better future."

After hesitating for a few moments, Brody nodded. He looked off toward the trees and sighed. "But what's going to happen to my dad? He won't go along with it. What will the Council do to him?"

His fear and sadness touched Rosie, and she bit her lip. Despite all the things Marcus had put Brody through, the kid still loved his father.

"That's not for me to decide," Rosie said. "I don't know what will happen to him. But I can tell you that no matter what, you won't be alone. Lucas loves you. The whole Beckett pack loves you. You'll never be alone, Brody."

Tentatively, Rosie rested a hand on Brody's. He flinched but relaxed as she sent calming energy to him. The tension left his shoulders, and some of the sadness left his eyes.

The chipmunk ran up Rosie's arm and perched on her shoulder. She held her hand out, and it moved down her arm and paused in her hand. She lowered her hand to Brody, and he held his out. The chipmunk tentatively climbed into Brody's hand. His eyebrows disappeared behind his curtain of hair as he smiled at Rosie.

FIFTY-TWO
ROSIE

IN THE BACK SEAT OF THE CAR, BRODY PLAYED A game on his phone. In the driver's seat, Lucas looked at him in the rearview mirror for the millionth time and screwed up his face in anger. Rosie hid a smirk. Brody had spent all night and all morning begging Lucas to let him come along. Lucas had adamantly said no. Then Brody had finally switched tactics and asked Rosie.

Lucas glared at her. *"I still can't believe you said yes."*

"This is a historic moment, Lucas. He should be there."

"It's dangerous."

"You'll keep him safe."

He glared at her again.

"The Council said they wouldn't bring their bodyguards." Rosie glanced behind her and smiled at Brody. That she was winning cool points with Brody might have swayed her decision a little, too, but she wouldn't admit that to Lucas. *"They promised. If the bodyguards were going to be there, I would think twice about it. But it's just the Council. We'll have the entire Beckett pack, the entire Hart*

pack, and five witches there. What can possibly go wrong?"

"Don't *say that.*"

Rosie rolled her eyes. *"Don't be superstitious."*

"You know, it's funny. You've always gotten your way. I thought maybe when I became alpha, that might change."

"You're right. That's funny." Rosie gave him her sweetest smile.

As they neared the gated entrance to Hart House, her stomach sank. She'd been optimistic about things when she woke up that morning, but as they neared Hanks Hollow, nerves took over. The plan was so huge. What if it didn't work?

She felt Lucas looking at her and plastered a big, fake smile on her face. He frowned. He knew her too well.

They pulled up the driveway and parked in front of the house. A caravan of cars followed closely behind, carrying the remainder of the pack and the sisters.

Sam emerged through the front door, followed closely by Daniel, Greta, and Michael. As they came down the stairs, Rosie ran up the sidewalk to greet them. She gave each of her former pack members a tight embrace. She had found her home, but God, she missed the guys.

"Where's Becca?" she asked.

Sam frowned. "I didn't want her here. Too risky."

That was probably best. The Council was making a lot of concessions, but performing pack business in the presence of a pregnant human might be going too far.

Roger stepped forward and embraced Sam. "I'm proud of you. I know your dad would be too."

"Thank you, Roger." Sam nodded. "It's good to see you."

As Sam and Lucas each took turns introducing their pack members to one another, the witches in the group did their own introductions, each feeling out the energies the others projected. Rosie stifled a laugh. It was like dogs sniffing butts.

They were about to go inside when the final vehicle made its way up the driveway. The Council had arrived.

FIFTY-THREE
ROSIE

As a group, they waited to greet the Council. The large SUV parked next to Lucas's car, and the three Council members climbed out of the vehicle. The back door stayed open as a fourth person slid out.

Lloyd Abrams moved slowly as he stood to his full height. A large, balding, elderly man with wrinkled dark skin. He was tall and husky, though he looked like he had been very lean and muscular in his prime. His expensive suit was pressed and clean but somehow still looked casual and cool. He leaned heavily on a cane as he limped forward. Jagger held out a hand to help him, but the old man swatted it away.

As he neared, his wrinkled face came into view. The effort it took him to move across the sidewalk brought droplets of sweat to his forehead. They all waited silently for him to move to the base of the steps. There, he finally accepted Jagger's help and took them one at a time.

"I hope Sam's cool with us spending the night, because I think it's going to be midnight before the old man makes it to the top of those stairs." Lucas's snark

was hidden well from his face as he watched the world leader with cool indifference.

"*Stop, Lucas!*" Rosie gave him a kick.

When they finally all made their way inside, Sam invited them to sit in the living room. He offered the armchair by the fireplace to Mr. Abrams. Stuart used to read to Rosie in that chair when she was little. As he sat, she was reminded of her great uncle and why they were all here today.

The three United States Werewolf Council members sat on one couch, and Greta and the sisters sat on the other. Rosie stood beside them, with Lucas and Sam next to her. The rest of the pack members found seats or stood around the room.

"Mr. Abrams, you haven't met all the pack members here today. I believe some introductions are in order," Jagger said.

"Ack." Lloyd waved a hand. "That will take all day. I just want to meet the witches."

Jagger cleared his throat. "Very well." He nodded at Rosie. "If you will, please, Ms. Hart."

The thump of her heart became loud in her ears, and she took a shaky breath. Lucas reached for her hand and squeezed it.

"*You've got this. Do your thing, Rosie.*"

His voice in her head reassured her.

Rosie stepped forward and cleared her throat. "The Chosen were created to protect mankind, but mankind changed. When that happened, the purpose of the Chosen did too. Instead of being revered for their gifts, they were shunned for them. They were driven away from one another. There is so much disagreement about how it happened and who is to blame. We'll never know exactly how it all played out, but what we do know is that the witches were forced into hiding, and the werewolves were left without a way to carry on their legacy.

"The actions the werewolves took to carry on their lineage kept the witches away. Now, many werewolves are finally realizing things need to change. The witches are ready to join those werewolves who are ready to put the past behind them. Together, we can create a new generation of Chosen."

"How do you know all this?" Lloyd leaned forward and narrowed his eyes at Rosie.

Rosie felt like a bug under a microscope, but she went on to explain everything about her parents and her dreams.

"I didn't believe it at first, but I see it now," Rosie said. "Witches are being drawn to territories run by packs that have moved past the old ways."

"It's true," Greta said. "I've lived my entire life in Nebraska, but I had this sudden urge to come here. To this tiny town in the middle of nowhere. I can't explain it. It was like something called to me."

Tia cleared her throat. "We've lived in Chicago all our lives. We have strong ties there. We never intended to leave." She looked at her sisters. "But we all had the same strong urge to come here."

"So you're here," Roland said. "So now what?"

"Now they're finding what my parents had," Rosie said. She looked at Lucas. "What Lucas and I have."

"What's that?" Lloyd seemed amused.

"A mate bond. It's stronger than love. It's stronger than anything in this world."

"So it's true," Lloyd said. "The bond between witches and werewolves exists."

"But the rumors," Roland hissed. "The evil witchcraft she's been performing. What about that?"

"What evil witchcraft?" Sam crossed his arms. "Who's been spreading these lies? Rosie has lived here her whole life. She's never done anything but make plants grow, calm me down when I'm angry, and heal hurt animals."

Garrett dropped his hand into his lap and cocked his head to the side. Skepticism poured from him. "You can heal?"

Rosie strolled forward and knelt in front of Lloyd.

"What are you doing, witch? Get away from him!" Roland stood. "She'll kill our world leader!"

Rosie looked into Lloyd's face, praying he would trust her. She held her hand above his leg. "May I?"

His eyes searched hers, and she felt his hope blossom as he nodded. She hadn't sensed any pain. He just didn't seem to be able to use it. A stroke, maybe? Placing her hand gently on his leg, she let her healing energy flow into him. His leg jerked forward, catching her in the middle and sending her backward, onto her butt.

"Oh my goodness!" Lloyd's eyes rounded, and he laughed. "I'm sorry!"

Rosie laughed with him.

"I haven't been able to move this leg in years." He stood slowly.

The other Council members rose, and Roland spluttered out his objections once again.

"Enough, Roland," Lloyd scolded him.

Roland snapped his mouth shut.

Lloyd took a few moments to walk around the room, testing his leg. He closed his eyes and smiled. When he opened them, he turned toward the witches. "I will go back to the Council and put an executive action on the floor."

An executive action wasn't something done often.

Both the United States Werewolf Council and the World Werewolf Council were supposed to be democratic, but they each had a leader who had final say.

"If what you say is true, we need to stop dancing around the subject and meet it head on. The World Werewolf Council will ban the nonconsensual use of women for procreation. And we'll ban the killing of humans who don't pose a threat to our existence."

Elation spread through Rosie. They'd done it. They'd really done it. As she turned toward Lucas, the sound of shattering glass made her flinch.

"Look out!"

She wasn't sure who'd shouted, but Rosie ducked and turned her head just as a ball of flame came hurtling toward her.

FIFTY-FOUR

LUCAS

Flames. That's all Lucas saw before he lunged for Rosie, crashing into her and pinning her to the floor. Shouts all around him were too loud. He couldn't hear her. Was she okay?

"Rosie?" He braced himself on his arms to look down at her.

Her eyes were like saucers as she stared into his face. "What the hell was that?"

Another crash sounded, and another ball of flame came hurtling through the air.

Sam shouted over the chaos, "Fire! Everyone outside!"

The curtains around the window were already a raging inferno, and the flames spread to the doorway that led to the front door.

"Out back. Come on!" Sam steered everyone through the hallway.

Lucas helped Rosie to her feet and frantically searched the room for the rest of his pack. He spotted Shawn dragging Brody out to the hall. Brody was screaming for Lucas, reaching out toward him.

"I'm coming, Brody. Don't worry!" Lucas choked

on a cough as smoke burned his throat. Yelling was a bad idea.

He took Rosie's hand and led her toward the hall. The thick smoke collected quickly as fire spread. Sam trailed behind them as they ran down the hallway, through the dining room, and out the patio door.

The rest of the packs and the Council members were standing on the patio. Why the hell were they just standing there instead of moving away from the house? As Lucas dragged Rosie outside and sucked in a lungful of fresh air, he got his first look at the backyard and the answer to his question.

William Cramer stood on the lawn with his pack. They all held torches. Next to William was Marcus Beckett with his own torch. The old alpha's eyes went straight to Lucas, and he sneered.

"William, what are you doing?" Roland barked at his nephew.

"Thanks for the intel, uncle," William said. "I assumed the Cramer pack's invitation to this meeting got lost in the mail. I thought I'd take it upon myself to show up anyway."

Roland hung his head. "I told you about the meeting so you could come and speak your mind, William. Not so you could try to kill us. Don't be a fool."

"The time for talking is done!" William shouted. "We won't stand by while Lloyd Abrams orders us all to bury our traditions." His eyes trailed over everyone on the patio. "Anyone who wants to join us may do so now. It's your last chance. Before we kill you."

On the patio, no one moved.

"Brody!" Marcus shouted. "Come here, son!"

Brody turned to look at Lucas, tears in his eyes.

Lucas held his hands out to him, and Brody fell into him, squeezing his waist.

"I want to stay with you, Lucas!" he cried.

"Brody!" Marcus's frantic scream echoed off the trees.

Lucas squeezed Brody's shoulder then moved him aside. He stepped off the patio, onto the lawn.

"He doesn't want to come with you, Marcus," Lucas growled. "Back off."

"You." Marcus's eyes were wild. He handed his torch to William and stomped across the lawn toward Lucas. "You've poisoned his mind. I've had enough of you."

Though Marcus was a large man, his actions were fluid as he moved forward and shifted into his enormous wolf form.

Lucas leaped, shifting. Rosie and Brody cried out behind him, begging him not to go, but his rage spurred him forward. He ran across the grass, the blades whipping at the pads of his paws. He didn't break Marcus's gaze, holding firm until they collided. Pain flared through every part of his body. Marcus was like a concrete wall.

Lucas rolled across the grass but quickly jumped to his feet and charged again. He took Marcus off guard as he went for his head, grabbing his ear and ripping through the flesh.

Marcus cried out, and Lucas tasted blood. He tried not to gag as he held on, whipping his head back and forth until the ear gave way, coming off in his mouth. Lucas fell backward, half of Marcus's ear still in his teeth.

Marcus howled and cried, pawing at his torn ear. Lucas took the opportunity and leaped again, going for his exposed throat.

"No, Lucas! Don't!"

The desperate cry made him pause. He stayed crouched, but he glanced toward the patio. Brody stood in the grass. Tears streamed down his face as he sobbed.

"He's my dad, Lucas!"

God, he couldn't kill the kid's dad right in front of him. What was he thinking? Lucas relaxed his muscles and turned to Marcus. Blood matted the side of the giant's head as he watched Lucas back slowly toward the patio. Fire continued to engulf the house, and the flames reflected in Marcus's hateful, piercing eyes.

"No takers, then?" William *tsk*ed. "Well, then. I guess it's time for you all to die."

As William spoke, a dozen more werewolves emerged from the forest and slowly moved to his side.

Behind Lucas, the heat from the house forced the group of werewolves and witches from the patio, onto the lawn. They were pinned between the raging fire and the furious wolves. And they were highly outnumbered.

FIFTY-FIVE
ROSIE

THE HEAT FROM THE FIRE SCALDED ROSIE'S BACK,
and she tried to breathe through plumes of black
smoke.

The werewolves were lined up on either side of
the Cramers—William, George, Bruce, and Calvin.
Ethan and Ian must have been left behind.
Thank God.

She watched Calvin. His gaze flitted between
William and Rosie. He met her eyes, and something
in his seemed to ask her for the courage William had
taken away from him. He set his jaw, and the uncertainty turned to determination.

"Wait!" Calvin looked at his father as he stumbled forward. "I don't want to fight for you."

"Get back in line, you coward," William sneered.
"It will be quick. You won't get hurt."

"No!" Calvin yelled. He put his head down and
started across the lawn, toward the burning house and
the doomed werewolves and witches. "I'll fight with
them."

"Get back here!" William's face reddened.
"Damn you, then! Die with the rest of them!"

Bruce and George shifted. William was the only

one left standing in human form in the center of what looked like about fifteen or twenty werewolves. He held his torch up. "Kill them!"

"We're outnumbered!" Sam shouted. He looked at the others standing around him. "I don't know about the rest of you, but I don't intend to go down without a fight."

Without another word, Sam was gone, and his wolf was running across the lawn toward the charging werewolves.

"Sam!" Rosie screamed, and a sob rushed through her as she watched Lucas go after him. "Lucas! No!"

The other werewolves followed, shifting and running headlong into danger. Even the Council members joined in. When Brody started forward, Rosie grabbed him from behind and held firmly to his shirt.

"Let me go!" he shouted. "I want to help!"

Scanning the lawn, she watched helplessly as her family, her entire life, fought a losing battle.

Michael and Daniel went straight for Bruce Cramer. She could feel Michael's elation from hundreds of feet away when he got the satisfaction of sinking his teeth into Bruce's neck. Her cousins took Bruce down in seconds, but they were quickly overcome by three other wolves.

It was hopeless. Her family was going to die.

In the distance, Rosie spotted movement. She squinted, and two figures became as clear as day. Her mother and her father. They stood by the oak. Her oak, which had somehow been restored.

Her mother's voice echoed in the breeze. "Don't forget, Rosie."

Slowly, determination replaced the hopelessness. She could help. She wouldn't stand idly by while her family was murdered. She pushed Brody toward

Leslie, who grabbed him and hugged him tightly to her chest. Rosie focused all her energy on the forest and made the call. It was the loudest, most desperate call for help she'd ever made.

It started with mice—hundreds of them. They came like a swarm of bees and crawled up the legs of the Cramers and their party. Barks and whines pierced the air. Two werewolves that had Daniel pinned to the ground jumped off him and went running for the trees.

Next came the bugs, the spiders, the ants, then the badgers, squirrels, and racoons. None of them so threatening on their own, but when they came by the dozens, by the hundreds, they were deadly.

With the critters, Rosie's family was starting to gain the upper hand. Sam and Lucas had three werewolves pinned with the help of some racoons that bit at their heels and tails.

It wasn't enough, though. There were so many of them. She needed more, but her energy was waning. She squeezed her eyes shut and concentrated all her energy on her call.

A hand slipped into her right one, and another slipped into her left. Her eyes popped open. The witches, minus Leslie, who still held onto Brody, had formed a circle.

"Use our energy, Rosie!" Tia shouted. "You can draw more from us."

Rosie closed her eyes again and made another call.

More small creatures came, followed by bigger ones. Foxes, coyotes, and bobcats. Then the deer came. Dozens of them. They leaped through the yard in herds, pummeling the werewolves with their hooves.

It was working. The werewolves that hadn't been beaten to the ground ran for the woods.

William Cramer stood in the center of the yard, his furious growl roaring over the noise. "Witchcraft! You all see the witchcraft!"

A large buck charged out of the forest. His broad shoulders and enormous crown of antlers crashed through the trees. His powerful hoofbeats thundered across the ground as he ran straight for William Cramer. He reared, and Rosie could have sworn she saw a flash of the God of Hunting in his form before the heavy feet came crashing down on William's head.

FIFTY-SIX

CONCLUSION

Gone. Hart House was gone. Smoldering black embers and soot littered the ground where it had once stood.

The cacophony of noise around Sam barely penetrated his awareness. The Council had been scarily fast in dealing with the aftermath of the battle. The few bodies that littered the lawn were swept away by helicopter to be disposed of somewhere else. The deceased included William and Bruce Cramer and a few werewolves Sam had never heard of from neighboring states.

None of the casualties had come from their side. That was all that really mattered to Sam.

The Council vowed to spend an enormous amount of time and resources tracking down the werewolves who had escaped. And they banished Roland Cramer.

"It's just a house, Sam." Michael's voice was low. He sniffed. "Just a house."

"Yeah." Sam took a deep breath and coughed on the fumes.

Out on the lawn, Daniel sat in the grass, holding

Greta. She cried softly in his arms. Sam remembered her words from earlier. *"There is evil here."*

Rosie used to be afraid of the basement. She said it held voices from the past. Maybe it did.

Becca had asked him how he could stay in Hart House while knowing the horrible history that lived right underneath him. She was right. As long as they had that reminder of the past right beneath their feet, it would always cling to them and haunt them. He was being given the chance to wash away the horrid past and start fresh. He would take the good memories with him and leave the evil behind. Future generations of the Hart pack wouldn't have those remnants of a shameful history.

"I think it was time to rebuild anyway."

~

~Lucas~

Sitting on the patio steps, as he had a hundred times before, Lucas studied his pack. Christopher and Shawn sat with Tia and Sophie in the grass. Shawn had been nursing a broken jaw right after the battle, but Sophie wasted no time in healing it.

The witches had made their way to everyone, making sure all injuries were mended. After that, Leslie had disappeared somewhere with Calvin. Something had sparked between them. Lucas was pretty sure he would lose one of his bottling employees to the new Cramer alpha.

Roger was on the patio, talking with Shawn, Jagger, and Garrett.

Rosie sat on the steps next to Lucas. Her face was covered in soot, and her curls were a tangled mess. She leaned into him with a long, exhausted sigh. He rubbed her back, trying to sooth some of her tension.

Brody sat on his other side, staring off toward the woods. Lucas nudged his shoulder.

"You okay?"

Brody turned to him and gave a hint of a smile before turning his gaze back out to the trees. "Where do you think he went?"

Rosie squeezed Lucas's hand before she stood. "I'm going to take a walk."

She stepped off the patio and moved slowly across the lawn, toward the forest. Lucas watched her go as he thought about Brody's question. In the years to come, the kid would have a lot of questions he wouldn't know how to answer. About his father and the beliefs he, the Cramers, and the other werewolves had tried so adamantly to protect. What was it about tradition that held such power? Why were people so willing to fight for traditions they had to know deep down weren't right?

A sense of belonging? Of nostalgia? Were people so intent on carrying on the behaviors of their ancestors simply because "that's the way it's always been done"? Did they hold themselves and their traditions in such high regard that they couldn't bear the thought of someone else daring to question it?

"I don't know," Lucas whispered and dropped a hand onto Brody's shoulder.

Behind Lucas, the sound of chairs scraping against the patio surface came a second before Roger called to him. Lucas turned. His father stood with Shawn, Jagger, and Garrett.

Lucas squeezed Brody's shoulder then stood and walked across the patio to greet them.

"We've been speaking with your father," Jagger

said. "After today, we don't know who to trust in the Great Lakes region. Many of the werewolves never shifted. We didn't see faces."

Lucas narrowed his eyes, not sure where they were headed with this. "Yes?"

"We need a new Council member from the Great Lakes region," Garrett said. "Until we know where everyone else stands, a member of the Hart pack or the Beckett pack would be our only consideration for membership. We've asked your father to join us."

A proud smile stretched across Roger's face for a second before he tried to hide it behind a mask of indifference. "I told them I wanted to talk to you first. I won't do it, son, if you need me in Beckett Falls."

"Dad, I..."

"I think you've got this, Lucas." Roger stopped trying to keep the pride out of his smile. "Both alpha and managing the brewery. You're smart. You're capable. You don't need me."

"I'll always need you, Dad." Lucas didn't care if it sounded cheesy. "But I think the Council needs you more right now. You're the right man for the job."

~

~Rosie~

Rosie hadn't stepped foot in the forest since the day she discovered her oak had been chopped down. When she'd looked to the trees earlier and had seen her parents, she'd seen the oak too. It stood to its full height, shading and protecting them.

She let hope light in her chest, but it died as she neared the trees and saw the indentation where the oak had once stood. Still gone. She moved closer until she could see the dead stump.

Kneeling in front of it, she touched the bark, letting her fingers brush over the bumps and grooves. She closed her eyes and breathed. Something thumped against her hand, and she blinked her eyes open.

A small tendril of life pulsed behind the bark. Just barely. Her lips tipped up in a smile, and a tear dropped down her cheek as she let her energy feed the life in the roots. She closed her eyes again.

The pulse strengthened until it thumped wildly against her hand. The familiar energy filled her, and she sobbed. "You're alive."

She opened her eyes again and smiled. A carpet of lush moss grew over the stump, and vines slowly sprang in all directions, full of rich green leaves and fragrant white flowers. They curled down the side of the stump, sliding along the bark toward the ground.

One of the vines snaked up her arm, past her shoulder, and brushed her cheek, wiping away a tear.

She held out her hand and let the vine coil delicately around her fingers.

"Thank you, old friend."

EPILOGUE

O_{NE YEAR LATER}

"He's so tiny." Little toes curled under teeny-tiny feet, and Rosie thought she would burst. "And so darn cute."

"He's not as cute when he keeps me up half the night." Becca yawned. "But still cute enough to keep me from throttling him."

"You'll just have to call Auntie Rosie to babysit a little more often." The baby-talk voice Rosie used made her cringe. Since when did she do baby talk? "Yes, you wi-ill."

"Maybe if Auntie Rosie didn't live so far away." Becca stuck out her lower lip.

"Come on." Rosie nudged Becca's shoulder. "I'm here almost every weekend."

"I know." Becca frowned. "I still miss you, though."

"Are you getting out of the house enough?" Rosie eyed Becca. "Getting to town to see your dad?"

"Yeah, yeah." Becca waved a hand. "I get out plenty. I just miss my best friend."

"Aww." Rosie smiled. "I miss you too."

The new Hart House was enormous and beautiful, and best of all, it sat a few hundred feet away from the old Hart House foundation and had a new basement with no traces of a horrid past.

The sisters had told Rosie they knew a blessing that would release the spirits trapped in the old basement. Sam granted the witches permission to gather and perform the ceremony. It had been an experience Rosie would never forget. The relief as the old, trapped, tortured spirits flew free was like nothing she'd ever felt before.

After the ceremony, Sam had the cells torn apart and the old basement filled with concrete. Rosie and Lucas had joined the pack as they watched it get poured into the old foundation, sealing off the evil that had once lived there.

Sam strolled into the room, and Rosie snapped back to the present. She gave him a hug after he crossed the large marble floor toward them. "There's my big brother, father of Wisconsin's youngest werewolf."

"Not for long." Sam grinned. "I just got off the phone with Calvin. Leslie is due in a couple of months."

"They didn't waste any time, did they?" Becca's gossip tone rang out, and Rosie laughed.

"Well..." Rosie frowned. "I would love to stay, but I really need to head back."

Sam wrapped Rosie in a quick hug. "Already?"

"Yeah. I need to stop and pick up some inventory from Grandma on the way. Lucas is going to meet me at the store and help me shelve it. He doesn't like me driving at night through the woods." Rosie rolled her eyes.

"He's right." Sam scowled. "You'll hit a deer."

"Your confidence in my driving skills is touching."

Sam shrugged. "Just be careful."

"I will." Rosie bent down to give her nephew a kiss on the forehead. "See you guys next weekend?"

"We'll be here." Becca stood to give Rosie a hug. "Love you."

After a little wave goodbye, Rosie headed out to her Jeep and climbed inside. The vehicle was a much newer model than her old one but had the same feel. Her new Betty.

She drove through Hanks Hollow to her grandmother's place on the outskirts of the other side of town. Fresh potted mums sat on the porch steps, and they bloomed brighter as Rosie skipped up the stairs.

"Grandma?" With a quick knock, Rosie opened the front door and stepped inside.

"Just finishing up, dear." Clara closed a box on the kitchen table and taped it up. "These are soaps. Over there are the oils, and on the floor is the incense." She pointed at each set of boxes. "Your car is going to smell heavenly."

"Your stuff has been selling like hotcakes." Rosie picked up a box from the floor. "Everyone loves your homemade remedies."

"Be careful, dear." Clara patted her shoulder. "Don't hurt yourself."

"They aren't heavy, Grandma. It's okay."

After Rosie got the boxes packed away in her Jeep, she returned to the house to say goodbye. She'd been coming to see her grandmother every weekend, yet it still felt like a lifetime passed between each visit.

"You tell Lucas I said hello," Clara said.

"I will."

"And you drive safely."

"I will."

"And... I'm proud of you."

A smile tugged at Rosie's lips. "For what?"

"So many things, dear." Clara's eyes brimmed with tears. "You got your GED, you got your massage license, and you opened your very own massage shop and herbal remedy store in Beckett Falls. You've made a home there. And you did what the gods asked you to do. You brought the Chosen back together." Her grandmother shook her head. "I have an amazing granddaughter."

Rosie's vision blurred as tears welled. "Grandma."

"You go now." Clara wiped her eyes. "Get on the road before it gets dark, or you'll hit a deer."

~

THE SUN SET JUST below the horizon as Rosie pulled the Jeep in front of her shop on Main Street in Beckett Falls. She spotted Lucas across the street in the park, helping Stanley, the village maintenance manager, with the park display. They were busy untangling the Halloween lights.

She climbed out of the Jeep and shivered. Late September had brought an early frost. She crossed the street toward Lucas, and as she approached, she called out to him.

"Rosie!" Lucas's face brightened, and it warmed her heart. The way his eyes lit when he looked at her would never get old. He stood and gave her a peck on the cheek. His warm lips felt good on her already-cold skin. "Sorry, I guess I lost track of time."

"Hey, Rosie," Stanley muttered as he continued untangling lights. "How's business?"

"It's great, Stanley. Thank you."

Rosie watched Stanley closely. He hunched over,

his brow creased in concentration. She could feel the faint whisps of his pain from where she stood.

"I wish you would come by and let me see if I can help you with that arthritis," Rosie said. She had been trying to get him into her shop for months.

"Ah, I'm not into all that new-age herbal-remedy mumbo jumbo. You know that, Rosie."

"I know, Stanley," Rosie said patiently. She had learned to let the naysayers' remarks slide off her back. "You know where to find me if you change your mind."

"Yeah," he said, waving a hand dismissively.

Lucas put the strand of lights on the ground. "Good luck, Stanley."

They crossed the street to Rosie's shop, and Lucas grabbed a couple of boxes from the Jeep as Rosie unlocked the shop door. The bell above the door jingled, a sound she'd grown to love.

After a couple of trips back and forth from the Jeep, they had the boxes unloaded, and they went to work unpacking them and filling the shelves that lined the front of the shop. A counter with a cash register sat along the wall, and in the back, a private room provided a space for Rosie to give massages to her clients. She simply closed the shop during appointment times.

Business had been good. Her reputation as the masseuse with magic fingers had grown quickly, and she booked appointments daily. Of course, no one knew how true that reputation really was.

"Essence of... I can't pronounce this... Where does this go?" Lucas held out the jar.

"Oh." Rosie looked at it. "I don't know. Haven't seen that one before. I'll have to ask Grandma what it is. Put it behind the counter for now. I don't want someone to ask me what it is before I know how to answer them."

"I think that's the last box." Lucas tossed it toward the storeroom. "You ready to go home?"

"Yes." Rosie stretched, a long yawn falling from her lips. "I'm tired."

"I'll drive your Jeep," Lucas said. "It's dark."

"What about your truck?"

"Christopher dropped me off in town earlier."

"Okay." Rosie rolled her eyes. "Let's go."

Lucas took the keys with a triumphant smile, and they made their way outside. Lucas fired up the Jeep, and they made the short drive out to the Beckett property. As they traveled up the driveway, Lucas honked when they passed the pack house, and they both waved to Christopher and Roger, who stood on the deck, each with a beer in his hand. Behind them, Travis was making out with Sophie.

They travelled down the newly laid driveway to their house.

After Lucas parked the Jeep, they shuffled through the front door. Rosie flipped the light switch, and soft light bathed the living room. She moved to the base of the stairs and peered up toward the top. Light from Brody's bedroom split across the top of the stairs.

"Brody!" she called up to him. "We're home!"

"What do you want to do tonight?" Lucas asked as he moved toward the couch. He collapsed onto the cushions, grabbed the remote, and turned on a sitcom. "You want to go for a run?"

Everything about the evening had seemed perfectly normal. Soon, Brody would come down the stairs and sit in the armchair with his book while Rosie and Lucas sat on the couch to watch television.

Later, they would all have dinner then go to bed. They'd had nights like it a dozen times. It was the normal she'd always craved but with their own spin. Rosie loved it. She relished every single second.

"No." She climbed into his lap, and he wrapped his arms around her. "I think tonight, I just want to sit here with you."

ALSO BY RACHELLE KAMPEN

The Hanks Hollow Series Continues...

Moon Over Hanks Hollow

Witch in a Wolf Den

Lost in Hanks Hollow

THANK YOU!

Dear Reader,

THANK YOU for reading *When Witches Wake*! These characters have become such a big part of my world, and I really hope you enjoyed meeting them. If you liked the story, please consider leaving a review on <u>Amazon</u> or <u>Goodreads</u>. Reviews and ratings help me so much, and I would be so grateful for the support!

For updates, follow me on Facebook, TikTok, or Instagram, and be sure to sign up for my newsletter!

https://linktr.ee/rachellekampen
https://www.facebook.com/rachellekampen
https://www.tiktok.com/@rachellekampen
https://www.instagram.com/rachellekampen/

ABOUT THE AUTHOR

Rachelle Kampen grew up on a farm in southern Wisconsin with three brothers and two sisters. In a rural setting with no cable television or internet, options for things to do were limited, so she read—a lot.

Though she's been writing stories from the time she learned to pen a sentence, she didn't take the leap into publishing until she started writing the Hanks Hollow series. The beloved characters and unique world of Hanks Hollow unite some of Wisconsin's fun quirks with a magical paranormal adventure.

She lives outside Madison, Wisconsin with her husband, daughter, two dogs, and two cats. Even now, with cable and internet at her fingertips, she loves a good book to pass the time.

You can find author Rachelle Kampen at:
    https://linktr.ee/rachellekampen
    https://www.facebook.com/rachellekampen
    https://www.tiktok.com/@rachellekampen
    https://www.instagram.com/rachellekampen/